a PORTHKENNACK
CONTEMPORARY

WAKE UP CALL

JL MERROW

RIPTIDE
PUBLISHING

Riptide Publishing
PO Box 1537
Burnsville, NC 28714
www.riptidepublishing.com

Wake Up Call

Cover art: Garrett Leigh, blackjazzdesign.com
Editor: Sarah Lyons
Layout: L.C. Chase, lcchase.com/design.htm

ISBN: 978-1-62649-541-8

First edition
April, 2017

Also available in ebook:
ISBN: 978-1-62649-540-1

a PORTHKENNACK
CONTEMPORARY

WAKE UP
CALL

JL MERROW

RIPTIDE
PUBLISHING

With thanks to all those who helped with this book: Penelope Friday, Pender Mackie, Kristin Matherly, L.C. Chase, and my fantastic editor, Sarah Lyons. And especial thanks to Alex Beecroft for creating the wonderful world of Porthkennack for me and my fellow authors to play in, and giving it such a rich and inspiring history.

TABLE OF
CONTENTS

CHAPTER ONE

"You all right, mate? Mate?"

The bloke didn't answer, just carried on half-sitting, half-lying there on the bench, eyes glassy behind his Aviator shades.

Dev glanced back at the Square Peg Café. He'd been sitting outside drinking the world's crappest latte, wondering if he should've gone for the cream tea, when he'd noticed the man on the other side of the road. The bloke had slumped down onto the bench all of a sudden, and not like his feet had been killing him and he couldn't wait to take the weight off. No, this had been jerky, unnatural—more like he hadn't been able to stand up any longer. After a split second waiting to see if someone else was going to deal with it, Dev had jumped up and jogged over the quiet street.

Now he was here, though, he still wasn't sure whether to call an ambulance or call the bloke a wanker for pissing him about.

There were only two other people who'd been daft enough to join Dev at the outside tables under the cloudy skies, a middle-aged couple in matching walking gear, and neither of them bothered to look up from their phones. The skinny waitress stopped clearing tables long enough to roll her eyes at Dev and make a scornful drinking-up gesture.

Great. That was well public-spirited, that was. So what if Dev's Good Samaritan act turned out to be over the local alco? Even alcoholics got ill. Had strokes and stuff, didn't they? Like his mate Mal's uncle, who staggered around everywhere these days looking wasted even on the rare occasions he wasn't on the piss.

This bloke looked way too young for that sort of crap, mind. Midthirties, tops, although the full, dark beard made it harder to tell for sure. Pretty fit too, with a lean build and broad shoulders. Dev reached over to grasp one of them and give it a gentle shake.

Dev wasn't even certain if that was what had done the trick, but a second or so later the bloke roused and blinked, life coming back into deep-blue eyes. "Sorry," he said, frowning up at Dev. "Did I . . .? Sorry."

"'S all right, mate." Dev realised he was still hanging on to the bloke's shoulder and let go in a hurry. His hand felt cold, after, and he shoved it in the pocket of his hoodie. "You okay now?"

"Yes. Thank you." His voice was clipped, like he was angry about something. "Sorry to disturb your . . . Sorry."

Dev couldn't help a laugh. "You're gonna wear that word out, mate."

For the first time—at least, that was what it felt like—the bloke focussed on Dev properly. He smiled, his lips twisting up in a mocking way that turned him from some random bloke on a bench into a guy it might be interesting to get to know. "Sorry," he said again, laying on the irony with a shovel.

"Wanker." Dev grinned, then wondered if he'd gone too far. His foster dad was a drinker, and that bastard's moods could turn on a sixpence. He took a step back without even thinking about it.

Bench bloke's smile buggered off like the bloody Cornish sun had done ever since Dev got here, and he stood up.

"Thanks for your concern," he said frostily. Then he strode off up the road without even a backward glance.

Huh. There was gratitude for you. Dev watched him stalk off for a mo, decided he probably wasn't going to fall over anytime soon, then shrugged and went back to his table.

"You're wasting your time with that one," the girl from the café told Dev as she gave him back the mug she'd just that minute put on her tray. At least, Dev hoped it was his mug she'd given him. "Don't talk to nobody, he don't. Some posh bastard from the Home Counties or God knows where, thinks he's too good for the likes of us. Only come here to drown himself in a bottle."

Dev glanced up at her sideways. "Yeah? Funny how he didn't smell of drink, then." He took a sip of his half-cold coffee and wondered why he'd bothered.

"Give 'im a good sniff, did you?" She straightened, hands on her back like Dev's foster mum had done when she was pregnant with the twins, although this girl wasn't carrying any extra weight around the middle. She wasn't carrying *any* weight around the middle. A white girl—pale white, like she hadn't seen any more sun lately than she'd seen square meals—she looked a fair bit younger close up. He could see there weren't any lines around her eyes, only dark smudges that could've been old mascara but Dev reckoned weren't. She was wearing a name badge on her Square Peg Café T-shirt that said *Ceri*.

Dev huffed out a laugh at it, and her dark eyes narrowed. "Somethin' funny?"

"Only that your mum couldn't spell neither. I'm Devan. With an *a* instead of an *o*."

"Is that Indian? Sounds Indian. And *Ceri*'s Welsh and so's my mum, on her mum's side, so she spelled it just fine, which shows how much you know."

"Make a lot in tips, do you?" All right, he hadn't meant to say that out loud.

"Bugger all. It's all tight English bastards we get here." She gave him a sharp look. "So is your mum Indian or what?"

"No." He knew that much.

"Your dad?"

Dev shrugged. Like he was going to tell someone he'd only known five minutes how his mum had given him up for adoption before he'd drawn his first breath and had never bothered to leave a single bit of info about his dad.

Christ, when was even thinking about it going to stop being like ripping off a scab?

Kerry spelled-Ceri cocked her head, not fazed by his lack of communication. "Your skin's not that dark, but your hair's more black than brown, and it's not curly like if you were African or Jamaican or summat. And you've got those big, dark eyes like a lot of Indian lads do. Nice eyelashes too. Could be. You still gonna be here in half an hour?"

Dev bristled. "Why? Not like you need the table, is it?" The place was three-quarters empty, even inside, and out here there was room for half a coachload more. Even the his 'n' hers hikers looked like they were about to bugger off.

She rolled her eyes again. "That's when I finish work. You want to get a drink or something?"

Okay, he had *not* seen that coming. Dev gave her a sharper look, taking in the tension in the way she held herself, and wondered why he hadn't noticed how brittle that hard shell of hers was till now. Wasn't like he hadn't seen that kind of thing before, was it? "Sorry, love, I don't do girls." He tried to say it gently.

Ceri scowled at him like he was something she'd scraped off the bottom of her shoe. It was weirdly reassuring. "Like you were going to be doing me, anyway. I said *get a drink*, not *make a bloody sex tape*. Or do you only bother talking to people you're hoping to shag?"

"All right, then." Dev gave her a steady look. "But I'll see you back here. I'm not numbing my arse on this seat drinking cold coffee for half an hour."

"Suit yourself. I'll see you at five. Or I won't." She swept away and started clearing the tables inside.

Dev gave his coffee a wry smile. Then he stood and left it on the table with relief.

He checked his watch as he made his way along the street, not really heading anywhere in particular. It was more like forty minutes until five o'clock—must've been a bit of wishful thinking on Ceri's part. He wasn't sure, if he was honest, why he'd agreed to go for a drink with her, seeing as he'd never had a right lot of female friends, and this one had a chip on her shoulder the size of the Severn Bridge . . . Fuck it. He knew exactly why. This way, at least he wouldn't be drinking on his own, which was all he'd reckoned he had to look forward to after Mal had bailed on him for a better offer, the tosser.

When he knew bloody well how much this trip meant to Dev. Christ. If Dev thought too much about all *that* crap, he was going to end up like that sad bastard on the bench. Dev wondered how it'd started with him—the drinking and all. If that was what it was. Still, Ceri was the local here. She ought to know if the bloke was a drunk or not.

Shame, though. Him being so fit and all.

Dev grinned at himself. Hoping for a bit of holiday romance, was he? Like that was ever going to happen. He'd checked out the local gay scene online before he came—just for something to do, because that wasn't what he was here for—and there wasn't one. Oh, plenty of places that reckoned they were "gay friendly," but that was it.

Well, that and a listing for a public toilet that was supposed to be "popular with young dudes," but that had turned out to be in Australia. Porthkennack Street, Melbourne, to be exact. Dev wondered which ex-pat had named that street in fond memory of the old place, and how horrified he'd be to see what it was famous for these days.

If he kept walking this way, Dev realised, he was going to run out of town. His feet had carried him down towards the beach and a short way along the coastal road that bordered it, sometimes closely and sometimes farther away, like it'd been laid out by a bunch of drunk navvies. A sign up ahead told him he was on the right track to get to Booby's Bay and the Round Hole—where did they even get these place names? Dev amused himself imagining a gang of old Cornish smugglers and pirates, all wearing tricorn hats and eyepatches, not to mention a parrot or two, sitting round a barrel of rum and laughing themselves silly as they marked up a map.

Of course, some of them could have been his ancestors. Dev stopped smiling. Shit. What was he even doing here?

Dev turned on his heel and started walking back the way he'd come. He was walking into the wind now, and it carried the fresh, briny scent of the ocean. It reminded him of Southend, where he'd been taken for day trips when he was little, except it was different, too. The air here smelled cleaner. Wilder. A gull screamed overhead, white boys on surf boards chased the waves in the bay, and an almost overpowering sense of *not belonging* swept over him. For a moment he was fiercely tempted to run back to the B&B, chuck his stuff in his rucksack, jump on the Hornet, and roar off home to London.

Then a trio of girls in bright, summery hijabs and jeans walked past, one of them flashing him a smile and the whole lot of them breaking into giggles a minute later, and Dev felt somehow better. Yeah. Why the hell shouldn't he be here? This place might be a lot whiter than he was used to, but it'd always had new people come in, hadn't it? Like all those Turkish sailors the tourist bumf had been on about, who'd built Cornwall's first mosque right in the centre of town.

Speaking of town . . . Dev glanced at his watch. Shit. He needed to get back, or he'd be late to meet Ceri. He quickened his pace into a half jog, dodging round families dawdling on the seafront with their ice creams.

Slowing down at the end so he wouldn't be out of breath, Dev got back to the café dead on five. It was just as well because Ceri was already waiting outside. She'd changed out of the frumpy black skirt she'd worn for work and pulled on a pair of skinny jeans that were living right up to their name and no mistake. They could've been made for a seven-year-old. Dev gave her a look. "Don't they feed you at this place?"

"Fuck off with the body-shaming. Sexist bastard. I wouldn't eat that shite we serve to the grocks. And like you've got a leg to stand on, anyhow, mister skinny fucking latte and no scones."

"Yeah, well, I hear they're shite here. What's your problem? You're off work now. Cheer up."

"I'll cheer up when you get me to that bloody pub and buy me a drink. And no, not the sodding Slug and Lettuce. That'll be full of grocks all thinking they know me from somewhere and that it gives 'em the right to grope my bum."

"You ain't got no bum to grope. So where are we going, then? And what's a grock when it's at home?"

"You are. Bloody tourists."

Dev laughed. "You're unbelievable, you know that? It's bloody tourists like me what pay your wages, remember."

"Bloody rubbish tippers, the lot of 'em."

"Maybe you should try smiling once in a while, yeah?" Dev held up his hands to ward off her poisonous look. "Oi, just a suggestion. Done it meself, ain't I? Waited on tables. Punters like service with a smile. The end of my shift, my face used to ache like I'd been deep-throating King Kong, but I made a packet in tips."

"Bet you did. Bet you got your bum groped a few times too, you with your dark eyes and all."

Dev grinned, because yeah, he had. Mostly by girls drunk off their heads at hen parties, but still.

They walked in silence for a bit, because they were going right through town and the pavements were too busy with dawdling tourists to make conversation easy. Ceri dodged round them with tight-lipped impatience, making Dev have to hurry to catch up.

It was a flipping long way to go for a drink for someone who'd been on her feet all day. It wasn't like they hadn't passed any other pubs, either. There'd been a tearoom, too, that'd looked way nicer than the Square Peg Café, and Dev thought he'd caught a glimpse of the mosque, but Ceri had dragged him onwards before he could be sure. They were right out the other side of Porthkennack now, and if they went much farther they'd end up in the sea. Maybe that was Ceri's plan. Maybe she was the local serial killer and was bringing him all this way so she could shove him off a cliff unseen.

She'd be out of luck, then. There were still plenty of tourists swarming the streets like ants at a picnic, even this far away from the main beach, and family cars idled past them as they walked down the road.

"So where are we going?" Dev asked as they rounded a sharp corner and headed down a side street. "You still ain't said."

"Here." Ceri stopped abruptly and pushed open a door.

Here, according to the flaking sign that creaked as it swung in the cooling sea breeze, was the Sea Bell, and first sight of it wasn't promising. Dev hadn't visited any of the pubs in Porthkennack yet—he'd only got here this afternoon—and he hadn't had a clear idea of what he was expecting, but this dingy place, with its threadbare carpet and walls and ceilings still tobacco-stained from before the smoking ban a decade ago was definitely not it. Didn't they *want* to catch the tourist trade?

One of his mates, Baz, had been joking last week about how it wasn't safe to go to these remote places—anything west of Middlesex being remote in his book—because they probably sacrificed newcomers to the sea gods or burned them in wicker men or something. Right now Dev could believe it. A few heads turned towards them as they walked in, then turned away again, clearly unimpressed.

Ceri didn't even seem to notice. She led the way to a corner table. "Sit down there. What're you having?"

"I'll get 'em," Dev said quickly. "You've been on your feet all day."

She looked surprised and a bit suspicious at that, but she sat down. "Vodka and Coke, then."

Dev marched up to the bar, a bit of extra swagger in his step for the benefit of those tossers giving him the evil eye. At least he got served quickly, probably because most of the other punters had been scared off by the bad vibes. "Vodka and Coke, please, mate," he said to the miserable old git behind the bar, who grunted and nodded. "Tell you what, make it two," Dev added a moment later. He'd planned on having a pint of something local to blend in a bit better, but sod it, he was paying. He didn't give a monkey's what they thought of his choice of drink.

And it saved him having to work out how the hell he was supposed to pronounce *Chough's Nest*. If it was how he thought . . . Well, he'd never been one for anything that came from *that* area, ta very much.

The barman plonked the drinks on the bar. He didn't offer ice or lemon. Dev flashed a smile he'd been told was deeply annoying and said chirpily, "I'll have ice with 'em, yeah? Cheers, mate."

Dev might have been imagining it, but he reckoned there was a glimmer of respect in the old bloke's eye as he lumbered over to get the ice.

Ceri wasn't on her phone when he got back to the table, which was weird, because that was what you *did* when you had to sit around on your own for a bit in public, wasn't it? Get onto social media sharpish. It was like holding up a sign saying *Oi, I got mates, they just ain't here right now.*

"Here you go," he said, putting the cleanest-looking glass in front of her, because he was a proper gent, he was. He sat down. "So, you come here often?"

"No." She took a sip, then blinked. "You got 'im to put ice in it."

"Yeah, but no slice. Didn't wanna push me luck. Cheers, love." He raised his glass and took a gulp, surprised to find the Coke wasn't flat and didn't taste like shite. "So how long you lived around here, then?"

"All my life."

"What, and you ain't found nowhere better to drink than this shithole?"

"Fuck off. I like it in here. Food's good too. They have a folk night, Thursdays. My grandad always used to come down with his violin."

Her mouth went sort of tight and wobbly, so Dev reckoned he'd better not ask what the old bloke was up to these days.

"Hope they have a few more punters in then. I've seen roadkill with more life in it than this place."

"What d'you expect, half past five in the afternoon? Everyone's still finishing work, aren't they?"

"S'pose." Dev took a thoughtful sip of his drink. "So are all your family from round here? Like, generations back and all that shit?"

She nodded. "Well, on my mum's dad's side. She's an Ede. Well, was. Till she married my dad."

"And that's s'posed to mean something, is it?"

"Been Edes fishing here long as anyone can remember. They're one of the old Porthkennack families."

Dev's interest picked up. "Like the Roscarrocks?"

"*No*. Nothing like those bastards."

It came out so harsh Dev stared at her in amazement. Her face was flushed.

"Why? What they done?" he asked, a prickle of unease making his drink roll uncomfortably in his stomach.

She looked down. "Nothing you'll need to worry about." She said it with a flat kind of certainty that didn't make Dev feel any better.

He was glad of the interruption when a couple of men in their thirties or so barged into the pub like they owned it, one white and one with skin darker than Dev's, both of them calling out loud greetings to people already there. The barman and the other miserable tossers who'd given Dev and Ceri the evil eye now broke into smiles and cheerful insults for the newcomers. Dev listened for a mo to their soft, rolled *r*'s and thick vowels. Ceri sounded a bit like that when she talked, but a bit different too.

"You've got a funny accent, you know that?" he said without thinking, and braced himself for the fallout. "I mean, different to that lot."

For once, Ceri didn't take offence. Dev half thought she was doing it to mess with his head. "My mum's half Welsh, like I said. And my dad's from Brizzle, and I grew up here, so."

"Brizzle?"

"*Bristol*. Don't you know anything?"

"I know you ain't winning any popularity awards with an attitude like that." Dev grinned as he said it, meaning no offence meant or taken, but her eyes flashed like warning lights and she put her glass down so hard it must've dented the table, not that you'd be able to tell.

"Yeah? What about you, then? Coming on holiday all on your lonesome, Mr. Billy-No-Mates himself?"

"Oi, I got mates." Dev shrugged. "S'posed to be here with one of 'em, ain't I? We had it all planned."

"So what happened to him?"

Dev thought about lying for a brief moment, but sod it, it wasn't like he had anything to prove to her, was it? "Got a better offer, didn't he? Fortnight in Portugal with some of the lads from work. They had a place in a villa come up, so he only had to spring for the flights."

"Wanker." She still sounded pissed off, but not at Dev any more.

He laughed. "Yeah, that's what I said. Ah, shit. Can't blame him, really. Wasn't like this trip was ever gonna be a barrel of laughs."

"Why not?"

He should have guessed she'd ask. "I just . . . got stuff to do here, that's all."

"What stuff?"

"*Stuff*, all right?" Dev huffed, exasperated. "Family stuff. Okay?"

She frowned. "You got family round here?"

"You know you ask a fuck-ton of questions, right?"

"Well, 'scuse me for making conversation." She curled her lip and nodded at his glass. "Same again? Or is that *another* question you don't want to answer?"

"Yeah. Ta. Uh, that was to the drink, right?"

Ceri rolled her eyes and stood up.

Dev was ready with a change of subject by the time she got back from the bar carrying their drinks plus a couple of packets of crisps, one of which she chucked at him when she'd got the glasses down safely onto the table. Dev caught it inches from his face and opened it up. "Cheers, love. So what's the deal with the bloke on the bench? He the town drunk?"

"Told you, didn't I? He's new. Moved into one of the old cottages up on the cliffs a couple of months ago. Dad reckons he's a drinker, and so does Mrs. Hammet, my boss, but I dunno for sure. Could all be talk." She flushed for some reason, then gave Dev a sharp look. "Why, fancy him, do you?"

"Not if he's a pisshead, I don't." Dev wasn't going to end up like his foster mum, jumping every time the front door opened on a Saturday night in case it was his foster dad coming home in a drunken rage—and then lying her teeth off about it all to Dev's case-weary social worker when she came round for a visit.

"I told you, I dunno if that's true. He's too good-looking, anyway. Well, you know. For his age. Good-looking men are bastards."

Dev laughed. "So is this you insulting my looks, or my personality? 'Cos from what you just said it's gotta be one or the other."

"You're gay. It's different."

"Trust me, it ain't that different." He chucked a handful of crisps in his mouth and crunched noisily.

She shrugged, like she didn't believe him. "So do you fancy him, or what?"

Dev almost choked on his ready salted. He washed the crisps down with a mouthful of vodka and Coke, buying time, but there didn't seem any harm in telling her. "Maybe. He's interesting, you know?"

"What's that when it's at home?"

"You know. Different." Dev shifted in his seat. "Like, not the same as all the blokes I know at home. And I reckon he's got a sense of humour."

"You could tell all that from the way he was lying on that bench, could you?"

"Shut up. Maybe I just like a bloke with a beard, all right?"

Ceri half laughed at that. "You ever think about growing a beard? I reckon it'd suit you. Even one of they bushy lumberjack ones."

"Nah, get real. Dark-skinned bloke with a full beard? All I'd have to do would be to get on the Tube with me rucksack, and someone'd be calling the cops before you could say *Daesh*."

"Yeah, there's been some of that round here and all. Muslim girls getting picked on for wearing headscarves. Not a lot, but still. It's grocks and old folks, mostly."

Dev nodded. "Tell me about it. Well, not the grocks 'cos believe it or not, we don't get a right lot of tourists round my neck of the woods. But yeah. Old folks, defs. My boss, Masood, he reckons it's a lot better now than when his mum and dad came over from Pakistan in the sixties."

"S'pose it would be, at that. What do you do, Devan-spelled-with-an-A?"

"Mechanic. Work in a garage. Do a few odd jobs on the side, you know how it is. How about you? Is the caff it for you, or is it just a summer thing?"

"It's just for the summer. Dunno what I'm gonna do come autumn. Go on benefits, most like. Or move away. Where are you from?"

"Can't you tell? South London. Got a flat in Balham. Arse end of the Northern Line."

"On your own?"

"Nah, I share with me mate, Mal."

"What, the one who's not here?"

"Yeah, that's him." Dev glared halfheartedly at his half-drunk vodka and Coke, then downed it in one. Which wasn't a good move seeing as the Coke here was well gassy. Dev belched loudly, just glad he hadn't got bubbles right up his nose.

"That's disgusting."

"Anytime, love."

Ceri looked like she was about to say something, but she turned as the street door opened and a noisy crowd of newcomers lowered the average age in the place by ten years at a stroke.

There was a mob of around half a dozen of them, all in their late teens at Dev's guess. Fresh out of their first year at uni, maybe—they had that student look about them, the lads in Jack Wills shirts and the girls with minimal makeup and unfussy hair. Not like the girls—and some of the lads—he was used to back home, all done up like pop star wannabes. Plus they had that relaxed, lazy air you got when you had three months of freedom, not the desperate overexuberance Dev was used to from his own mates, who only got two weeks off in the summer and were going to have fun if it bloody well killed them.

The uni mob were all looking right at Dev and Ceri. And not like they were pleased to see them.

CHAPTER
TWO

"Mates of yours?" Dev asked.

Ceri flushed and turned her head away. "No." Her voice had an ugly, harsh tone.

"You know, we could head off somewhere else. I ain't had me tea yet," he reminded her.

"No. We was here first, and they *never* come in here." She sounded furious that they'd dared change their routine, and now she mentioned it, Dev could see a few of the regulars sending the uni mob dark looks too. "You stay where you are. I'll get another round in."

Like Dev was going to let her go up to the bar with that lot there. "I'll get 'em," Dev said, standing up. "It's my round anyway."

"So? I got paid today."

"Yeah, but I'm on me hols, ain't I? Got money to burn. Same again, right?" He swept off without waiting for an answer and headed to the opposite end of the bar from Ceri's not-mates.

The old git had disappeared somewhere, to change a barrel or maybe to drink one, so the bar was now staffed by a middle-aged-to-elderly barmaid who looked like she'd run out of fucks to give a week ago last Tuesday. Dev wondered if she was Mrs. Old Git. It'd certainly explain why she looked so bloody fed up. Standing there trying to keep one eye on Ceri to make sure no one bothered her while simultaneously trying to catch the barmaid's attention with the other, Dev supposed he shouldn't have been surprised he didn't notice the redheaded girl sneaking up on him.

"You're new," she said right in his ear and nearly made him drop his wallet. "How long you known Ceri Harper?"

See, that sort of crap got Dev's back right up. He spun to face her. She was a pretty girl, and he reckoned she knew it, with her carefully natural makeup and her off-the-shoulder top that showcased creamy pale skin. With her red hair falling in waves over her shoulders, she looked a bit like that actress who'd played Demelza in *Poldark* (shut up, he only watched it for when Aidan Turner got his shirt off), and Dev reckoned she knew that too. Her accent wasn't right for the part, though—it was local still, but a bit on the posh side for Demelza the kitchen maid. "What's it to you, love?"

"Just here to give you a friendly warning." She smiled, and it was good. Almost as good an imitation as her French manicured fingernails and those stencilled-on eyebrows. "You want to be careful with that girl. She's not right in the head. Imagines things. You'll end up in trouble if you hang around with her."

"I can take care of myself, ta very much. And if you ask me, it ain't Ceri who's going around causing trouble." If anyone wasn't *right* around here, Dev reckoned it was this girl, with her dire warnings like she'd walked out of some gothic romance.

Demelza-like shrugged her bare shoulders. "Suit yourself. But if you ask me, a good-looking lad like you could do a *lot* better." Half-turned away, she glanced at him over her shoulder, and what got Dev then was that her expression seemed real, genuine. Concerned. "I mean it about the trouble. The bad kind. *Police* trouble. You'd better watch yourself."

Dev snorted to show her what he thought of that, and turned back to the bar because Christ, he was never going to get served at this rate. Luck was finally in, though, as the barmaid glanced his way almost immediately. Dev ordered and paid for his and Ceri's drinks, took a gulp of his own because he needed it after that, and started to make for their corner table.

It was now occupied by a trio of spotty lads sipping their pints with furtive looks and an air of triumph that said all too clearly the barmaid hadn't bothered to ask them for proof they were over eighteen, which it was also pretty clear they wouldn't have been able to provide. Dev had been there, done that. But where the hell was Ceri?

Maybe she'd nipped off to the ladies'? Except who in their right mind left a table in a quickly filling pub until they had someone to hold it for them? Dev leaned against the wall anyway and drank his vodka and Coke, feeling like a right tool, with the uni mob glancing over his way every now and then.

Ceri didn't appear. Dev started on her drink, having finished his own.

When Demelza-like put down her glass and looked like she was about to come over, Dev left.

He'd had enough drama for one night. Time to hit the chippy.

Shit.

Where exactly *was* the chippy, from here? And how the hell was he going to find his way back to his B&B without Ceri? Dev got out his phone and stared at the pitiful number of bars, trying to will the signal strong enough for him to actually use the GPS.

Like that ever worked. You'd think Cornwall was Outer flippin' Mongolia as far as his network was concerned. First thing tomorrow he was going down the tourist information place and getting a map.

CHAPTER
THREE

From his house on the cliff, Kyle gazed out at the darkening sea, its waves at this distance no more than ripples on an endless, featureless pond. The sky's sunset bloom was muted by the lowering clouds, their silver linings a lie. He waited for the sense of relaxation he usually got from the view to wash over him. Calm him.

It was slow to come tonight.

For God's sake, just when he thought he'd settled in here. Had got himself enough of a reputation that people would *leave him alone.*

Of course, he probably shouldn't have come somewhere with a continual influx of tourists, then, should he?

Like the young man from the café this afternoon.

The attack had come on suddenly—Kyle barely had time to get to the bench before he was out like a light.

He'd come round to the sound of a concerned London accent. When he'd opened his eyes, he'd half thought he was still asleep and dreaming. There'd been a young man bending over him, his brown eyes impossibly large, staring right at Kyle from only inches away. His hand had been on Kyle's shoulder, his grip firm. Warm.

He was breathtakingly handsome. Light-tan skin—genetic, not from a tanning bed or out of a bottle. Black hair, cropped aggressively short at the sides and gelled up on top. Casual clothes. Here on holiday, of course, although he didn't seem the sort to be a family man.

His face had looked somehow familiar. Not in itself, but in its lines, its features. Maybe his mixed-race ancestry included some Turkish blood, like a lot of the darker-skinned residents of the town.

Not that it was any of Kyle's business.

The young man had laughed and joked with him, as if Kyle's humiliating collapse was nothing to worry about. For a moment, it almost hadn't been. For a moment, Kyle had almost believed it was something that could be taken in stride. Just another part of him. Something to joke about.

He hadn't felt so normal, so *light* since he'd come to Cornwall. No, since he'd been diagnosed and realised he wasn't ever going to get better.

Then it had all gone wrong somehow. Something Kyle had said, something he'd done, had made the young man take a step back, his face suddenly wary. The weight had settled on Kyle's shoulders once more.

He'd left as soon as he could marshal his wretched, treacherous limbs to carry him.

The young man had had an interesting face, though. A strong jawline, almost belligerent, that was at total odds with those soft, dark eyes of his.

Kyle reached for his sketchbook and pencils almost before he knew what he was doing. He frowned, very deliberately sat down and, with a soft pencil, sketched out the scene before him, devoid of all human life.

Then he tore out the page, crumpled it, and threw it blindly at the bin behind him.

CHAPTER FOUR

Once he'd actually managed to find the place again, Dev slept all right that first night in the Spindrift B&B. If he didn't count the dreams where Bench Bloke somehow turned out to be his long-lost dad and Ceri was his *mum*, for Christ's sake, which was rich seeing as she had to be younger than he was. And everything was pink, but that was a direct result of the room. The B&B advertised itself as gay friendly, which was why he and Mal had chosen it, despite them not being actually a couple or even mates with benefits except on nights they got *really* wasted. Or lonely, or horny, or all three. Which was great, yeah, but for some reason the owners had decided that meant the whole bloody place had to look like an explosion in a Barbie factory. Dev wondered if Mrs. Quick would be offended if he started wearing his Ray-Bans indoors.

She'd dished him up an awesome cooked breakfast, described as "full Cornish" but which seemed pretty identical to a full English to Dev—there was fried egg, bacon, sausage, beans, and grilled tomato. The only difference seemed to be potato cakes instead of fried bread, and something called hog's pudding where you'd normally get a slice of black pudding nobody in their right mind would touch with a bargepole. Dev ate the lot, including the hog's pudding, which the lesbian couple from Glasgow he'd got talking to over breakfast told him tasted a lot like haggis. Dev had never had haggis, and he'd always reckoned it was one of those things everyone hated but ate because it was traditional, like Brussels sprouts at Christmas, but this stuff was actually tasty.

Huh. Maybe he'd pick up a haggis next time he saw them on offer at Tesco. Of course, he'd have to find out what neeps and tatties were if he did that, seeing as Val from Glasgow had said they were the only proper things to eat with haggis and then changed the subject before he could say, *You what?*

"And what will you be up to today?" Carol, the younger and prettier one, asked him. She was small and blond and talked a bit different from Val, like maybe she hadn't always lived in Glasgow, but Dev didn't know enough about Scottish accents to tell for sure. "Will you be doing a wee bit of surfing?"

Dev patted his belly with a grimace. "After eating this lot? I'd flippin' sink. Probably cause a bloody tsunami on me way down and all. Nah, thought I'd take a wander up to Big Guns Cove and have a look around. What about you two?"

Carol glanced at Val and smiled. "We'll be paying a visit to the Round Hole and the castle up on Caerdu Head. It's steeped in Arthurian legend there, you know."

Val snorted into her tea, although she somehow managed to make it sound fond. "Black knights and sea serpents, I ask you. When you know full well that castle was nae built till long after Arthur's time. You stop your havering, and we'd best be away now, or we'll not get anywhere. You have a good day, laddie, and we'll see you tonight."

Dev watched them go off smiling and hand in hand, and felt a bit melancholy for some reason. Of course, he was disappointed he hadn't got to hear more about the black knights and sea serpents. Had they meant, like, *black* knights, meaning Turks or Saracens or whatever the fuck they'd called them in those days, or was it just a saying, like they'd had black hair or black flags or black hearts or something? And sea serpents were well cool, obviously.

Dev had half a mind to run after Val and Carol, say he'd go with them—except what kind of a git barged in on someone else's couple time? No, he'd stick to his—hah—Big Guns and head off in the opposite direction.

At least he'd feel he was getting somewhere. Sort of.

First, though, Dev decided as he headed down the drive of the B&B, he was hitting the Square Peg Café. Not for another shite cup of coffee. To find out what was going on with Ceri. It'd make the round trip far enough to think about taking the bike—but sod it, it'd only be a couple of miles or so. And he really needed to walk off that breakfast. His jeans were tight enough already.

As he made his way through the town, Dev could hear church bells ringing, although they sounded a fair way off. For some reason, he'd forgotten it was a Sunday. Funny that. Second day of his hols and he'd already lost track of what day it was. That'd be St. Ia's, then—the tourist info had mentioned that as one of the attractions. Maybe he'd find out where it was and pop in sometime, but not today. Dev wondered how he was supposed to pronounce it. Saint Eye-yah? Saint Ear? Why did they have to have all different saints around here anyhow? Most of the churches he knew back home were called Balham (Insert Denomination of Choice) Church, but even the sainted ones had names you recognised and knew how to say, like St. Mary or St. Anselm. He'd never even heard of a St. Ia, and he wasn't *that* unreligious. Okay, so he never went to church except when someone he knew was getting hitched or had popped a sprog and was getting it christened, but he'd done years of RE in school.

Then again, he had failed his GCSE. Mostly due to arsing about during lessons, which had been a bit of a feature of his school career if he was honest. He hadn't really got his head screwed on straight until he'd left the place and started at college, where they'd actually treated him like an adult, not a really dim, annoying toddler they'd be glad to see the back of.

Ceri was back in her frumpy skirt at the Square Peg Café, dishing out coffees with a surly grunt before moving on to clearing tables.

Dev marched straight up to her. "Oi, what was that all about?"

"What?" Ceri didn't even look at him. She just carried on stacking plates. Badly.

Dev picked up a knife that'd skittered off a plate and onto the ground, and handed it to her. By the jam-smeared blade, because he was a gent like that. "You. Blowing me off last night." He licked strawberry-flavoured sticky stuff off his fingers, and tried to ignore the sniggering coming from a couple of twin lads aged about twelve sitting round a table with Mum and Dad.

He briefly thought about explaining he hadn't meant *blowing me off* in the sex sense, but decided it'd probably make them snigger even worse. Then he saw what they were eating and did a double take.

Seriously? Dev liked a clotted cream tea as much as the next Brit, but not at ten o'clock in the flipping morning.

No wonder Ceri didn't think much of tourists.

"Didn't think you'd want me around no more, did I?" Ceri muttered. "After what *she* said to you."

"Yeah, well, whoever she is, she can go . . . stuff herself." Dev glanced guiltily at the kids, which nearly made them piss themselves. Dad carried on stuffing *him*self with his over-laden scone, oblivious, while Mum heaved a pointed sigh. Dev looked away again quickly. "You off at five again, yeah? I'll see you then, all right."

"Want to hear my side of the story, do you?"

"No. Far as I'm concerned, there ain't no story. Just some ginger bi—bit of fluff stirring up sh—stuff, that's all. I'll see you later. And oi, smile a bit, yeah? I want two bags of crisps tonight."

She did smile at that, so yeah, job done. Dev strolled off to reward himself with a cup of coffee from somewhere decent.

Not that he actually deserved a reward, seeing as he hadn't done the first bloody thing about the whole reason he'd come here yet. But, well. He had three weeks, didn't he? Plenty of time. And, yeah, this was his holiday, wasn't it? Only one he'd be getting all summer. So he deserved a bit of relaxation, right? It'd put him in a better frame of mind for . . . stuff.

Dev found a place near the tourist information office that served him a proper Turkish coffee, thick as used engine oil but way tastier. Trouble was, all that caffeine left him keyed up and jumpy as he walked out of town on what he later realised, looking at the map the lady at the tourist information place had given him, was the wrong path. He'd come down the same way, he reckoned, that Ceri had taken him to the Sea Bell last night, but before he got as far as the pub there was a fork off to the right leading back the way he wanted to go. Dev took it, and a few minutes later found himself looking across a broad, sandy cove.

There was a lifeboat station with a weird, curved roof directly below him, which according to the map made this Mother Ivey's Bay. The sea stretched out forever in front of him. Under the clear skies—so different from yesterday Dev wouldn't have believed it—the water was a rich, deep blue it hurt to gaze at. Salt-laden air ruffled his hair, which he hadn't bothered to gel, and drenched his lungs, so fresh it made his chest catch.

The beach looked better than Dev could ever have imagined for somewhere in Britain. If the weather kept shaping up warm, he was going to be back here later with his trunks on. There was a broad stretch of golden sand on which a few families had already staked their claims, loomed over by dark, craggy cliffs. There wasn't anyone in the water yet, except a couple of toddlers paddling with their dad at the water's edge, shrieking and running as the waves broke gently on their little legs.

Dev wandered along the narrow road that hugged the contours of the cliffs, its edges bordered by scraggy little bushes that might have been gorse or heather or something. He wasn't all that good on plants, all right? The beach ducked in and out of sight with the bends in the road, but the view was never less than seriously awesome.

He'd heard places described as "unspoilt" before, but he'd never really got what it meant until he saw this cove. All right, so up top where he was right now, there was a road and a car park and stuff—a few odd shops and a pottery, it looked like—but down on the beach there was nothing except what nature had bunged down there. No public lavs, no kiosks, not even anyone hiring out pedalos or windsurfers.

Dev was used to a beach being somewhere you went to muck about and have a laugh with your mates, or sleep off your hangover after clubbing all night. This place, though . . . It was about as different from Magaluf as, well, Porthkennack was from Balham.

And maybe this place really was in his blood, because for a moment the thought of going back home to the dirt and the smells and the endless, soulless brick, concrete, and tarmac of London seemed almost unbearable. Even the cries of the gulls overhead seemed less earsplitting today, more just part of the scenery.

Then one of them shat on his bare arm, the droopy-beaked bastard.

Christ, that was gross. And he had sod all to wipe it up with. Fucking *marvellous*. Dev glanced around—any mums up here with young kiddies? A baby wipe would be magic right now, ta very much.

No such luck. They were all either on the beach already or still in their holiday homes spooning goo into tiny mouths. Dev did see someone up on the cliff with him, though. Was it . . .? He blinked. Yeah, it was him all right.

Bench Bloke. The drunk from yesterday. He was standing on the cliff a hundred yards or so ahead, round past the end of the beach where the cliffs climbed up to the Big Guns place. And he was too bloody close to the edge for Dev's liking. For Christ's sake, there was a warning sign and everything.

Of course, if you were planning to jump . . .

Ah, sod it. Dev looked at his arm. The bird shit was already starting to dry in the sun. He crouched down, wiped it off quickly and ineffectively on one of the least scratchy-looking bushes, and jogged on over to Bench Bloke. With all this good karma Dev was storing up, he was going to come back as a bloody billionaire in the next life.

"All right, mate?" he called out.

The sea-blue eyes seemed a lot more alert today as they swung round to focus on him. A frown formed a crease between them. "You're . . . from yesterday. In town."

He didn't look like an alcoholic. He didn't have the bloodshot eyes, the reddened complexion, and the broken veins Dev remembered from Mal's uncle. He just looked tired. He'd trimmed his beard since yesterday. Dev was relieved to see it. He couldn't be that far gone if he'd bothered to get out the trimmers. Anyway, the more groomed vibe suited him, and weirdly, didn't make him seem any less at home here on the wild, craggy clifftop.

"Uh, yeah. Listen, mate, you wanna step back from the edge a bit? I'm getting vertigo just looking at you."

"Worried I'll fall?" He sounded bitter.

"No, I'm worried the sea spray's gonna mess up your hair." It came out a bit sharper than Dev meant it to. "Course I'm bloody worried you're gonna fall," he added in a softer tone, then ruined it all by adding an automatic, "you tosser," on the end.

Shit. Then again, maybe not, because the bloke actually smiled at that, the half smile Dev remembered from yesterday.

Then he stepped away from the edge, thank Christ. "Happy now?"

"Over the fucking moon." Dev had meant it to sound sarcastic, but it came out mostly relieved. "I'm Dev," he added quickly before the bloke could pick him up on it. "From London. Here for a few weeks. You?"

The bloke blinked, like he hadn't been expecting conversation. "Kyle," he said at last. "From Epsom in Surrey, although I live here now."

Dev nodded, then realised that'd look a bit odd. "Yeah. I heard."

Aaand there went the smile. Fizzled out like a ciggie in a urinal, and Dev had been the one who'd chucked it there. Bugger it. "Heard a lot about me, have you?" If Dev had thought Kyle sounded bitter earlier, his tone now could curdle clotted cream.

Dev forced a cheeky smile. "Yeah, mate. Didn't you know? You got your own page on the Tourist Info website."

Result. The smile was back. Except it was a bit more twisted than Dev would've liked. "On display for a limited time only: the incredible collapsing man."

"Hey, we all got our problems. Listen, do you wanna go for a—" Dev broke off. Shit, had he really been about to offer an alcy a *drink*? He stared at Kyle, appalled. "Shit, sorry, no, course not—"

Kyle stared back for a mo, eyes wide—then, which was weird as fuck, burst out laughing.

And fell over.

CHAPTER FIVE

hat.
The actual.
Fuck?

Dev was too shocked to even catch him on the way down.

Kyle had just sort of crumpled from the knees, exactly like a puppet with its strings cut, which Dev knew for a fact because he'd had to take his foster sister, Tasha, to a kiddies' party once, and they'd had a puppet show there, and it had been boring as fuck until the villain puppet actually got out a big pair of scissors somehow and cut the strings on the hero puppet and half the kiddies started crying, and Christ, why was he remembering that *now* instead of doing something useful?

Dev shook himself and dropped to his knees beside Kyle. Recovery position, right? Kyle was pretty much in that already, the way he'd fallen. Maybe he'd had a lot of practice. Falling. Shit. Focus. Was he breathing? Dev bent close, and he'd have sworn on his life there wasn't a hint of alcohol on Kyle's breath, which seemed to be coming just fine, thank God. Was he epileptic? Christ, was he likely to swallow his tongue? Dev pulled down Kyle's slack jaw, hoping he wasn't, like, tearing muscles or dislocating joints or anything. Kyle's tongue was exactly where it ought to be.

Right.

Sitting back on his heels, Dev took a deep breath and pulled his phone out of his pocket to call 999—but even as he did, Kyle blinked and stirred.

"Mate," Dev said with feeling. "You all right? You nearly gave me a bloody heart attack. Shit—did *you* just have a heart attack?"

Kyle swallowed, struggling up to a sitting position on the grass. He shook off Dev's offered hand and said something that came out way too garbled for Dev to make out. He closed his eyes for a long moment, rubbed his jaw, then tried again. "I'm fine."

Christ, he sounded tired. "You're fine? Does that word mean something different around here? 'Cos last time I looked, *fine* didn't include collapsing on the bloody ground with no warning." Ice flooded Dev's veins. "Shit, if you'd still been standing on the edge . . ."

"I'd have . . . I'm *fine.*" Kyle's voice was angry. Frustrated.

"So what was it?"

"Haven't you heard?" Kyle made the same drinking-up gesture Ceri had made yesterday.

"No. No way." Dev shook his head slowly for emphasis. "Mate, I've seen falling-down drunk—fuck it, I've *been* falling-down drunk—and that is *not* what this looks like. So what is it? Epilepsy?"

Again the eyes closed, like Kyle wanted the world to go away. Or maybe just Dev. "Cataplexy," he said at last.

"What?"

"I have narcolepsy with cataplexy. I fall asleep at odd times during the day. And sometimes I just fall." Kyle spat out the words like foul bits of gristle from a cut-price supermarket's value-brand pack of sausages.

"Shit. You know, you oughtta have one of those medical bracelets or something."

Dev trailed off as Kyle held up one hand. On his wrist was a chunky black leather band Dev vaguely remembered noticing yesterday. He'd thought it was a fashion statement. It had a stainless steel plate engraved with a symbol of . . . Dev frowned. "A pole-dancing snake? What's that mean when it's at home?"

"It's the Rod of Asclepius." He pronounced the weird word with annoying precision. "The international medical symbol. The information's on the other side."

"Huh? What's wrong with the flippin' red cross? Everyone knows what that means. And, mate, I hate to be the one to break it to you, but *that* symbol could get seriously misinterpreted in certain company." Like Dev's, for instance. First sight, he'd thought it looked well gay.

Kyle stood up smoothly, although he swayed a bit when he got there. "You can go now. It won't happen again. And my house is just up there." He nodded to a row of bright-white cottages along the cliff, far enough back from the edge that at least *they* didn't look in any danger of toppling over.

"Yeah? You got anyone there?"

"No. But I'll be fine."

"You sure? You want me to call a doctor? Your family?"

"There'd be little point. They're in Australia." Kyle started walking towards the path that led up to the cottages.

Dev fell into step beside him. "*All* of 'em?"

"My parents. My sister and her family. I said you can go. I'm fine."

Dev ignored the last bit. "You don't sound Australian." Not to be suspicious or anything, but he wasn't sure the bloke wasn't pissing him about.

There was an impatient *huff.* "My sister moved out for work, taking her family with her. Mum and Dad moved out there to be near them. Satisfied?"

"What, they moved halfway round the world with you ill and all? Jesus."

"I hadn't been diagnosed when they went out there. Not that it's any of your business."

Shit. "And they never came back when you got ill?"

"They don't *know* I'm ill."

Dev actually stopped walking and turned to stare at him. "You haven't *told* them? Your own mum and dad? Are you serious?"

Kyle took a mo to answer, seeming to struggle with his temper. "They don't need to know."

"*Don't need to know*? Are you fucking serious? Jesus, you got this illness that makes you fall over all the bloody time, you live on your own, and you've moved somewhere you don't know anyone, and you're saying, what, you don't need your family?"

Christ. Families were *wasted* on some people.

"What the hell is your problem?" Kyle was breathing hard, fists clenched by his sides. Dev took a step back in case the guy decided to throw a punch. They were pretty evenly matched, weight wise, but Kyle was a couple of inches taller so he had the reach. And yeah, definitely some anger issues. "You think because my life is ruined, I should ruin everyone else's too? Is that the kind of selfish thing *you'd* do?"

Okay, so maybe Dev had some anger issues of his own. At least, *now* he did. He balled his fists and stepped back up in Kyle's face. "What, like hanging around on cliff edges until you manage to fall over and kill yourself ain't gonna ruin their lives anyway? You wanna talk about fucking *selfish*? What about the poor bastards who have to scrape your body off the rocks and stuff it in a coffin for your mum to cry over, eh?"

"That's not . . ." Kyle stared at him, openmouthed. Then he looked away, his face screwed up. "I'm not suicidal," he said at last.

"Bollocks. What was all that pissing about on the edge, then?"

"I was safe. No, listen—the attacks don't come without warning. Usually. When I fell down just now it was different . . ." Dev's face probably showed what he thought of that, as Kyle spun away with an angry gesture. "I'm not explaining this well. Just now . . . It was because you made me laugh."

"You're shitting me."

"Trust me. Narcolepsy is one thing I *never* joke about. Unlike the rest of the world." God, he sounded bitter.

And yeah, Dev could remember when Tasha had been into that Shrek movie where all Sleeping Beauty did was have nap attacks all over the shop. And there was that old film with the bloke who did *Mr. Bean*—Christ, what was it called? *Rat Race*, that was it—where he'd done the same.

It'd seemed pretty funny at the time. Although maybe not to anyone who actually suffered from that sort of thing. "Fucking hell."

"Yes. It is." Kyle's words were clipped, but Christ, there was plenty of feeling behind them.

He strode off again.

"Hey, that's the way I'm going," Dev said, half jogging to catch up with him, only partly to annoy the git. The cottages were on the way to the Big Guns place, after all. "I'll walk with you."

"Suit yourself."

They strode on in silence a few paces, and Dev started to feel a bit bad about it all. Here the poor bastard was, dealing with really shitty health issues, and Dev had gone and got all up in his face about it.

"So, you lived here long?" he asked, even though he already knew the answer from Ceri.

"A couple of months." He side-eyed Dev. "As you seem to know already."

"Uh, yeah, might have heard something..." Dev rubbed the back of his neck. "They didn't say much, though. Just that you're new round here. Where are you from, then? No, wait, you told me that. Surrey, yeah? Bit different round here, innit?" Not that Dev had a fucking clue, apart from being fairly sure Surrey didn't have any coastline. Wait—he'd been to Guildford once. That was in Surrey. Of course, he couldn't exactly remember a right lot about it, mind, seeing as it'd been a mate's stag weekend.

"Yes."

"I'm from Balham, me. South London. It's a bit shit, but it's home, you know? I'm here on holiday. Got a few weeks off, thought I'd grab some fresh air and all that bollocks. Ain't never been to Cornwall before, but it's all right."

Kyle didn't say anything, but his shoulders had relaxed. Dev snuck a glance at the man's face. With the beard and all, even neatly trimmed, he had a sort of wild look. Like he belonged out here, with the cliffs and the sea and all that dodgy history of smugglers and wreckers.

It was a bit of a turn-on, if he was honest.

"So which one of these houses is yours?" Dev asked. "Hey, why'd they build them up on the cliffs like that? Weren't they worried about, you know, erosion and stuff? I've seen that on the telly—houses falling in the sea and all."

"Apparently not. Which they clearly didn't need to be, given that the houses are still standing centuries later. And mine is the farthest one. The Zelley cottage."

Wow, actual extra info he hadn't had to push for. "Zelley the bloke what built it, was he?"

"No. He just bought it."

"So why'd it get named after him?"

Kyle huffed again, but Dev could almost swear it was less pissed off and more fondly exasperated than last time. "There's this thing called the internet, you know. You can look up all kinds of information on it."

"Yeah, but reading history's dead boring, innit? Much more fun hearing someone's take on it. So go on, tell me about this Zelley bloke."

"He was an artist."

"Yeah? What did he paint, then? Naked women with wobbly bits?"

That almost got him a laugh, there. Then again, given what'd happened last time Kyle had laughed, maybe it was a good thing the bloke was such a moody git. "Landscapes, mostly. Some portraits. And we're here now." There was a clear subtext of *so you can piss off and stop asking me all these bloody questions.*

The Zelley house was what Dev was already coming to think of as traditional Cornish style: whitewashed walls and a grey slate roof. So it wasn't a proper cottage, was it? Because those were supposed to have thatched roofs. Dev hadn't seen a right lot of cottages in his time, but he knew that much. It didn't have roses round the door, either, but there was a small, overgrown garden in front, with a riot of bushes and flowers of different colours that filled the air with scent and had Britain's last remaining bees buzzing around them.

And this was where they were going to part company.

"Wanna ask me in for a coffee?" Dev blurted out. "Always wanted to see an artist's cottage. They have, like, good light, innit?"

Fuck him, what the hell *was* all this shite coming out of his mouth?

Kyle stared at him. "You're . . . I'm not interested in anything," he said at last.

Jesus. That was a slap in the face and no mistake. How had the bloke known Dev was even gay? He wasn't obvious. Was he? Maybe it was the earring? Maybe round here it meant something it didn't mean in London? No, even places like this, blokes wore jewellery. Probably. "Uh, right. No problems, bruv. I ain't gonna come on to you or nothing." Dev backed off a step, holding his hands up.

"I didn't mean . . . It's not a problem. But I'm not . . ."

"Interested. I got it." Christ, he *got* it, all right? No need to keep banging on about it. "Fair 'nuff. Just, I'm here on me own, thought it'd be cool to hang out for a bit, that's all. I didn't come here looking for a bloke."

Of course, he wouldn't say no if one happened along for the duration. Say, a bit taller than him, with a beard and mysterious blue eyes that gazed out to sea like they were witnessing the end of the world . . .

"What are you looking for?"

Dev had the daftest urge to actually tell him the truth. "Cup of coffee and a history lesson," he said instead, because Kyle had his own problems. No way would he want to hear about Dev's. "Unless you've told me all the good bits already. Then I'll just take the coffee."

Kyle was staring again. "Why?"

Someone, somewhere must've really done a number on him if he couldn't imagine why anyone would want to spend an hour or so in his company. Dev felt a surge of sympathy for the poor bastard. Of course, telling the bloke *that* would get him the cold shoulder again faster than he could say *fuck off, I don't need your pity*. Inspiration hit. "I got told off, didn't I? By this girl I met yesterday. For only talking to people so I could get 'em into bed. So this is me proving I'm not like that, all right?" The logic seemed a lot shakier out loud than it had in his head and from Kyle's look, he probably agreed. Plus Dev had probably made it sound like he was bi, which he wasn't.

Ah, sod it. Dev thought he'd better change tack, and went for the sympathy vote. "'Sides, I'm all on me own here, like I said. Me mate couldn't make it. You really gonna leave me with no one to talk to for three weeks straight? I'll go loopy. Start seeing mermaids and chatting up the seagulls and stuff."

Kyle drew in a deep breath, then let it out again. "Fine. But I've only got decaffeinated."

Dev grinned, because as last-ditch attempts to put him off went, it was pretty feeble. And he could be philosophical about decaff. Yeah, it'd taste like shite, but it wouldn't give him the jitters, which after that wicked strong Turkish coffee was a serious risk if he had any more caffeine in a hurry. "Lead on then, mate. And go on, give us the guided tour."

The front door was at the side of the building, around the corner from a slate plaque that proclaimed the place to be *Mother Ivey's Boudoir*, not Zelley House at all. "Bit racy, that," Dev commented. "So who was Mother Ivey to old Zelley? His bit of stuff?"

"No. His alter ego. She was a nineteenth-century drag queen."

"Shut *up*." Dev was fucking delighted. "I didn't know they even had 'em in them days."

"Thought gay culture was invented in the twenty-first century, did you?" Kyle sounded amused.

"No, but seriously . . . they had laws back then, didn't they? Two years hard labour just for having a limp handshake and a lisp." One of Dev's ex's had been mad keen on Oscar Wilde. They'd seen the film several zillion times, until Dev had started having disturbing dreams about Stephen Fry with floppy hair, and put his foot down.

"It's surprising what you could get away with, provided you did it on a stage in front of a paying audience. This is the living room."

It was pretty bleeding obvious what it was, seeing as the front door opened directly onto it and it had comfy chairs, a stone fireplace, and a smaller-than-average telly. Plenty of space, though, as it stretched the entire depth of the house, and the large windows opposite him had a seriously awesome view of the bay. They faced due north, Dev reckoned, which meant the room wouldn't overheat in the summer. Could be bitter in the winter, though, with the wind blowing straight off the Atlantic.

He wandered past mismatched armchairs to squint out of the nearest window. "This place must've set you back a fair bit."

"I'm renting." Kyle gave Dev a sidelong look. "If you're casing the joint, I regret to tell you most of my valuables are back in Epsom."

Dev flipped him a finger. "Tosser. So how long are you planning to stay? Just for the summer?"

There was a pause. "I haven't made plans. There's an option to buy on the place. The dining room's through the far door."

Huh. "You know, you can tell me stuff. I ain't gonna take it down and use it in evidence against you." Dev kept his tone light, moving into the dining room as he spoke to show willing.

Then he sort of wished he hadn't said it. Went two ways, that sort of thing, didn't it? It'd serve him bloody well right if Kyle started grilling him on why he'd come here.

"What did you do, back in Surrey?" he asked, because jobs were always safe ground.

"I was a barrister."

The flat tone, with a slight emphasis on the *was*, told Dev he'd better rethink his position on jobs never being a minefield.

"You like the place?" Kyle asked, like maybe he'd realised he wasn't exactly being chatty. "The furniture came with the house, but I think it suits it."

"Yeah, it's cool. Homey, you know?" Dev flashed him a smile, but Kyle looked away.

The dining room was a lot like the living room—it wasn't as wide, but it still stretched the whole depth of the house and looked like it'd been put together by a real person going to shops and buying stuff they liked, not from a furniture catalogue or the Ideal bloody Home Show. There was a pine table and chairs, but the cupboards and sideboard were all different shades of wood. The open staircase leading to the next floor was pine, again, but a deeper shade than the furniture. An actual real oil painting on the wall—Dev could see the splodges and everything—showed what could only be a Cornish fishing village, its squat, rough-looking men setting out to sea in old-fashioned boats while white-aproned women, who were also a bit on the squat and rough-looking side, watched them go, probably wondering if this was the trip that'd widow them.

"That's Porthkennack how it used to be, right?" Dev asked.

"An artist's impression of it, anyhow. The painting's modern—not a Zelley."

"Yeah? Too bad. Won't bother nicking it, then. Well into their gender roles back then, weren't they?"

Kyle gave an intriguing little smile. "Not all of them. Mother Ivey, remember? Coffee?" He paused, his posture stiff for some reason. "It's getting on for lunchtime. I could knock you up a sandwich?"

"Nah, I'm good. Ate a whole bloody farmyard for breakfast. You go ahead, though, yeah? Seriously, mate." If a bloke had a habit of keeling over anyhow, adding low blood sugar into the mix probably wasn't the best idea. Maybe narcolepsy was like diabetes, and he *had* to eat at certain times?

Dev reckoned he'd guessed right when Kyle's shoulders visibly relaxed. "Come through, then," Kyle said, leading the way to the door at the other end of the dining room.

The kitchen was pretty small, probably built in the days when no one had fridges or dishwashers or washing machines. Christ, how had they even *lived*? Dev leaned on a counter while Kyle switched on the kettle and started putting together a couple of cheese and pickle sarnies. Dev liked that he was getting on with his lunch even though Dev wasn't eating—like you would with a mate, not just a guest.

There was a mug tree on the counter, so Dev grabbed a couple of mugs and set them by the kettle to show willing. They were solid, chunky, earth-coloured things with a stylised fish carved into the surface and a dribbly glaze that looked deliberately random, not the plain blue-and-white-striped stuff he'd seen in gift shops in town. "These from the local pottery?" he hazarded.

Kyle's pause made him look up.

"I made them. Back in Epsom," Kyle said in the end.

Dev's eyebrows shot up before he could stop them. "You never. Thought you were a barrister, not a potter."

"I'm not either, these days."

"How come? I mean, yeah, I get the barrister thing—no one wants a lawyer who's always kipping in court—but you could do the pottery thing, couldn't you?" He thought about it. "S'pose it could get a bit painful if you face-plant on the wheel, but you reckoned you get warning, didn't you? And these are dead good. I mean, people'd buy 'em and everything."

Kyle gave him a funny look. He'd finished making the sandwiches and now cut them both into quarters diagonally, posh café style. "Are you some kind of counsellor? Social worker?"

"Fuck *off*," Dev said fervently. "Why'd you say that?"

"You seem unusually good at listening. And…making suggestions. All right—police, then?"

"Fuck off and *die*. Nah, mate. I'm a motor mechanic."

Kyle seemed amused, though fuck knew why. "Handy profession to be in," was all he said, though.

"You're not wrong, mate. Way I see it, anywhere you go, people are always gonna want their cars, right? And I was never gonna get some job where I had to ponce around in a suit." A thought hit him. "Oi, barristers, right? They still wear those naff little wigs like on the telly? That'd put me right off." Dev shrugged, and added honestly, "Well, that and all the studying. Do my head in, that would."

"Actually a lot of barristers like the *naff little wigs*. It makes them less recognisable on the street." Kyle sounded distracted as he spooned coffee into the mugs from a jar that managed to look expensive even though the coffee inside was just instant, and poured on the hot water.

"Huh." Dev had never really given a thought to barristing, or whatever the fuck you called it, being a potentially dangerous occupation. But yeah, if you sent someone down for twenty years or whatever, chances were his mates weren't going to be happy. "You ever get beaten up for putting someone in jail?"

"No, but a friend had her wig vandalised once."

Dev laughed. "Seriously?"

"Seriously." Kyle's tone was trying to be solemn, but his face wasn't having any of that shit. "Some people see the wigs as a symbol of the dignity of the profession. Although I think some of my older male colleagues just appreciate having hair again," he added drily. "Milk?"

"Yeah. Ta. No sugar." Some blokes, when you looked at them, you could easily picture them bald. Kyle, though? Dev couldn't imagine that thick, dark hair even thinning. He could see it with a daft white wig on top, though, the black beard below making it look even more unreal. He looked away to cover his smile. "We going back through?"

Kyle nodded, and Dev carried the mugs back into the dining room. Like the living room, it had a large window with a fucking epic view of the bay. Dev couldn't imagine actually *living* anywhere like this. It was, like, sea views were for holidays. Not for real life. He made sure he took the seat with the best view, the sun not in his eyes or anything. Kyle could look out at this shit *every day*.

Kyle made it through to join him without keeling over and dropping his sarnies, which was a relief. Grated cheese would've got *everywhere*. "How often do you get those attacks, anyway?" Dev asked, then realised it was a bit personal. "Shit. No, forget that. None of my business."

"It depends," Kyle said after a long pause. "So where are you staying?"

Yeah, Dev could take a hint if you bashed him over the head with it. "B&B on the edge of town. It's nice. The landlady makes a wicked breakfast, which is why I ain't helping you out with those sandwiches."

"No? I made extra in case."

"Sorry, mate, they're all yours." Despite how good they smelled. "So how do you like it here? Got to know a lot of people?"

Kyle looked out to sea. "Not really," he said after a long while. "Although apparently I've been around enough to get a reputation." The bitterness was back.

"Uh, yeah. You know, you oughtta tell people you ain't an alcy. What if, like, you really need help some day and no one bothers 'cos they think you're drunk?" Like that time Tasha had a hypo while she was in the pub, and none of the useless twats she was with even noticed.

"I don't want their pity. Or yours," Kyle added, though he didn't seem quite so certain on that one.

"It ain't pity, mate," Dev said earnestly, leaning forward. "It's, like . . ." Shit. What *was* it like, except that Dev liked the bloke and yeah, felt sorry for him having to deal with this shit? Kyle had already made it pretty bloody clear he didn't want anything to do with either of those reasons. "We're both new around here, yeah? And we're both on our own. We oughtta stick together."

Kyle gave another crooked smile. "The two of us, united against the Kernewek?"

"The what now?" Dev's eyebrows were getting a right workout today.

"It's Cornish. Meaning *Cornish*."

"Yeah? That's like Welsh, innit? I mean, I seen signs up in town and it looks sort of the same. Lots of *y*'s and stuff. I've been to Wales. We had a school trip." Dev's case worker had buggered up the forms to get the council to pay for it, but his geography teacher had found funding somehow. He'd got really good marks in geography that year, but the following year she'd left to go back to Scotland and he'd failed all his exams.

Dev found he'd absentmindedly picked up a sandwich and taken a bite. Huh. Maybe he wasn't all that full from breakfast anymore, after all. It was good too. Decent quality Cheddar, and bread that tasted like it came from a baker's, not a supermarket. He took another bite.

Kyle was nodding. "They have a common root. They're not as similar as they might look, though."

It was times like this Dev wished he'd paid a bit more attention in school. "Can you speak Cornish?"

"No. I only know a few words."

Dev swallowed his mouthful. "Yeah? Go on. Say something." He grinned at Kyle's trapped expression. "Go on. Anything."

Kyle glanced out the window again, as if he hoped someone might be doing a fly-past trailing a big banner with Cornish phrases on it. For all Dev knew, maybe they did sometimes. "All right, here goes, but I warn you, my accent is probably atrocious. *Bràmm an gàth.*"

"Meaning?"

"Cat's fart."

Dev burst out laughing. "Shut *up*! Why'd you wanna learn *that*?"

Kyle looked amused, if a bit sheepish. "The website said it was an authentic Cornish curse."

"What, particularly smelly round here, are they? Must be feeding 'em too much seafood. Mind you, my mate Baz's farts are well rank, and he can't stand fish. So are you doing, like, evening classes in Cornish or something?"

Kyle shook his head. "Just online."

"Yeah? Don't they do classes round here, then? That ain't right. It's important, innit? Heritage and all that." Stuff like that shouldn't get forgotten.

"They do. They run courses at the Institute of Cornish Culture in town. But it didn't seem worth signing up for them," Kyle said, gazing out to sea. "I'd probably miss most of them anyway."

That didn't seem right, either. Was his . . . what, illness? Condition? Was it really as bad as all that? Not that Dev had a fucking clue. He took a gulp of his coffee, surprised how cold it'd got. How long had they been yakking away here? It was time he was getting on, really. Between them, they'd finished all the sandwiches. He put down his mug.

Hesitated.

Now it came down to it, he didn't want to go. He liked Kyle, despite the darkness about him. Maybe because of it. Like eating really posh dark chocolate that was never sweet like proper stuff made by

Cadbury's or whatever. First bite, you didn't like it, but after a while you got to appreciate the bitterness and the dryness of it, and if you went back to the normal stuff it tasted sugary and bland.

Of course, maybe he was missing a trick here anyway. "You ever have anything to do with them over at the big house?"

"The big house?"

"You know. Roscarrock House, up on Big Guns Whatsit up the hill."

"Why do you ask?"

Dev gave him a look. "There's this thing called conversation, see? People use it to find out stuff about each other." He laughed out loud when Kyle, straight-faced, gave him the finger for that.

Then he broke into a smile, and Dev cringed.

"Shit, I'm not gonna make you pass out again, am I?" He had got to remember to be more careful about making jokes.

"I didn't pass out. I fell over. And *no*." Kyle seemed to think about it a bit. "Probably not."

"Good." Dev took a deep breath. "So do you? Have anything to do with them?" Dev wiped his hands on his jeans. It was stupid, getting so worked up over just asking a bloody question, but apparently his body hadn't got the memo.

"The Roscarrocks? Not so far, no." Kyle stared down at his mug for a moment, then looked up at Dev. "There is a connection, though. Well, sort of. I suppose that's why I came here, rather than anywhere else. You see, my mother's family were from around here, originally. Until they moved away, sometime in the nineteenth century. Which was quite unusual for those days, of course. People didn't move around nearly so much as they do now. Unless they had good reason."

Dev suddenly knew what it must feel like to be a car that'd just had its air con recharged and switched on at full blast. "So what's that got to do with the Roscarrocks?" It sounded a bit off even to Dev. Too sharp.

Kyle frowned, so apparently he'd noticed too. "Oh, it's nothing. There's always been a family legend about a link. A bit of a joke, really. Supposedly one of my forebears was a Roscarrock bastard."

Dev's chair scraped queasily on the tiled floor, and he found himself on his feet before he'd even thought about it. What were the odds? What were the *fucking* odds? This was bollocks, this was. "Listen, mate, I'm gonna tell you this once, okay? Don't mess with me. Do *not* fucking mess with me. Shit." He ran a shaky hand through his hair. "I gotta . . ."

He had to get out. Right now.

Kyle didn't try to stop him. Dev was out of the house and stomping back down the cliff path before his head had even cleared.

CHAPTER SIX

Kyle stared after Dev in shocked bewilderment. What the hell had he done *this* time?

He played the conversation back in his mind as best he could and still utterly failed to account for Dev's behaviour. What had he *said*?

Should he go after Dev? Apologise? He stared at the picture on the wall, irresolute.

Kyle blinked in the bright sunshine. He was standing in his front garden with, for some reason known only to his subconscious, the cheese grater in his hand. And no shoes on. Dev was nowhere in sight, which in the circumstances was just as well.

He had absolutely no memory of leaving his dining room. Well, this was what he got for thinking he could live a normal life. For ignoring the way his brain had fizzed and ached after the cataplexy attack on the cliff.

How long had he lost? He looked at his watch, which was utterly pointless as he hadn't been keeping track of the time before the sleep attack happened. It'd probably only been a few minutes, based on prior experience. Plenty of time for Dev to be lost to him. Kyle cursed, and turned back to his front door.

Locked. And he hadn't brought a key out. He picked up the large stone by the door, enjoyed for a moment the thought of hurling it through the nearest window, then put it back down and used the key that had been underneath to let himself back into his house. He didn't forget to put the key back under the stone for next time.

Because there *would* be a next time, damn it.

And then it hit him. Oh God. He must have had an attack without being aware of it while Dev was there. He must have drifted off into automatic behaviour and said something when he wasn't in his right mind. *That* was why Dev had stormed off.

A thick, heavy fog of depression threatened to crush Kyle, and he sank down onto the sofa under its weight. It had been going so well. Dev was easy to talk to—more than that, he was *fun* to talk to. Even if Kyle himself wasn't. And for some reason Dev had persisted, past all Kyle's monosyllabic answers and downright rudeness.

Even though Kyle had said he wasn't interested in . . . anything, as though it were a given that Dev would be interested in *him*. That had been the old Kyle's ego talking. From the days BN—Before Narcolepsy.

The old Kyle had been a whole person. One with a future.

Sometimes he hated the old Kyle. There had been a feature in a newspaper he'd flicked through a day or two ago: the journalist's advice to his younger self. He'd thought even then that if ever he met his younger self, he wouldn't bother giving him advice. He'd just punch the arrogant git in the face.

Well, maybe he'd tell him not to bother spending half his life studying for a qualification he'd barely get to use before everything was ripped away. He'd *certainly* tell him not to waste days and nights angsting over whether he could spend his life with a man who didn't want children, given how Jeffrey had broken up with him at the first sign of trouble in any case.

No, that wasn't fair. The breakup had been Kyle's fault. He'd pushed Jeffrey away. Accused him so many times of wanting Kyle gone it was hardly surprising Jeffrey had eventually come to believe it too.

And now he'd driven Dev away. Well, he was nothing if not consistent.

But what had he *said*?

He'd thought there had been an odd sharpness in Dev's tone when Dev asked about the Roscarrocks. Maybe his subconscious had reacted to that? Said something about . . . What? Bastards? Called *Dev* a bastard?

Jeffrey had told Kyle often enough he'd become too sensitive. Too easily affected by the way other people spoke to him. Always taking things the wrong way. Would it be that surprising to find his subconscious was the same?

God, he hated this. Hated not being able to trust his memory. Not being able to trust *himself*. He'd never know what he'd said to Dev, if he'd had an attack and carried on talking with only his dreaming self at the helm. Not unless Dev told him, and how likely was that?

But what if his memory wasn't playing him false, this time? What if there really had been something upsetting Dev about the subject?

Could Dev be in the same situation Kyle was, regarding his ancestry? Perhaps he too had a great-great-grandfather or -grandmother who'd been a Roscarrock by-blow? God knew, from all accounts there'd been plenty of them. The man at the museum had joked how the Roscarrocks all took care to marry out of Porthkennack, for fear they'd end up committing incest without knowing it.

But if that was the case, why would Dev get so upset about it?

A religious objection, maybe? God, he was clutching at straws, here. Dev had given absolutely no indication of being a particularly devout *anything*.

Then again . . . He'd been so keen to help, hadn't he? Maybe it was all religious duty rather than the attraction Kyle had been egotistical enough, *deluded* enough, to ascribe it to. Because Kyle was such a *fucking* catch these days, wasn't he?

No. No, Kyle couldn't believe it. Dev was gay. He'd admitted it—or at least, hadn't protested his heterosexuality when Kyle had made a point of turning down advances that had never actually been forthcoming, which was as good as admitting it. Wait a minute. He'd mentioned a girl, hadn't he? So maybe he was bi. Whatever. It didn't matter. The point was, his sexuality made him unlikely to be any kind of religious zealot.

But for him to react so strongly . . . Kyle frowned. Could Dev be a Roscarrock by-blow himself? It'd explain why he'd taken the matter so personally.

No. Kyle was jumping to conclusions here.

But it'd explain why Dev had come here—and why he hadn't changed his plans when his friend dropped out of the trip. Young men Dev's age weren't known for taking solitary holidays, after all—and Dev was definitely not the solitary type.

Kyle stood up.

And if that *was* the case, perhaps he'd been psyching himself up to go to Roscarrock House and confront, presumably, the father he'd never known? What he'd said about going Kyle's way could have been the truth.

God. No wonder he'd got upset over Kyle describing the situation as a *joke*.

It fit. It was a tenuous web of reasoning, perhaps, but it fit. And if it was true, it at least meant the situation wasn't Kyle's fault.

His spirits lightening along with his burden, Kyle wondered what to do with the sudden burst of energy. Maybe take a walk down to the pottery, see if they'd be willing to give him the use of their facilities now and then? Dev had been right. There was no reason he couldn't keep up his hobby, and he'd missed it more than he'd realised until Dev had remarked on the mugs.

He could handle explaining his humiliating situation to the potters there. Probably. It'd be worth it to feel the clay take shape under his hands. To actually produce something useful once again.

Maybe not on a Sunday, though. There was a good chance there'd be nobody around with the authority to make any decisions. He'd drop in tomorrow.

There was somewhere else he could go, though. And Sunday afternoon would be a good time for a friendly visit, wouldn't it?

Kyle slipped on his shoes, grabbed his keys, and set off up the cliff path to Roscarrock House.

It wasn't far—the walk up there took barely long enough for misgivings to set in. Kyle steeled himself to push open the gate. To walk up the garden path and knock on the front door.

He stepped back to admire the E-shaped frontage as he waited. Built in an attractive pale stone, the Elizabethan property was a comfortable-looking display of wealth. The twin cannons guarding the lawn gave a nod to the source of the family's riches. It must be a pleasant place to live, if perhaps a little draughty in winter. Almost half the frontage was made up of rectangular, mullioned windows, so apparently the family coffers had been deep enough to weather the window tax of the eighteenth and nineteenth centuries. At some point in its life a large wing had been added to the western end of the property, but the extension had been sensitively done, its architecture so entirely in keeping with the main building Kyle couldn't have hazarded a guess as to its age.

He could almost see the Roscarrocks of centuries past in their archaic finery, strutting across the lawn while an army of servants toiled in subterranean kitchens.

Kyle's introspection ceased abruptly as the door was opened by a tall, blond man of around his own age wearing a beard and a scowl. No fine Cornish courtier in doublet and hose, he. There was a faintly Viking air about him—unless Kyle was letting the man's unwelcoming attitude influence his perceptions. He looked exactly the sort to enjoy cutting open someone's rib cage and ripping out their lungs, which, given that his ancestors had been government-sponsored pirates of the sixteenth century, probably wasn't all that surprising.

"Yes?" His voice didn't fit the picture—even in the clipped tones of a single syllable, the courtier with doublet and hose suddenly became more plausible.

Kyle wondered what had happened to his Cornish accent. It had probably been mislaid sometime around the man's first term at public school, if Kyle had to guess.

"Hello," Kyle replied in his best courtroom voice. He'd been told it radiated competence and trustworthiness, in that order. "I've recently moved into the Zelley house down the cliff, and I thought it was about time I introduced myself. Kyle Anthony. I'm renting the place for the summer, but I'm seriously considering buying, so we may well be neighbours for a while." He smiled.

The Viking's frown took on a worried cast. Without a word, he stepped back into the hallway and yelled out, "Bran?"

He wasn't looking at Kyle anymore, but he'd left the door open. Kyle debated whether to step inside, but decided to wait for an invitation—if one ever came. He wondered what would happen if he had a cataplexy attack. He couldn't imagine the Viking carrying him into the house and making sure he was okay. More likely he'd be dragged out by the heels and thrown over the garden wall.

"I hope I haven't called at a bad time," he started to say, just as another man appeared. Much shorter than the first, he was unlike him in every other way, too—with hair so dark brown it was almost black, much like Kyle's own, and clean shaven, without a hint of five-o'clock shadow despite it being already midafternoon. The only thing they had in common was a distinct lack of welcome.

"Can I help you? Bran Roscarrock." He thrust out a hand in Kyle's direction.

Kyle took it mechanically, arrested by the sudden thought that, if he'd guessed right, this could be Dev's father. He didn't look old enough, though—surely Bran couldn't yet be forty?

Bran's already sharp gaze turned a little sharper, and Kyle realised he'd been silent too long. "Kyle Anthony," he said hastily, releasing himself from Bran's too-firm handshake. "I've recently moved into the Zelley cottage down the way."

"Ah, yes. So I'd heard." Bran moved on swiftly before Kyle had time to enquire what, precisely, he'd heard. "And you've met my brother, Jory."

His brother? Kyle couldn't help flashing a glance at the big, blond man, who was hovering in the hall as if preparing to repel boarders. Could *he* perhaps be Dev's father, then? Kyle couldn't for the life of him see a resemblance—and in any case, Jory was definitely far too young.

His interest didn't go unnoticed. "No comments about the milkman, please," Bran said with a laugh that was anything but amused.

"Ah—" Not knowing how he was going to finish that sentence, Kyle was grateful when Bran interrupted him.

"I take it you've settled in all right?"

"Yes. Thank you."

"Glad to hear it. Well, I'd love to invite you in, but we're rather busy at the moment. But it's been good to get to know you. Good day."

The door was shut gently but firmly in his face. Kyle stepped back, fighting down a bitter laugh.

His reputation had apparently well and truly preceded him.

Well, his social interactions were all going swimmingly today, weren't they? The thought was more painful than bitter, and apparently Kyle was a glutton for punishment, as he found himself looking at his watch while hastening back down the cliff path to his lonely sanctuary. It wasn't all that long after 3 p.m. That meant . . . 10 p.m. in Perth. Still just about early enough to call.

He pulled out his phone and hit Call with one hand while fumbling for his keys with the other. Before he could change his mind.

As usual it was Mum who answered. "Kyle? That was good timing. We've only this minute stepped in the door."

"Church social?" he guessed.

"Not this time. Just a little get-together at a neighbour's house. Margaret and Bob—you remember I told you about them . . ."

Kyle let her voice wash over him, informing him of all the latest mundane exploits of people he only half remembered from previous phone calls. When he could finally get a word in edgewise, he asked about his father.

"Oh, Dad's fine. Says he wishes we'd moved over here years ago. But what about your young man? Don't tell me Jeffrey's out again. He always seems to be out when you call us. I feel like I haven't spoken to him in months. The poor boy will be thinking we don't love him anymore."

Kyle's heart sank. It had always been so easy to give her an excuse, before. To tell her Jeffrey was working, or out at a meeting, or at the gym. Now, for some reason, Kyle was tugged by a guilty compulsion to tell her . . . not the whole truth, maybe. But part of it.

"Mum, things haven't been going so well with Jeffrey. I think . . . I think we're splitting up."

"Oh, Kyle, no. No, I can't believe that. It's spending so much time apart, isn't it? I told you, building your career is all very well, but you need to take some time for each other. Have you tried going to see someone at Relate? They do all kinds of couples these days. You don't have to be married to get counselling. Oh, darling, I hope it's not really that serious."

"It is. I'm sorry."

"What about taking a holiday together? It could help you both to remember why you first fell in love—"

"*Mum*. It's too late for that."

"Oh, Kyle. Do you want me to come over?"

"No." God, no. He'd never been able to keep anything from her when they were face-to-face. Not as a boy, and not as a man. "It's fine. I'm fine."

"How can you be? Darling, it's not weak to be upset when a relationship ends. I know, why don't you come over here? Flights aren't that expensive at the moment. And we've got so much to show you. Lauren and the boys would love to see you too, I know they would."

God help him, he was almost tempted. But it was impossible. "I . . . can't. Too much to do at work," he added, hating himself for the lie.

"You work too hard. Making a success of your career is all very well, but there's no point if you end up making yourself ill. Even your father realised that in the end."

"Mum, I've got to go. Something's come up."

"On a Sunday? Still, I suppose you're preparing for a case tomorrow."

Funny, how being saved from a lie by Mum's suppositions made the guilt even harder to bear. Kyle said his good-byes and hung up feeling worse than he had before he'd called.

CHAPTER SEVEN

Of course, once Dev's head cleared, he felt like a total cock. Christ, what had he even been *thinking*? It wasn't like anyone here even knew why he'd come. It was just some weird coincidence, that was all. Kyle hadn't been making fun of him. How could he even have thought that?

And he was walking the wrong way. Away from Big Guns Cove and Roscarrock House. Sod it.

Dev left the road and picked his way over the scrubby grass to the end of a finger of rock that poked out at the edge of the beach, pointing to the sea. He sat down at the end. The sun was high now, and getting warmer all the time. Blokes below had their shirts off, but there was still a stiff breeze blowing up here. Even in this short time, more people had arrived at the beach. There was a family below him, Dad setting out towels on the sand and weighing the corners down with rocks while the kids ran around getting in his way and Mum unloaded plastic boxes from a cooler bag. It brought back memories of Southend, and Dev could almost taste those plastic ham sandwiches on cheap white bread that always seemed to end up with sand in them somehow. They'd used to crunch when he bit them, and if he got unlucky the sand would grind between his teeth and make him shiver.

It hadn't been like it was for the family below. Dev had never had a dad to pick him up and dangle him upside down, shrieking with laughter. He'd never had a mum to fuss around him, slapping on sunblock so thick people could barely see what colour the kid's skin had been to start with. At least, not that he could remember.

Dev stood up. This was all getting him precisely fucking nowhere. He didn't even *know* why he'd reacted like he had.

No.

That was bollocks. He knew all right. It'd been that phrase. *Roscarrock bastard.* Said in that sharp, mocking tone of Kyle's.

It'd just... just done his head in, for a mo. That was all. Dev shoved his hands as far as they'd go in his jeans pockets, which wasn't all that far seeing as they were well tight. He retraced his steps along the coast road, his pace quickening as he passed Kyle's house and slowing again once he was a safe distance beyond it. He didn't know *what* he was going to do about Kyle, seeing as the bloke probably thought he was a total nutjob now, and he wasn't sure he could face doing it today anyhow.

So he might as well get something done today, even if it felt like the last thing he wanted to be doing. He wasn't sure whether to be glad or sorry he'd nicked those cheese sarnies at Kyle's; his stomach was churning anyhow.

This could be it.

It probably wouldn't be, mind—after all, just because it said on the website that some of the family still lived there, didn't mean they all did, now did it?

But it could be.

He pulled his hands out of his pockets and carried on up the hill. Should he have worn a proper shirt, instead of his vintage Bowie T-shirt?

No. No, he was fine.

Roscarrock House was set high on the cliffs right at the end of Mother Ivey's Bay, where the land jutted out into the sea between this bay and the next. The Roscarrocks must have even better views from their bedroom windows than Kyle had from his living room.

Dev had lived in a few places in his twenty-four years, flats and houses and group homes. The views from his bedrooms had pretty much all had a common theme of brick walls.

He felt like an orphan from some Dickens adaptation on the telly as he looked at the big house through the bars of the iron gates. There wasn't a big, long, winding driveway like some posh houses had, to stop the family inside from having to see the plebs passing by, so Dev could practically look in the windows from where he was standing. He even thought he caught a glimpse of someone moving around inside.

The house was built of grey stone, with big, rectangular windows and fancy curvy bits on the gables. There was enough ivy growing up the walls to give it a bit of character without you having to worry about nature taking over the place anytime soon. On the lawn sat a couple of bloody great cannons—the Big Guns, Dev guessed—pointing straight at him, as if just setting the dogs on unwanted visitors wasn't good enough for the Roscarrocks.

Course, they wouldn't sink a right lot of ships, pointing inland. Maybe they'd moved them, after times had changed and the government didn't let you shoot bloody great iron balls at foreign shipping anymore? Or maybe there were some more cannons around the other side. Maybe the Roscarrocks just liked the idea of being surrounded on all sides by weapons of mass medieval destruction. Christ, what must it be like living in a house like that? You'd grow up thinking you owned the whole world. Or this part of it, anyhow.

There was a discreet sign on the gate showing when the place was open to the public. Dev scanned it and saw *Sunday & Monday: Closed*.

Guilty relief broke over him like the waves crashing against the rocks way down below. Reprieved. For the next day or two, at least. All right, so he could still go and knock on the door—but no, that had never been the plan. Scout the place out first before he actually tried talking to anyone; that had been what he'd decided, and he was going to stick to it.

So he'd probably better scarper before anyone inside noticed him and came out to see why some mixed-race yobbo was leaning on their gate and lowering the property value. Dev snapped a quick shot of the opening times with his phone—it'd be quicker than looking it up online later—and headed off.

He kept his eyes pointing straight ahead while going past Kyle's house on the way down, and for safety's sake didn't turn his head until he'd passed the last of the white cottages. The sun was still high, and Dev wondered what to do now. He'd been meaning to get to the museum and check out a bit about the history of the area—with a focus on one family in particular—but bugger that when the weather was so good. He pulled his T-shirt up so he could remind himself what underwear he'd put on this morning. A plain black elastic band showed over the tops of his jeans, with a hint of equally plain black cotton underneath. Result. Yeah, he could get away with these on the beach, as long as no one looked too close, and if they were staring at his dick, they deserved all they got, didn't they?

Dev found the top of the path that led down to the beach, and made his way along it, his spirits lifting. When he made it to the golden sand, he toed off his trainers and then had to hop around for a mo, doing the sock-stripping dance. Hopefully no one noticed. Well, hopefully Kyle hadn't been looking out of his window at the wrong time and noticed. Dev didn't give a monkey's about anyone else seeing him looking daft.

The sand was faintly warm underfoot, not cold like he remembered it from Southend or baking hot like in Magaluf. Dev looked around. Plenty of space—so which bit to claim for his own?

There were a couple of girls a bit younger than him not far off who looked like they'd settled on their towels for the long haul, bikini straps undone and pale, white backs gleaming with cheap sun lotion that probably wasn't going to stop them burning.

Yeah, they'd do. Dev sat down on the sand about six feet away from them, and pulled his T-shirt off.

The nearest girl looked over, a bit awkwardly because she had to be careful not to move too far and accidentally flash a tit.

Dev gave her a slow smile. "All right, darling?"

She looked back at her mate and giggled.

Five minutes of the cheeky Cockney charmer act later, Dev was slightly ashamed of himself, but was also on his way down to the water in his skivvies with a promise from Chantal-from-Birmingham that she'd keep an eye out to make sure nobody nicked his phone, his watch, or his wallet while he was swimming.

Of course, he'd feel well daft if she nicked them herself, but she hadn't seemed the sort. He could usually tell, when he asked someone to look after his stuff, if they were going to be honest about it. Slowing down as he reached the water line, Dev eyed the waves breaking on the shore. It was going to be a bit colder than the Med, round here, wasn't it? Probably best to run in quick, rather than arse about going in on tiptoe, shivering all the way.

Dev took a deep breath and ran into the sea. It was all right for like half a second—then the temperature registered, and he stopped dead, cursing under his breath. A wave slapped him in the stomach, making him gasp with the icy sting. Christ, that water was a *lot* colder than the Med. Dev wouldn't have to worry about giving Chantal-from-Birmingham and her mate an eyeful when he got out of the water again. His balls would have shrunk to fucking grains of sand—if he didn't lose them to frostbite first. Despite the sun, he was one bloody big goose bump.

Sod it. There was nothing else for it. He braced himself and dived in headfirst.

Fuck, that was cold. Dev broke the water gasping and flailing. It was a different sort of cold, though—too cold to shiver anymore. More like an icy clench around his whole body, but he could already feel it easing as he got used to it. The goose bumps disappeared, and he shook the water out of his eyes and settled into an easy front crawl.

Dev was a good swimmer—his secondary school had been close to the leisure centre, so they'd had lessons there. He'd never been all that great at other sports, but in the pool, he was awesome. His spirits lifted with every strong, even stroke as he swam parallel to the shore, heading towards the Big Guns cliff.

Of course, it was a bit different with waves smacking him in the face all the time, but the salt didn't sting his eyes half as much as the chlorine in the pool used to, so he didn't care he hadn't got his goggles. Remembering the sea had currents and sandbars and stuff, Dev made sure to keep a steady distance from the shore, especially when he ran out of beach and was swimming past cliffs. Nearing Big Guns Point, or whatever they called the bit where the cliffs stuck out into the sea bordering the cove, he stopped and trod water for a bit, looking up. Roscarrock House was up there, although he couldn't see it from this angle. He could make out some shapes that might be those extra cannons, pointing out to sea—hard to tell from so far below, squinting into the sun. Of course, this was pirate country, wasn't it? Pirates and smugglers, running their dangerous trade at dead of night.

It was hard to imagine it, in the bright summer sun. Which was daft, when he thought about it, because they'd had plenty of sun in *Pirates of the Caribbean*, hadn't they? Dev grinned to himself. That film—and more to the point, Johnny Depp's Jack Sparrow—had been what first made him realise he was gay, although he hadn't seen it until a couple of years after it'd come out.

Cornwall's pirates probably hadn't been quite like that, though. Shame.

Dev turned and headed back the way he'd come. It was easier, swimming this way, and he wasn't tired yet so he overshot a bit and then came back again, the current much more noticeable this time. Good thing he hadn't gone too far.

When he walked up, dripping, to where he'd left his stuff, Chantal and her mate had turned over to do their fronts. Dev wasn't sure if they'd fallen asleep, but Chantal's eyes flickered open as his shadow fell over her.

She smiled. "Good swim?"

"Yeah, you should try it. Water's lovely."

"Nah, I'd ruin me hair. We're going clubbing tonight," she added, maybe worried Dev would think she was being vain for the sake of it. Fair dues, her long, straight blonde hair looked like it'd frizz right up if she got it wet.

Dev gave her a one-shouldered shrug. "Yeah? Didn't know there were any clubs round here." It wasn't strictly true, but once he'd realised there weren't any gay bars or clubs, he'd sort of lost interest.

"Course there's clubs. We're going to Piskies, down by the front— you interested?"

The other girl woke up at that, and there was a furious whispered conversation between them. Dev didn't catch it all, but he was pretty sure he caught the words *Worrabout Cal?* from Chantal's mate, countered by *He's not here, is he?* and had to stop himself from smiling.

"I'll have to see what my mate wants to do," he said when there was a break in the whispering.

"You got a mate here? What's he like?" It came with a strong subtext of *Reckon he'd fancy my mate?* if Dev wasn't mistaken. He grinned.

"She. Her name's Ceri. She works in the Square Peg. We're meeting for drinks tonight."

"Oh," Chantal said flatly. "Well, maybe we'll see you, then."

She closed her eyes.

"Maybe," Dev said cheerfully. He hadn't done it on purpose, but it looked like mentioning Ceri had done a good job of getting him out of having to let Chantal down gently.

Dev sat on the beach gazing out to sea until the hot sun had dried him off enough to get his kit back on. His kecks were still pretty soggy—not to mention sandy, because there was a limit to how long he was prepared to stand there in public dusting off his own arse—but that couldn't be helped. Anyway, even if a wet patch soaked through onto his jeans, hopefully people would assume he'd been in the sea rather than that he'd peed himself.

Energised by his swim, Dev set off along the path that led up to the cliffs. When he'd reached the top, he cast a glance over at the white cottages. Should he go knock on Kyle's door and apologise for being a dickhead?

He looked at his watch. Huh. He'd spent more time in the water than he'd thought. It was getting on for four o'clock now, and he was supposed to meet Ceri at five. No, there was no point running up to Kyle's when he'd have to run off again five minutes later. Particularly not with suspicious wet patches on his jeans. Might as well head back to the B&B for a shower and some dry underwear.

He'd talk to Kyle tomorrow. Explain stuff. Or, well, not. But he'd apologise, anyhow.

He just hoped the bloke would be all right about it.

Ceri was waiting outside the Square Peg again when Dev got there, despite it being only five to by his watch. She was wearing the same skinny jeans and, for all he knew, the same white T-shirt.

"Ain't they got a problem with you skipping off work early?" he asked, as they fell into step walking away from the seafront.

She shrugged. "Weren't that busy. It's Sunday, innit? Everyone has a big lunch, and then they don't want a cream tea in the afternoon."

Dev frowned. The café had looked pretty busy to him. Still, none of his business. His stomach rumbled, reminding him *he'd* only had half a round of cheese sarnies for lunch and a cream tea would've gone down a treat, ta very much. "You hungry? Wanna get some fish and chips or something?"

"You can get that at the pub," she said, offhand like it didn't matter to her if he did or he didn't.

"That's where we're going, is it? The Bell again?"

"The *Sea* Bell. The Bell's down Harlyn way. We'd need a car to get there. You got a car?"

Uh? "No, I ain't, and I don't even want to go to Harlyn. Wherever the hell that is. The Sea Bell's fine, but what if that crowd from last night turn up? You gonna bail on me again?"

"They won't." She sounded certain and a bit smug.

"What, chucked 'em all off a cliff, have you?"

She smiled at that, but it wasn't a nice one. More like she'd be happy to see the lot of them fall screaming to their deaths. Dev started reconsidering that serial killer theory. "Uncle Jago said he told them they were barred. Said they'd never have got served if he hadn't been called away just before they got there."

Dodging round a family of five as they dawdled past the posh tea rooms, Dev missed his step and almost fell off the kerb. "The landlord's your uncle? You never said."

"Not a real uncle. But him and my grandad were mates since they was lads."

"So how come we got all them dirty looks when we walked in?"

She stared at him like he'd told her he'd been abducted by aliens or something.

"We did," he insisted. "Like they was all just two pints away from bashing us over the head and, I dunno, putting us in the pasties or something."

Her what-are-you-on expression got even worse. "You get too much sun today?"

She was close as fuck to laughing out loud at him. Dev could tell.

"Shut up," he muttered. "I know what I saw, all right? I was there. It happened."

Ceri's face changed and she looked away.

What the hell had he said to upset her? Dev played it back in his mind, but maybe his mental MP3 was fucked, because he still had no clue.

He wasn't going to push, though. Especially not while they were still walking through packed streets. "So how come we don't get free drinks, then? If you're in tight with the management?"

He'd meant it jokingly, but she snapped back at him. "Because I'm not a freeloader, that's why."

Christ, at this rate the evening was going to be about as much fun as a trip to the dentist. Dev gave it a break until they'd got past the centre of town, then tried another subject. "I saw that bloke again today. The one from yesterday, you know? What you thought was a drinker. He ain't. He's got a condition." Yeah, and he probably wouldn't appreciate people spreading it around, Dev realised as soon as he'd said it. "He's a bit touchy about it," he finished, trying to get *but I shouldn't have told you that* across to her without actually coming out and saying it.

"What, like Parkinson's or something?"

"Yeah. Sort of." Dev found himself glancing over his shoulder. "Look, forget I told you, all right? Just . . . don't go spreading that story about him being a drunk, 'cos it's all bollocks."

Ceri was silent for so long Dev thought he'd somehow managed to piss her off again. Then she spoke in a low voice, still not looking at him. "You're right. I won't." There was another pause, then she exploded with, "People are *bastards*, aren't they?"

The insult sounded even worse in her accent, all the *r*'s rolled out to Land's End and back. A white couple in matching shorts who'd been frowning at a map shot her a worried glance and sped up as they walked away.

"Oi, I hope you mean present company excepted," Dev said, keeping it light.

"Yeah. You're all right. So you like him, then, do you? This bloke."

"Kyle," Dev said quickly. "That's his name. And I dunno, all right? Ain't like it's going to come to nothing, anyway."

"Why? You live in London, not the other side of the world."

"Yeah, but . . . he said something, and I took it the wrong way. So now he thinks I'm, I dunno, some weirdo or something."

"What did he say?"

"Ah . . . Doesn't matter. I took it wrong, all right? Stormed out of his house like some bigoted old bat who'd stumbled into a Pride parade on her way home from having tea with the vicar."

"You were in his house?"

"Yeah . . ." Shit. Dev sighed. At least they were out of the crowds now. He gave her a massively edited version of what had happened on the cliff, leaving out all references to death wishes and the actual phrase he'd been such a fucking idiot about.

All she said afterwards was, "And you still like him?"

Dev frowned. "Maybe. Why not?"

She shrugged. "'Cos most blokes run a mile when they find out the person they're into's got something wrong with 'em."

"Oi, now who's being sexist?"

"It's true, though."

"Yeah, well, I ain't like that. Don't matter anyhow. He ain't interested. He said so."

Yeah, just like he said he was fine.

Ceri gave him a knowing look, like she could read his mind or something. "Don't believe him, though, do you? You're lucky, you are."

"Why?"

"Both of you's blokes. Makes it easier."

Dev gave up trying to work out Ceri's logic. "Get any good tips today?" he asked instead.

"Maybe. Don't mean the drinks are on me, mind."

"You owe me one for last night. I bought you a drink and when you pissed off I had to drink it meself."

"And how does that mean I owe you? You got both drinks, didn't you? That means you owe me."

Dev frowned, not sure himself, now. "Ah, whatever." He pushed open the door of the Sea Bell. "Usual, then?"

She nodded. "I'll grab us a table."

As he walked up to the bar, Dev cast a sharp glance over the drinkers already there. Far as he could tell, it was the same crowd as yesterday—in fact, for all he knew, maybe they'd been here since then—but today none of them were giving him and Ceri a second glance. No, wait—one of them lifted his head and met Dev's gaze. Then he nodded.

A bit embarrassed, Dev nodded back.

The miserable old git at the bar didn't seem so bad if Dev thought of him as Ceri's Uncle Jago. *He* nodded at Dev too. "Two vodka and Cokes?"

"Cheers, mate." Then, because he never could leave well enough alone, Dev added, "Ice and a slice, yeah?"

Jago gave Dev a hard stare. "No lemons."

"No?"

"Ship sank." He turned to pour the drinks.

Dev was, like, ninety-nine point nine recurring percent sure the bloke was pissing him about.

Probably best not to call him on it, though. Dev waited for his drinks and, when he'd paid, bunged a penny in the tip jar. Just to make a point.

Jago's face didn't alter. "Very generous of you," he said with no inflection whatsoever.

"You're welcome," Dev said, and legged it back to Ceri.

They'd just got started on their second round of drinks when a man walked into the pub on his own. He was probably in his forties, of average height, average build, and pretty much average looks. Dev wouldn't have given him a second glance if it hadn't been for Ceri's sharp intake of breath. Oh, and the way he made a beeline for their table, pulled up a stool, and sat down without even asking.

That definitely got Dev's attention.

"Good day at work, love?" the bloke said.

"What do you want?" Ceri snapped at him.

The newcomer nodded at the bar. "Jago said you'd made a new friend. Thought I'd come and meet him."

"This is Dev. Now you've met him. Bye."

The bloke turned to Dev. "Here on holiday?"

"I said, *bye*." Ceri whipped her head around to Dev. "You don't have to tell him anything."

Jago's mate frowned. "Now wait a minute. If he's got nothing to be ashamed of, he won't mind answering a few questions about himself."

Dev didn't like his attitude. Or his face, for that matter. "Oi, what's it to you anyway?"

Ceri stood up. "We're going to get something to eat."

"You could—"

"Shut *up*." She almost yelled it, and heads turned as she grabbed Dev's arm and practically dragged him out of his seat. Jago's mate looked upset, but he didn't move to stop them.

"So who was that bloke?" Dev asked once they were through the door and back into the open air. He'd done a bit of thinking as they marched out of the pub, and that look on Jago's mate's face had seemed pretty familiar. He'd seen Mal's dad wearing it as he hauled Mal's drunk arse home for a lecture on not turning out like his uncle. "Is he your dad?"

She didn't answer.

"Ceri?"

"*Yes*, all right? He's my dad." She stormed down the lane ahead of him, heading for the cliffs as far as he could tell.

Dev ran to catch up. "Did you have to be so hard on him? Don't you think it's sorta nice, him wanting to look out for you like that?"

"*No*."

"Why not?" There'd been plenty of times Dev wouldn't have minded having a dad or a mum to look out for him. *Plenty* of them.

Then again, he'd known one or two girls who'd ended up in the system who could have done with a lot less *looking out for* from their dad or stepdad or whatever.

Take Tasha, for instance. Dev's mood darkened. "Oi, he ain't been doing nothing he shouldn't, has he?"

She stared at him. "*No*."

"Then what's it all about?"

"Because it's bollocks, that's why!"

"What do you mean?"

She spun around, her eyes wild. Dev had to stop in his tracks sharpish so as not to run into her. "Because what's the point? What's the fucking *point*? He can ask you all the questions he likes, can't he, but it don't make no difference in the end, 'cos whatever happens, no one's going to believe me, they'll say I'm after *attention* and all that crap, and don't I know how serious it is, going round making accusations, so why don't I just fuck off and shut up, 'cos no one wants to listen to me anyhow?"

She was panting after all that, her skinny chest heaving. Dev couldn't help thinking of a stray dog he and Mal found once, limping from some useless twats giving it a kicking. It'd bitten Mal when he'd tried to pat it, Dev remembered.

"I'll listen to you," he said cautiously.

"Don't you *fucking* patronise me!"

"I'm not, all right? I know there's some sick shit goes on in families, so if you wanna tell me stuff, I'll listen."

Her dad stepped out of the pub at that mo, and jogged down the lane towards them with a heavy, middle-aged tread. Dev put his arm around Ceri, drawing her back and putting himself between them.

She pushed him away. "Just leave me alone, both of you."

"Not until you tell me he ain't done nothing the police oughtta hear about." Christ, it'd come to something when Dev was threatening to call the filth on someone.

"*What?*" Her dad's voice was high and cracked on the word.

Ceri gave a short, incredulous laugh. "*Dad?*" She closed her eyes, then opened them again. "It's nothing like that, Dev. Promise."

"So what is it like?"

She didn't answer, and her dad stepped up. "Ceri's been having a difficult year. Found out a few friends weren't friends at all. Ceri, love, it'd make your mum happy if you came home for tea tonight." His voice was all thick. Gruff, that was the word.

Ceri looked close to tears. "I'm with Dev," she said, but it sounded uncertain, and she took a step towards her dad. Like, maybe, despite the way she'd spoken to him, she really wanted him to hug her like she was a little kid.

"You do what you want, all right?" Dev told her. "Don't worry about me. Look, gimme your phone a mo, yeah?" She handed it over, and Dev tapped his number in quickly before handing it back. "You need anything, you call me, got that?"

Ceri nodded, leaving her head down so her loose hair fell over her face and hid it from view. Dev was pretty sure that was deliberate.

Her dad put his arm around her, and she didn't push him away. "Come on home, love. It'll be all right."

Dev watched them go, Ceri looking even skinnier and more fragile than ever next to her dad. He hoped he'd made the right call, leaving her with him—except, it hadn't *been* his call, had it? It'd been hers.

He sighed.

Okay, so what to do now? Dev was hungry, but another night eating fish and chips on his own was about as appealing as walking back into the Sea Bell and asking to see their menu. Christ knew who bloody Uncle Jago would call if Dev showed his face there again, this time without Ceri.

He walked off, not sure where he was heading—away from the pub, yeah, but not back into town. The low whisper of the sea got louder as he walked and, sure enough, when the view opened up in front of him he realised he'd come out above the lifeboat station at Mother Ivey's Bay.

Not far from Kyle's place.

It'd still be light for hours yet. And he needed to apologise to the bloke anyway. What would he do if he went back into town now? Meet Chantal and her mate at Piskies?

Dev couldn't see that ending well. No, he might as well get the apology over with, right?

There were still some people on the beach, but the cool breeze off the sea had picked up and blown most of them back to their holiday homes. Probably all eating their dinners now, Dev thought regretfully, willing his stomach not to rumble.

Heh. Maybe if the apology went really well, he'd be able to cadge another cheese sarnie from Kyle.

CHAPTER
EIGHT

W
hen the knock came on the door, Kyle's first thought was
that perhaps it was one of the Roscarrocks, here with
ill-timed courtesy to apologise for the behaviour of their brothers,
sons, or whatever to him earlier. Cursing, he put down his wooden
spoon, turned the heat under the pans as low as it would go, and went
to answer the door.

He blinked in surprise to see Dev standing there with his hands in
his pockets, his shoulders tense. "Dev?" he said stupidly.

"Yeah. Uh. Came to apologise. Can I come in?"

"Yes. Yes, of course." Kyle waved him in with an awkward gesture.
"Um. I was cooking, so if you don't mind coming through—"

"Shit, sorry. Should have guessed. I'll come back another time."

Alarm jumped unexpectedly in Kyle's chest at the thought of him
leaving so soon. "No. It's fine. Have you eaten? You're welcome to stay."

"Yeah, but mate, I stole half your lunch. I can't nick half your
dinner as well."

"I've only just put the penne on. I can easily throw in some more
and cook it a little bit longer." Kyle stifled a laugh. "Unless you're a
pasta pedant and are now outraged at me for even thinking of treating
it this way."

Jeffrey would have been horrified. One time when he'd seen Kyle
throw pasta into a pan of cold water rather than getting it to boil first,
he'd sulked all evening. Despite the fact he'd never noticed all the
other times Kyle had cooked it like that.

Dev broke into a sunny grin. "You kidding? Anything up from
spaggi hoops out of a can is dead posh in my book." He stepped inside
as he spoke and closed the door behind him.

God, where did Dev get that gift of defusing tension? Leading the way into the kitchen, Kyle relaxed—then tensed up again as he realised there was something he'd have to say. "I need to warn you—I sometimes have odd . . . episodes. Automatic behaviour, it's called." He didn't look at Dev's face. He could imagine the blank expression quite well enough.

"That's where you sort of sleep standing up, right? Or, you know, carry on doing stuff like you're awake, but you're really asleep?"

He did look at Dev then, surprised. "You've heard of it?"

Dev half shrugged and stared at the floor. "Yeah, I, uh, I sort of looked it all up on my phone. Before I came here. Didn't wanna, you know, set you off again. I mean, I only did a quick search. There's a shit-load of stuff on the internet. Would've taken me all night to read it."

Kyle wasn't sure how he felt about that. Touched. Embarrassed. Irrationally annoyed. But mostly touched, he decided. "So you know I might do or say something . . . strange."

"Yeah. I know it ain't your fault." Dev was still refusing to meet Kyle's eye. As if *Dev* were the one with the humiliating condition.

Kyle swallowed. He had to ask. "Is that what happened just after lunch? Did I say something—"

"No. Shit, no." Dev took a deep breath. "That was all on me. Sorry. See, I—"

"You don't have to explain yourself to me," Kyle interrupted, a bit more sharply than he'd intended to. It was too much, too *intense*, and his blood sugar had plummeted. "Let's get on with the cooking, and we can eat and talk afterwards, if you like."

Dev sent him a relieved smile. "Good plan. What do you want me to do?"

Kyle bit back the instinctive response of *Nothing, thank you*. With Dev occupied, Kyle would be less on display. "There's salad in the fridge, if you wouldn't mind getting that out."

Despite all his talk of canned food, by the time Kyle had added some more pasta to the pan, brought it back to the boil, and set the sauce to simmer, Dev had assembled two colourful bowls of salad, even going so far as to grate some carrot, which Kyle could seldom be bothered to do. "No radish flowers and cucumber curls?" he asked lightly.

"Nah, not unless you want me belching all night." Dev stilled, his expression suddenly hunted. "Evening. I meant evening."

"Of course you did," Kyle agreed way too quickly.

Damn it. This was a different sort of tension, and Dev's presence in his home, so close he could reach out and touch him, was doing *nothing* to defuse it.

He swallowed and grabbed a wooden spoon to give the pasta a stir, trying in vain to banish the image of smooth, tan skin; soft brown eyes; and a determined jawline. When he turned round again Dev was gone, and Kyle thought for an appalled moment he'd had another attack and missed Dev walking out on him.

Then Dev came back into the kitchen. "I took the salad out to the dining room," he said carefully, his eyes on Kyle's face all the time.

God. He was falling to pieces. Kyle forced a smile. "It won't be much longer. I'm afraid there's only water to drink."

Apparently that was all it took for Dev to regain his relaxed, teasing manner. "Yeah? You know, mate, as an alcoholic you're a real disappointment."

Kyle gave a bitter laugh under his breath. "Just as an alcoholic?" His brief amusement fled, leaving only the bitterness behind, when he realised he'd said it aloud. Self-pity. How very attractive in a man.

Although why should he worry if Dev found him attractive or not? Sheer ego. Nothing was going to happen. He wouldn't allow it to.

"Well, so far, anyhow," Dev said easily. "Course, I ain't tasted your cooking yet."

Kyle had to fight down nervous laughter. It hadn't been *that* funny, and if he collapsed now it was likely neither of them would get to taste the cooking. "Don't worry. Even I can't easily ruin pasta with sauce out of a jar."

"You ain't trying hard enough. My mate Mal tried heating a jar of sauce up in a microwave once, 'cept the stupid tosser didn't take the lid off, did he? Think they heard the bang three streets away. We had the cops come round and everything." Dev laughed, a low, pleasing sound. "Course, when they got there the kitchen looked like your actual crime scene. Red splattered all over the shop. I thought for a minute we was gonna get nicked." He paused. "Anything else I can do?"

"Pour a couple of glasses of water?" Kyle nodded towards the cupboard with the glasses in. "I think it's ready."

He served out and carried their plates through to the dining table, where they sat down. Desperately in need of the calories by now, Kyle didn't try to speak until he'd shovelled in a few forkfuls of pasta.

Then Dev beat him to it. "You know," he said thoughtfully, "this is good. See, I can never decide if I like pasta best when it's soft or when it's chewy, and here, I don't have to."

Kyle looked up in shock, and Dev burst out laughing. "Your face, mate. Sorry. Is it my fault I never got brought up right?"

"Wanker," Kyle muttered, heartily relieved he'd been sitting down already. Dev laughed again. Probably because even in his own ears, Kyle sounded like a petulant child trying out the rudest word he knew. "I'm sure your upbringing was perfectly fine. You were just determined not to listen when they taught you about good manners."

"Yeah, well. Six of one, maybe, like Mal's Uncle Bob always says. Course, he's always pissed off his face, so it's probably bollocks. Nah, it's all right, this. Seriously. Interesting texture."

"Did I mention you're washing up?" Kyle gestured sternly with his fork, and a piece of wild rocket fell off and onto the table between them.

"Sweeping up and all, by the looks of things," Dev countered cheerily.

Kyle picked up the offending leaf with his fingers and ate it before it could cause any more trouble. "Did you have an enjoyable afternoon?"

"Yeah, it was well good. I went down the beach near here and had a swim. You're so bloody lucky, mate, living here. If I had your house, I'd spend all summer in the water." Dev's face, alight with enthusiasm, darkened. "Uh, you are all right to swim, aren't you?"

Kyle nodded, amused. "You've been in the water. Just how likely do you think anyone is to fall asleep in there? Trust me, the Celtic Sea is one of the few places I'm fairly safe from an attack."

"Uh, yeah. I didn't really think that one through, did I? Does it ever get any warmer?"

"I'm pretty sure it's at its warmest right now. Let me guess—more used to swimming pools?" Kyle could just imagine him on a sun lounger in his swimming trunks, displaying that fit physique to general admiration.

"That or the Mediterranean. Go on, tell me I'm a wuss."

"It'd make two of us, then. I have to confess, I need to work myself up to going in the water here."

"It's good when you're in it, though." Dev grinned. "Long as you keep swimming hard enough. Hey, maybe we should go sometime?"

Kyle looked at his plate. Was that a come on? Or was Dev just being friendly? "Maybe."

There was no harm in being flattered if he *was*, was there? As long as nothing actually happened.

They ate in silence for a moment, until Dev spoke again. "Actually, I sorta wanted to ask your advice on something." He stopped.

"Go on." Was he about to bring up the Roscarrocks again?

Dev fiddled with his fork before speaking. "You remember I mentioned I'd met this girl, yeah? The one who works in the Square Peg. Ceri."

Oh. That. Kyle nodded, and braced himself for a recital of Ceri's many talents, most of them no doubt only visible to a man in the throes of a crush. Well, that'd teach him to assume Dev was into him.

"I dunno what's going on with her, right? I mean, there's something wrong, but I dunno what it is."

"Why do you care?" Kyle made sure his tone was nonjudgemental.

Dev frowned. "You mean, 'cos I only just met her? Ah, I dunno." He stared out of the window at the sea. "I got this sister," he said finally, to Kyle's surprise. "I mean, we ain't related or nothing, but she was my foster sister, last family I was with. She's younger than me. Tasha. I used to take her to kiddies' parties and down the swings and stuff." He fell silent, picking at the remains of his food.

"Is she still with the family?"

"Nah, aged out, didn't she? When she turned eighteen just over a year back. She's living in a shared house now. I mean, I said she could stay with me and Mal, but there ain't a lot of room, you know? She wanted her own space. Don't think she realised how hard it'd be."

"And Ceri reminds you of her?" That was rather endearing.

Also somewhat chastening. Kyle was guiltily aware that, at Dev's age, he'd spared very few thoughts for the welfare of his own sister in day-to-day life. Although Lauren was three years older than him, and had already been settled in her career by then, of course.

"S'pose. I mean, they don't look nothing alike. Tasha's dad was West Indian, and she got his hair." Dev pulled his phone out of his pocket, and flicked through to show Kyle a picture of a girl who could have been any age from mid-to-late teens to early twenties, but must be on the younger end of the scale from what Dev had said. She had African hair and features, but her smooth, clear skin was no darker than Dev's. Her fresh-faced prettiness was rather appealing.

Kyle was never quite sure what he was supposed to say in these situations. A comment on the subject's looks didn't really seem appropriate. "Nice photo," he went with in the end.

"Yeah. She's great." Dev smiled softly, and Kyle was struck with the irrelevant thought that he'd no doubt be a wonderful father one day. It pained him, for reasons he didn't want to examine.

"And Ceri?" he prompted after a pause.

"Like I said, I dunno what's going on. There's this other girl, see, she told me Ceri was trouble, like, into something illegal. Least, I think that's what she meant." He frowned. "I thought she was just stirring the shit, you know? But earlier this evening, we went for a drink—me and Ceri—and her dad turned up, and it was well weird."

"Weird how?"

"She was . . . Well, she basically told him to piss off, but he was all friendly, like. Weird. I mean, I ain't never had a dad, but if I spoke like that to my foster dad I'd have been well in the shit. But he just gave her a cuddle and took her home for tea."

Kyle's blood chilled. "You don't think . . .?"

"Nah. Well, I did, but she said he ain't doing nothing like that. And I'm pretty sure she wasn't just saying that. I dunno, though. It was like he'd, well, failed her or something."

"What did he say?"

"Not a lot. That she'd been having a rough time. Had some friends screw her over. He didn't put it like that, but that's what he meant."

Kyle thought. "Maybe she got mixed up in something and is now regretting it? Drugs, perhaps?" It was the obvious answer.

"Fucked if I know."

"So what did you want my advice about? Whether to . . ." Kyle shied away from saying *get into a relationship with her*, and finished weakly with, "continue your friendship?"

"What? Nah, I ain't gonna drop her or nothing." Dev looked affronted. "I just thought, did I oughtta try and get her to tell me about it? See if it's something I can help her with? Or, you know, carry on minding me own business?"

How big was the age difference between Kyle and Dev? Less than ten years? More? Apparently it was enough for Dev to see him as some sort of father figure, suitable only for the dispensing of sage advice. Wonderful. "Well, you said she was being looked after by her father—she went with him willingly?"

"Yeah."

"Then she's probably getting all the help she needs. It still wouldn't hurt if, next time you see her, you let her know you'll be there for her if she wants to talk. But I wouldn't pressure her into anything." There. That should be sage enough for anyone.

Dev was nodding. "Yeah. Cheers, mate. That'd be best."

Kyle sent him a wry smile. "I'm pretty sure you knew that already, though."

"Yeah, but . . ." Dev stretched. Kyle resolutely didn't stare at the way his T-shirt rode up to display a pleasingly hirsute midriff. "I ain't always made the best decisions, you know? Sometimes you wanna check with someone who's—"

"Older and therefore supposedly wiser?"

"I was gonna say smarter, 'cos you've probably got more letters after your name than I've got in mine, but hey, if the cap fits . . ." Dev grinned and put his hands behind his head, leaning back in his chair. "How old are you anyhow? Hit the big three-oh yet?"

"It's pretty obvious you haven't. I'm thirty-three." Never mind that he felt more like sixty-three some days. Kyle stood up, fighting the tiredness that had suddenly assailed him. "Do you want a coffee?"

"Only if you're having one."

It wouldn't be a good idea. Even decaffeinated coffee tended to disturb Kyle's sleep pattern, such as it was.

Which was probably why the craving for the stuff was suddenly almost unbearable. "No," Kyle said shortly, and picked up their plates in an attempt to distract Dev from how strange it must have sounded.

"I'll get those," Dev said, practically grabbing them out of his hands. "You go and sit down."

Feeling uncomfortably like a guest in his own home, Kyle went through to the living room and settled himself on the sofa.

Kyle woke up to find Dev sprawled at the other end of the sofa, flicking through TV channels with one hand while texting with the other.

Great. Some host he was being. "Sorry," he said, his mouth unpleasantly dry. "Have I been asleep long?"

Dev turned to give him a blinding smile. "Nah, just over an hour. Don't worry. The sex was brilliant."

Kyle froze, and Dev's expression turned stricken.

"Shit. That wasn't funny, was it? Sorry, mate. Wasn't thinking." He shoved his phone back in his pocket. "You want me to go?"

This was all moving way too fast for Kyle's sleep-fogged brain. "No?" he managed.

"Nah, it's okay. I should let you get to bed, whatever." Dev stood up, looking unhappy.

"No." Kyle said it more positively this time. "You don't need to go. I should be alert for at least another couple of hours. Please stay."

Dev wavered visibly—then sat down again. "Long as you're sure. And I'll try not to say anything so fucking stupid again."

"Don't beat yourself up about it." Kyle attempted a smile, but was aware it probably came out a little twisted. "You'd be amazed how few people I know *haven't* said something insensitive since I was diagnosed. It's funny, really. If you lose a leg, everyone feels bad for you. If you lose your ability to sleep normally, it's all a big joke."

"Not though, is it?" Dev stared out of the window, and Kyle followed his gaze. The sky had turned inky blue, and the moon had risen, an almost perfect silvery disc. "Is it really shit, living with it?"

Absurdly, Kyle found he couldn't say yes. It *was* . . . but there were so many worse things too. It wasn't like it was actually going to kill him, was it? "I don't think I'm dealing with it very well," was what he said in the end.

"How long's it been since you got ill?"

Kyle had a vivid memory of sitting in the chair at his doctor's surgery, the window blinds half open to show a jet-black sky. He'd always insisted on early-morning appointments so they wouldn't eat into his oh-so-important working day. Dr. Grey had been brusquely sympathetic in the face of his devastation—of course, she probably had to tell people far worse things every week. He'd listened halfheartedly to her list of available resources and walked outside in a daze to find the sun had still not risen.

It had been a dark month in more ways than one. "I was diagnosed in January this year."

"This year? Seriously? And since then you've lost your job and moved halfway across the country, away from everyone you know. You honestly think *anyone* would be dealing well with all that?" Dev was silent a moment. "You oughtta give yourself a break, mate."

It was just as well Kyle hadn't mentioned the relationship breakup, or Dev would no doubt have thrown *that* in his face too. "And you're the world's expert on coping with narcolepsy, are you?"

"No, but you remember I told you about my sister?"

"She's a narcoleptic?" Kyle didn't even try to keep the disbelief out of his voice.

Dev flushed. "No. She's got diabetes. But she went through some rough times in her teens, dealing with it, and the restrictions and all."

"Great. So I'm coping as well as a teenager. Thanks for the compliment."

"Christ . . . I just meant, everyone has problems, that's all. And you shouldn't call yourself *a narcoleptic*, all right? You're a person with narcolepsy."

"What the hell is supposed to be the difference?"

"The difference is, if you say you're *a narcoleptic*, you're saying that's what defines you."

Unable to sit there any longer, Kyle stood up and took a step back from the sofa. "So? In case you haven't noticed, my condition *does* bloody well define me. It defines my whole *life*."

"Yeah, well, you ever think maybe that's 'cos you're letting it?" Dev had got to his feet too. He stepped forward, closing the gap between them once more.

Kyle *hated* feeling trapped. "You . . . I can't believe this. You're standing here, in my home, telling me this is all my fault? What the hell do you even know? You're young, you're fit, you're ridiculously attractive—do you even know what problems *are*?" Anger fizzed through his veins, a crescendo of heat, and for the first time in months Kyle felt alive.

Dev's fists clenched by his sides. Good. He wanted a fight? Then he could bloody well bring it.

"You know fuck all about me, about my life, about *anything*," Dev fairly spat at him. "So don't you fucking *dare* tell me I don't know shit. You think my life's been easy? Christ. You ain't got the first fucking idea."

His face darkening with rage, Dev took a deep breath. Kyle's skin tingled in anticipation of the punch that had to be coming—but then Dev let the breath out explosively, turned on his heel, and strode out of the house.

The comedown wasn't pleasant. Kyle's anger still burned—but without an outlet it turned rapidly sour and corrosive.

Walking into the kitchen to find Dev had, while Kyle was asleep, washed all the dishes and left them neatly stacked on the counter made it, somehow, even worse.

CHAPTER NINE

Dev stumbled down the cliff path in the dark, which didn't matter because he was too angry to see straight anyway. Where the hell did that bastard get off, telling Dev he knew fuck all about anything? What the fuck did he even know, with his nice family in Australia, and his sea views, and his comfortable house despite having no fucking job? Dev tried to imagine what *his* life would be like if for some reason he couldn't work. He'd be living in some crummy council flat with mould climbing up the walls and shopping in food banks. Christ.

To think he'd even stopped on the way and sat on the cliffs for half an hour so he could look up narcolepsy on his phone. And the other thing, cataplexy, which luckily the search engine had auto-completed for him, because he hadn't been certain he'd remembered it right. He'd *tried*, all right?

Unlike some privileged bastards who didn't even know how lucky they were.

Christ, he wished Mal was here. He was a good mate, Mal was. All right, so he wasn't the most reliable bloke in the world, but his heart was in the right place. Mostly. And he never let shit get him down for long. Dev wondered how much it'd cost to ring Portugal. But Mal was probably out drinking by now and wouldn't even take the call.

Now his eyes had adjusted, there was actually a fair bit of light around, which was well weird, out here in the wilds without a lamp post in sight. Dev glanced up at the sky, and then couldn't tear his gaze away. The moon was either full or near as made sod all difference, a perfect silver disc in the sky—but it was the stars that made him stare. There were so fucking *many* of them. Dev wasn't stupid, and he'd looked up before, all right? He knew Orion when he saw it, and the plough. But Christ, there were so many other stars all around and in between that just weren't *there* in London. He'd never known there were so many to see. How could there be so many stars out there?

He'd never really understood why people got excited about space flight and stuff. Here on Earth was where all the real stuff happened, wasn't it? But right now, looking up at, like, a million possible other worlds, Dev couldn't help feeling . . . something. Awe, maybe. And a bit of a stiff neck.

Hey, maybe on one of those other worlds there was a bloke looking up at the sky right now, thinking all the same stuff Dev was. Except he'd be thinking it in Klingon or whatever the local lingo was, and he'd have six arms and fourteen dicks or something. Which, now he came to think about it, probably wasn't the best ratio. Dev laughed softly at himself. Yeah, 'cos space travel was all about the porn.

Leaving the path, he headed towards the cliff edge, keeping his eyes on the ground and treading carefully because he'd feel well stupid if he ended up headlining the local news after one false step. He sat down near the edge on the short, dry grass and stared out to sea for a long moment.

The beach below him was empty, its golden sand painted silver by the moonlight. It felt peaceful here—but bleak too. Dev remembered his reading from before the trip. There had been wreckers and smugglers working this coastline, centuries back. Although maybe not on nights like this. They'd be way too easily spotted by the excisemen. A wrecker's moon was a dark one.

It felt weird, being so alone. Yeah, there were people in the houses up the path, but out here there was literally *no one*. Dev couldn't remember the last time he'd really been alone in Balham. It'd probably never even happened. In a strange kind of way, he sort of liked the solitude here.

But it would've been better with someone to share it with.

Tasha. She'd be in on a Sunday night, wouldn't she? Dev pulled out his phone, flicked through his contacts, and hit Call.

It rang several times before Tasha answered. "Yeah?" she said, her voice so loud it was almost a shout. "Dev?" He could hear people laughing and chatting over the phone, like she was at a party or something. Or the party was at her place, maybe.

"Yeah, it's me. You all right?"

"Yeah, I'm good. 'S up, bruv?"

"Just wanted to give you a call. See how you were."

"What?" There was loud laughter in the background.

Dev tried again. "I'm in Cornwall, remember?"

"Oh. Oh, *right*. Hang on a mo." Dev could hear her talking to someone else, telling them *Gotta go, it's my bruv*, and then the slam of a door that cut off a lot of the noise. "How's it going? You met her yet?"

"Nah. Plenty of time. Met a bloke, though."

"Yeah? What's he like?"

"Total wanker."

Tasha laughed. "That's blokes, though, innit? You shagged him?"

"Nope. Not gonna. So what are you up to? Ain't you got work tomorrow?"

"I'm round at Sal and Mick's. Gonna call in sick tomorrow."

"Oi, that's how you lost the last job, remember?"

"So? It's a shit job anyhow."

She was working in a call centre at the moment, so Dev couldn't argue with that. And at least Sal and Mick weren't as bad as some of her mates. Then again, from the sound of things, most of the rest of her mates were probably there as well. "You drinking?"

"Course I'm fucking drinking."

"Watching your blood sugar?"

"Jesus, Dev, get off my case, will you?"

"*Are* you?"

"*Yes*, all right? Look, I gotta get back, yeah?"

"All right, but you take care of yourself."

"Don't I always?"

No, she fucking didn't, but there wasn't a lot Dev could do about it from nearly three hundred miles away. "I'll call you in a day or two."

They hung up. Dev gazed out to sea a while longer, getting to his feet only when the rising wind made him shiver.

Time to head back to the B&B.

"Are you all right, laddie? Looking a wee bit peaky there." Val's voice was concerned. It was also way too bloody loud for this time in the morning.

Possibly picking up a bottle of vodka on his way back to the B&B last night hadn't been the best move. But the off-licence had been *right there*, its brightly lit windows looking all warm and inviting. Dev pulled out a chair to sit down at the breakfast table and winced at the sound it made on the tiled floor.

"Had a bit too much fun last night, did you?" she went on.

That was so far from the truth, it was bleakly funny. "If only." God, he hoped the food came soon.

"Best drink your orange juice," Carol said kindly. "That'll help. And if you ever want to talk about anything..."

"Cheers, but I'm good." God, the *last* thing he wanted to do was to talk. Mrs. Quick brought his breakfast, which didn't look half as appetising as yesterday's had. He pushed his hog's pudding around the plate, not sure his stomach was really up for it. "You ever get sick of it?" he demanded suddenly.

"Sick of breakfast?" Val asked.

"Nah, you know. People looking at you, thinking they know you." He waved a hand in Val's direction. With her cropped grey hair, lack of makeup, comfortable figure, and mannish clothes, there couldn't be anyone alive who wouldn't take one look at her and think *dyke*.

Val raised a grizzled eyebrow. "Trouble in town last night?"

"Nah. Just... There's this bloke, right? And he... Ah, shit. You don't wanna hear this." Dev felt torn in two by the need to talk about Kyle, and the desperate want to forget about the whole shit show. It was doing his head in. He'd checked out some more websites last night, and... yeah. Total fuckup.

But sod it. He'd been well out of order, yeah, he could see that now, but why the hell couldn't Kyle have just explained stuff to him instead of spouting all that crap about Dev's life? He'd thought... Well. He'd thought Kyle *liked* him. He'd been checking him out and everything. Dev was sure he had.

Carol reached across the table and patted his hand. "There are plenty more fish in the sea for a good-looking young man like you."

Which was sweet, yeah, but totally missed the point.

Val cut in before Dev could say anything. "Aye, and it sounds like this is one you should throw back in the water. Thank you, Mrs. Quick," she added, as a fresh pot of tea arrived on the table.

"It ain't his fault," Dev found himself saying. "He's got a lot on his plate."

"As have you, laddie," Val said. "As have you."

Dev was left wondering whether she was some kind of mind reader, or if she was just talking about his breakfast.

Well, at least one of those things he could do something about. He tucked in, and it did help, thank God, although he couldn't manage more than half the plateful. He felt almost human by the time he'd downed the last of his coffee.

Heh. Maybe if he hit that Turkish place again later on, he'd actually start feeling good.

When he got outside, it was looking set for another warm, sunny day. Dev wondered what to do with it. His feet made the decision for him, taking him down towards the seafront and the Square Peg Café.

Not that he was *worried* about Ceri, or anything. Just checking in. Being friendly.

Maybe looking for someone to off-load to, if she was in the mood to listen which, yeah, knowing her, he ought to give up on that hope right now. Although if he *did* manage to get her to listen, she'd probably be up for calling him a stupid tosser when he'd finished. It'd be good to see her, anyhow.

He didn't realise until he was literally a few feet from the café's front door that Kyle was sitting at one of the outside tables.

CHAPTER
TEN

Kyle's chair backed up almost to the building front, and he was sitting in shadow. As if, say, he didn't want anyone approaching to be able to spot him in time to veer off without being seen. He had a pot full of tea in front of him, and a plateful of scones. Didn't he know it made him look like a tourist?

Dev could tell there was no point trying to avoid a meeting. And anyway, he wasn't a bloody coward. He strolled up to Kyle's table as casually as he could manage, his gut only a little bit uncomfortable, and that was all down to eating too much for breakfast, wasn't it? "All right?"

"I thought you might come here." Kyle gave a tense little half shrug. He looked good, his hair a bit wild and his shirt a deep blue that brought out his eyes. It was weird, seeing him at a touristy café like this. The place didn't seem good enough for him. And it was way too tame. "I bought you scones."

Dev was pretty sure he could hear *I'm sorry* under there somewhere, which made him feel even more of a bastard. He pulled out a chair and sat down, swallowing his nerves. "Mate, I'm not a stray cat. You don't have to keep feeding me. And those are shite, anyhow. Least, that's what the waitress reckons." He looked around, but couldn't see Ceri either inside or out of the café.

"Your friend," Kyle said. It wasn't really a question. "You came here to see her? I'm not sure she's in this morning. I've only seen an older waitress."

"Huh." Maybe Monday was her regular day off? Dev had never got around to asking. He pulled out his phone to check for messages, and winced at the cracked screen. That'd happened sometime after the third tooth mug full of vodka, and around the time he'd read on the internet about how narcolepsy caused social isolation, stress, and depression. Oh, and that Kyle had just been stating facts when he'd said how much it affected his life.

There was no message from Ceri. Shit. Why the hell hadn't he made sure he got her number too?

"I'm sure she's fine," Kyle said, putting a scone on his plate and slicing it open. "You shouldn't worry about her."

Dev hadn't realised he'd been that obvious. "Nah, course not. Just, you know. Last night. Um." He fell silent, because no way could he say it wasn't only Ceri he was worried about.

"I . . . said some things, last night," Kyle said awkwardly, concentrating on spreading butter on his scone like he was doing open heart surgery or something. "They were unjustified. It was . . . well. The anger I felt wasn't all to do with you. Since I got diagnosed I've had to listen to a great deal of advice on how I'd be so much better off if I only *tried* a bit harder. But I shouldn't have taken it out on you."

Christ. Dev was just the latest in a long list of arseholes who thought they knew better than the bloke with the actual illness, then. He was lucky Kyle was even bothering with him anymore, let alone buying him scones. Dev felt even worse when he realised how tired Kyle looked. Like he hadn't slept much last night either. Which he probably hadn't—that had been another thing on the NHS website. How shitty must it be, falling asleep uncontrollably in the daytime, while being unable to sleep properly at night?

"'S all right. You weren't the only one. I was a dick. Guess I should try thinking before I speak next time, yeah? Sorry." Embarrassed, Dev took a scone to show he meant it. There was a spare plate, so Kyle hadn't been lying about hoping to see him here. Dev halved the scone and bunged on a generous helping of strawberry jam. Clotted cream didn't seem like the best idea this morning. When he looked up, he saw Kyle nudging a cup of tea his way.

Dev had to smile. "You realise this is, like, the most English apology in the entire history of the world?" He bit into the scone, which was all right, actually. Ceri had lied. Unless they were only shite when she made them.

"I live to be a cultural stereotype. Have you got plans for today?"

"What, you wanna show me your collection of Union Jack teapots? Nah. Not really. Thought I might wander over and have a look at that Round Hole and the castle everyone raves about." It was the first thing that popped into his head. "You, uh, wanna show me around?"

Kyle hesitated.

"Or we could do something else," Dev said quickly, then realised it might not be the planned destination Kyle had a problem with. "Or, you know, not."

"No—I mean, that would be . . . I'd like to." Kyle picked up his teacup, then put it down again. "I'm not sure how much use I'll be as a guide. You'd want a real local for that."

"I dunno. You seemed to know your stuff about old Mother Ivey. Can you tell me about the sea serpents?"

"You mean the Black Knight's pets?"

Dev nodded, pleased. "There you go. I knew you'd know all about it. You'll do. Course, it might be a bit of a risk, mind. Based on past experience, one of us is probably gonna end up getting the hump and shoving the other one down the hole."

Kyle's lips twitched in that way Dev was coming to recognise as controlled amusement. "Well, the sea serpents have been down there for quite a while. They're probably getting rather hungry by now."

"Shit, I'd better watch out, then." Dev grinned at Kyle's raised eyebrow. "What? Younger and tastier, ain't I?" Uh-oh. He hadn't meant it to come out sounding like a come-on. All that stuff last night, that'd made him think Kyle fancied him . . . Well, it all seemed a lot more like wishful thinking in the cold light of day. Had he gone too far?

From the way Kyle was avoiding his gaze, yeah, he probably had. Dev took a slurp of tea and bunged the cup down in the saucer harder than he meant to. "You ready?" he asked. The sooner they got out of the suddenly awkward atmosphere, the better.

Kyle blinked. "Yes." He stood up. "I'll go and pay."

Dev, who'd half got up, sat back down while Kyle strode into the café to settle up. Good job *one* of them still had a working brain. He had another gulp of tea while he waited, then stood up when he saw Kyle step back outside again.

"You, uh, know the way?" he asked, as they left the café tables behind them.

Kyle nodded towards a brown tourist information sign pointing the way to Round Hole and Caerdu Castle, with what Dev assumed were the same words in Cornish underneath. There were even little diagrams in case neither of those languages did anything for you: a line drawing of a crumbly turret and—imaginatively—a plain white circle.

"Oh. Right." Dev felt like an idiot for not having noticed it.

"I'm not sure it's actually possible to get lost around here," Kyle said, blinking hard as if his vision was blurry and he needed to clear it.

"You all right, mate?" Dev asked.

"Fine. So what do you know about the castle?"

Right. Dev could take a hint. "Uh, black knights, sea serpents . . . That's pretty much it. Oh, wait—something about giants?"

"The Black Knight was a giant. Possibly. Which would make sense, practically speaking, as you'd need a fair amount of strength to handle sea serpents. Legend has it that he kept them under the castle, and their struggles to get free tunnelled out the caves beneath."

"Aw, now you got me feeling sorry for the poor little sea monsters. Are there really caves there?"

Kyle nodded. "That's where the Round Hole comes from—it's really just a cave that's had its roof fall in."

Dev frowned. "That happen a lot? Like, it's not gonna happen when we're up top there, is it? Hey, can you visit the caves? That'd be well cool."

"Make your mind up. Are you scared of the roof falling in, or not?" Kyle sounded amused.

"Nah, I'm good. I just don't like the thought of the ground dropping away underneath me, that's all."

"Most people would be more worried about being buried alive."

"Yeah? Nah, way I see it, if ten tons of rock falls on your head, you're gone before you even know what's happened. If it goes when you're on top, though . . ." He shuddered. "Like them scenes in action movies where the heroes are running away from earthquakes, or they're on a roof and the building's collapsing. Give me nightmares, those do."

"Were you scarred for life by having *Alice in Wonderland* read to you as a child?"

Dev gave him a blank look.

"She falls down a rabbit hole?"

"Oh. Mate, you have seriously the wrong idea about how middle class my childhood was."

"Ah. Sorry."

"Nah, it's okay." Except it wasn't, not really. Dev eyed Kyle as he strode along beside him. He didn't get it. How could a bloke, who'd clearly grown up assuming having your mum and dad read you classic bedtime stories was just what happened to everyone, cut his family out of his life when he got older?

They'd passed the edge of town now and were as far as Dev had been on the cliff path before. Ahead of them, the view had opened up, all craggy cliffs and sea, and over them, a wide, blue sky with a few wispy clouds being blown by the strong sea wind. Gulls circled, and now he thought of them, Dev realised he could hear their screams—when had that become just part of the background noise?

Kyle had turned his face into the wind, which whipped his hair back and tugged at his clothes as he squinted far out to sea.

"You like it here, don't you?" Dev said without really knowing where it came from.

He thought Kyle's step faltered, but the impression was gone before he could decide if it was real or not. "I suppose I do," Kyle said, his tone uncertain as if he hadn't really thought of it before. "What makes you say that, though?"

And there was the sixty-four-million-dollar question, though what sixty-four million dollars had to do with anything, Dev had no clue. No way was he going to say Kyle just looked *right*, somehow, like he fit in with the landscape. "Dunno, really . . . Just, you've read up on the place, even bits you haven't been to. I dunno. You seem to find it interesting."

It sounded pretty thin to Dev, but Kyle was nodding. "What do you think of Porthkennack?" he asked.

"You're gonna laugh."

"I hope not," Kyle said drily.

"Uh, shit. No." Dev coughed. Yeah, giving the bloke two cataplexy attacks in about as many days probably wasn't the best idea. "It's just . . . It's like it's not real, you know? I mean, the real world's back home in London, with work and mates and stuff. I can't even imagine actually living here. Growing up here." And fuck knew he'd tried. "It's like nothing that happens here could possibly affect the real world." Even as he said it, Dev knew it was bollocks. Wishful thinking, at best.

"But your friend Ceri lives here, and grew up here." There was that flat tone again.

"Yeah, well, I told you it was stupid. But yeah, I like the place."

"Wait till it rains for three weeks solid and the wind's blowing it sideways in off the sea," Kyle said, but he wasn't fooling Dev.

"Think you'll stay? You know, when your lease is up?"

Kyle didn't answer. He was staring intently ahead, and Dev followed his gaze automatically.

"What are you—" Dev blinked. "Fuck me, is that like a geyser or something?" A waterspout had just spurted out of the ground ahead of them, and then died down again.

"That's the Round Hole," Kyle said. Something about his tone made Dev glance at him. He had a smile on his face that looked unconscious, as if he hadn't yet realised it was there, and he even sounded happy. As if life had gone for a ceasefire on the constant lemon bombardment, and chucked him something he actually wanted for a change.

Dev's chest tightened, for a moment, and he found he was smiling back. "How's that work, then?" he asked.

"It's connected to the cave system. I'd heard this sometimes happens at high tide—the water rushes into the caves, and pressure forces it, well, up the spout."

"Huh. Cool." They picked up the pace, Kyle seeming as keen as Dev to get there before the show stopped. Dev couldn't believe there was no one else around to see it—a whole bloody town full of people on holiday, and they were all either on the beach, or in a café, or traipsing round shops buying tourist tat. It was like it'd been laid on just for him and Kyle.

The Round Hole itself was a *lot* larger than Dev had expected—at least a hundred feet across, easy. "Fuck me, that's big," he said, right as another wave hit just right and spray spurted up from its inland side, the wind carrying it dangerously close to where they were standing. They backed off a bit, laughing. Well, Dev was laughing. Kyle had that weird look on his face Dev was coming to recognise meant he'd be laughing if he dared.

"I can't believe the path goes right by it." Dev shook a few drops of seawater off his hand. "There ain't even a fence or nothing. *How* many tourists do they lose a year?"

"I'm not sure, but there is a gruesome legend attached to this place. It involves another giant." Kyle stopped and looked at Dev, as if he thought Dev might not be interested.

Which was just crazy. Course he was interested. "Go on, then."

"Apparently the giant—or possibly just *a* giant—fell in love with a beautiful and virtuous maiden, and she told him she'd only be his if he could prove his love by filling up this hole with his blood. Being a giant, he thought he could manage that easily, so he opened up a vein. Unfortunately, it was low tide, so he didn't realise the hole was connected to the sea and could therefore never be filled, and he bled to death."

"Nice. That was well virtuous, that was, getting rid of a bloke she didn't fancy by having him top himself."

"I think in those days they had a rather blinkered view of virtue."

Dev grinned. "Yep. No shagging, and you're golden. Must've been bloody awful living back in them days." He sat down at a safe distance from the hole to wait for another waterspout, his arms resting on his knees.

After a minute, Kyle joined him, although he didn't so much sit on the grass as sprawl on it, propped up on one elbow. He still looked tired, so Dev wasn't surprised when after a couple of minutes, he lay down fully.

It was fucking awesome up here, with a waterspout on one side of them and the sea on the other. And yeah, a fit bloke by his side. More than that—a bloke who, well, was interested in stuff that wasn't just sport on the telly and having a laugh. Who made *Dev* interested in all that sort of crap. And who just might be interested in Dev too. He'd seen Kyle looking at him again, at odd moments through the morning. Like he was checking him out.

Dev tried not to think about how solid the ground under his bum really was—after all, if the Round Hole was connected to the sea, the chances were they were right on top of the hollow bit here . . . Nope, not gonna think about it.

He gazed over at the headland a bit farther on, where he could see what had to be the ruins of the Black Whoever's castle. What would it have been like living in that castle back in the day? It must have been even more remote then than it was now. Some bastard had plonked a big, ugly block of a house around a hundred yards from where they were sitting, on the inland side of the Hole and a lot closer to it than Dev would've been happy sinking foundations. It looked old, but weirdly modern at the same time.

He turned to ask Kyle about it—and saw he'd fallen asleep.

Dev had to smile. Kyle seemed comfy enough, lying there on the springy grass, so Dev didn't try to move him or wake him. He did shift around though, making sure he was sitting where his shadow would fall on Kyle's face. Wouldn't want him to get sunburned.

Then he took another long, long look at the view.

CHAPTER ELEVEN

Kyle opened his eyes to see Dev sitting so close they were almost touching. He was doing something on his phone, a half smile on his lips.

Still here, then. And not angry. Or at least, he'd had time to get over it.

"I hope you're not putting pictures of me asleep on the internet." Kyle's voice sounded rusty to himself, but Dev's smile still grew as he turned to look Kyle's way.

"Nah. Got a text from Mal. He got lost on the way back to the villa in the dark last night. Had to kip down on the beach. Got woken up by the tide coming in, and had to walk back soaking wet in his clubbing gear." Dev chuckled. "Typical Mal, that is. You feeling better now?"

Kyle sat up. "Yes." He was, actually.

Dev put his phone in his pocket. "You knew that was gonna happen, din'tcha? That's why you lay down."

Kyle tensed, even though Dev's tone had been friendly. Teasing. "It'd be more accurate to say I knew it would happen *if* I lay down." He took a deep breath. "Sometimes giving in to it can stave off problems later."

Dev was nodding. "Tell me next time, though, yeah? I felt like a right cock sitting here talking to myself."

"I— Yes. Sorry." Kyle felt wrong-footed. He'd expected . . .

Well, not to be left, perhaps. Dev had never seemed the sort to walk off and leave someone in a vulnerable position. Annoyance, though, would have been perfectly justified. Kyle should have told him. But he hadn't wanted to make a bloody song and dance about it.

And yes, maybe he'd been testing Dev. Just a little.

"Seriously," Dev went on, his cheerful tone at odds with his words. "You were out for nearly an hour. What if I'd needed a piss? I'd have been well stuffed."

"Sorry," Kyle said again. He didn't know what else to say.

"And that's another thing. What did I tell you about wearing that word out?" Dev stood up and stretched, not gracefully but with endearingly obvious relish. "Christ, my bum's numb. Tell me if me legs fall off, won't you? We hitting the castle now? I've been looking it up online, and I hate to tell you, mate, but all that Black Knight stuff is bollocks."

Kyle scrambled to his feet with even less grace than Dev had managed. He doubted there was anything endearing about it. "Next you'll be telling me sea monsters aren't real," he muttered.

"Nah, don't be daft. They got their own Wikipedia page and everything. Course they're real." Dev grinned. "But the castle's only fourteenth century, which is two hundred years after the Black Knight was strutting his stuff in all them legends of King Arthur. And get this—it was built by a Black Prince. No, wait. *The* Black Prince, son of Edward the Somethingth, 'cept no one knows why he's called that. Have I earned me history GCSE yet?"

"No, but I bet they'd take you on as a tour guide at the castle if you fancied a change of career."

"You know what, I'm almost tempted. That's gotta be a fun job. You could make up any old shite to tell the tourists, and no one would ever know. Hey, you know anything about that old house over there?"

"That? That's Varhak Manor." Kyle smiled. "Used to belong to a mad Victorian scientist. He used to kidnap the townsfolk to conduct unspeakable experiments on them, and disposed of the evidence in the Round Hole."

"Shut *up*. Seriously?" Dev's eyes went from wide to narrow with almost comical speed. "Wait, no way. Now who's making shit up?"

"Would I?" Kyle walked on, feeling almost light-headed with something he shied away from naming.

The knowledge crept up on him anyway. Happiness. He was happy.

There wasn't a huge amount left of Caerdu Castle, but at least it was more than just an oddly regular mound of earth, which was more than could be said for a few misleadingly labelled heritage sites Kyle had seen. Enough fragments remained of walls both internal and external, some with doorways, windows, and fireplaces, to give some sense that once, people had lived here.

Kyle was expecting to be dragged down to the caves after they'd taken in as much of the ruins as they could, but Dev seemed keen to call it a day.

He shrugged, hands half in his jeans pockets, when Kyle queried it, hating the thought that Dev was making allowances for him. "Had a bit of a rough night last night— Ah, shit. Sorry, mate. That's gotta be like telling a famine victim you're starving 'cos your tea's half an hour late."

Kyle stared at him. "Something like that, yes." He broke eye contact, gazing out to sea.

"All right, mate?"

He took a moment to answer. Gulls were circling high above the water, while windsurfers scudded across the waves and, from time to time, fell in. Stupid, to be so affected by something so small. "Most people don't understand about the tiredness. They see me falling asleep all day, and assume I'm getting twice as much rest as everyone else."

"Nah, I was reading about it on the internet last night. Like, there's this . . . thing in your brain that doesn't work right, so when you go to sleep, it's not the right sort of sleep, am I right? Some chemical you ain't got."

"Orexin. Also known as hypocretin." Kyle said it flatly. Maybe there was a certain amount of anger in his voice too, as when Dev spoke again his tone was less certain.

"I wasn't, you know, prying or nothing. Just wanted to understand." He paused. "It must drive you crazy."

Kyle had to breathe deeply, forcing down a bitter laugh. "Yes," he said tightly.

Dev put a hand on his elbow, his touch light. "I was well out of order last night. I shouldn't have said that stuff."

"Thank you." Kyle couldn't look at him. He felt twice as tired as he had only minutes ago.

Dev's grip on his arm tightened for a moment, but then released. "Wanna head back, then?"

Kyle nodded. "Would you like to get lunch somewhere in town?" He could definitely do with a boost in energy levels right now.

"Yeah, that'd be cool. What d'you fancy? Pub grub all right?"

"Fine. Although I won't be drinking," he reminded Dev.

"Nah, me neither. Not after last night. Bit more relaxed, though, innit? Not like, you know, going out for dinner."

Was Dev nervous? Why now?

Was it because going out for a meal was akin to going on a date?

And there it was again: old Kyle's ego, rearing its entitled head. "Slug and Lettuce all right with you?"

Dev grinned. "Long as that's the name of the pub and not what's on the menu, yeah."

It wasn't until they stepped inside the Slug and Lettuce that Kyle remembered why he usually gave chain pubs a wide berth. There was nothing *wrong* with the place, per se—it was simply utterly generic and devoid of character. It was also crowded and incredibly noisy.

Dev shot him a look as they hovered on the threshold. "Uh, bit busy, innit? Tell you what, I think there's a pizza place up the road— wanna see if that's got a table free?"

Kyle couldn't see how any of the ubiquitous Italian food chains would be any better, but in fact Dev led him along a side street to a small, cosy-looking restaurant that proclaimed itself a family business and smelled enticingly of garlic and basil. Although the place was almost full, it was infinitely quieter than the Slug and Lettuce, probably down to the way the interior was sectioned off into small, intimate areas connected by wide archways. "Remind me which of us is the local here?" he said as they took their seats at a table by the window. "I didn't even know this place was here."

"You need to get out more, mate. Nah, a couple at my B&B were saying they liked the food here, and I saw it when I was out the other night. This all right for you?"

"Fine. Perfect. If the food's as good as it smells, I'll have to remember this place." Kyle gave a wry smile. "For the rare occasions I get into town."

"S'pose it's a bit far to walk back all the time. You know, we're not all that far from my B&B. If you like, I could get the bike and give you a lift back to yours after we've eaten. I brung a spare helmet, just in case." Dev's face fell. "Ah, shit—sorry, are you okay to ride a bike? You won't fall off or nothing, will you?"

Kyle hadn't actually considered that before. But in any case, he didn't need to be ferried around like an invalid. "I can manage the walk. It's not that far. Only a couple of miles, if that." Although if he was honest, he was feeling drained from so much exertion.

Bleak depression settled on him like the heavy arms of a false friend around his shoulders. This should be the prime of his life—and here he was, worn out by a morning's sightseeing.

"You need your lunch, mate," Dev was saying. "You'll feel better with something inside you. Uh. That wasn't supposed to sound like a come-on."

He seemed a hairsbreadth away from coming over all *No homo, dude*. Somehow, Kyle's bleak mood lifted, and he shook his head. "I'm sorry. I think I gave you a false impression of me. You don't need to worry about . . . uh, saying anything gay. I'm not straight myself. Until a few months ago, I was in a relationship with a man."

"Yeah? Seriously?" Dev looked almost comically relieved. Then his face darkened. "So what happened? He found out you was ill and he left you?"

"*No.*" It came out more sharply than Kyle had intended. "It wasn't Jeffrey's fault."

Dev leaned back in his chair, hands raised. "Okay, bruv. None of my business, I get that. You ready to order?"

Kyle hadn't even noticed the waiter's approach. "Yes. Sorry."

"Mate, I keep telling you about that word." Dev turned and grinned at the waiter, who was young and darkly handsome. Kyle felt a surge of irrational jealousy. "I'll have the Penne Arrabiata, cheers."

"Spaghetti Puccini," Kyle said, picking the first pasta dish off the menu that wasn't either vegetarian or overly spicy. "And a bottle of water, please."

After the waiter had left them, Kyle gave Dev a wary look, wondering if any more awkward questions would be forthcoming.

Dev was playing with the plain blue ceramic vase in the middle of the table, which housed a single white chrysanthemum, its stem neatly stiffened with a spiral of thin wire. "How'd you get into doing pottery, then?" he asked, setting the vase back down so that the flower faced Kyle. "Was that, like, before or after you got ill?"

Kyle blinked, feeling absurdly like the flower was a camera turned on his face. "Before. I've always found it relaxing."

"Did you do art and stuff at school? I was always rubbish at that sort of thing. Well, that and the rest of it, to be honest. Couldn't see the point back then, you know?"

"Of art?"

Dev grimaced. "Of studying. Always knew I wanted to work with me hands, didn't I? Course, then I find out you need exams to be a mechanic and all."

"It must have come as a bit of a shock," Kyle said drily. He'd known a few boys like that at school and had secretly envied them their confidence that life would turn out well for them without any undue effort on their part. Even *before* he'd spent years obtaining qualifications that were now so much waste paper.

And there was the bitterness again. How very attractive.

"So did you?" Dev demanded, making Kyle jump.

"What?"

"Take art at school."

"Oh. Yes. Sor— I took A-level art," Kyle said awkwardly. "But I studied law at university, of course."

"Oxford? Cambridge?"

"Lancaster, actually. I'm not that much of an overachiever."

Dev gave him a sharp glance and looked as though he was going to say something—but didn't.

"What?" Kyle prompted.

"Nah, it's just . . . Do you reckon that's what brought on your narcolepsy? Working too hard?"

Kyle closed his eyes briefly. "Don't you start. That's the sort of thing my mother would come out with. No, the latest theory is that it's down to a genetic predisposition triggered by a virus."

"Huh. So you had shit luck twice. That sucks." Dev grinned suddenly. "Hey, do you ever play the National Lottery?"

"No."

"Pity. I was thinking I could ask what numbers you got, and make sure I never choose them ones."

Against all odds, Kyle found himself smiling as the waiter brought their food.

It was good, if fairly unimaginatively prepared and presented. Kyle felt better already after a few mouthfuls. He looked up from his plate to make a comment and found Dev with an uncertain expression on his face.

"Not to your taste?" Kyle asked politely.

"Nah—I mean, yeah, the food's great. No worries. Just . . ." He broke off and gazed out of the window for a moment.

Kyle waited, a prickle of unease damping his appetite.

"Look, I gotta explain something to you, yeah?" Dev said at last.

Kyle concentrated on the spaghetti he was twirling around his fork and managed not to comment on how ominous that sounded. Especially with the anxious look Dev was giving him. "Carry on."

"It's about yesterday. Why I got the hump when you was on about the Roscarrocks. I mean, I know you said I didn't have to explain myself or nothing, but it don't feel right, not telling you. Not after you been all . . ." Dev made a vague gesture that appeared to encompass Kyle, their meal, and presumably the whole morning as well, then he rolled his shoulders and took a gulp of water. "See, when my birth mum had me, she gave me up for adoption."

Kyle froze. Had his wild guesses as to Dev's parentage actually been correct? "And . . .?" he prompted.

"Well, she's here, ain't she? I mean, she lives here. In Porthkennack. I mean, I found out her name and I tracked her down. That's why I got a bit . . . See, her name's Roscarrock. Beaten Roscarrock. Think it's Cornish 'cos it sounds well weird to me, calling a kid Beaten, like you want them to grow up and get . . . Shit. That's why."

Dev took another gulp of water, looking like he wished it was something a lot stronger. Not sure what to say, Kyle couldn't stop himself from reaching across the table to grasp Dev's forearm.

He'd been right. Not on all the details, maybe, but in the broader sense, he'd been right.

"You ain't looking all that surprised," Dev said with an awkward half laugh that rang a few warning bells.

"I didn't know," Kyle said cautiously. "But I . . . speculated, after what happened at my house."

Dev bit his lip, playing with his fork in his bowl of penne. "How come you never asked?"

"It wasn't any of my business." Kyle hesitated. "Have you seen her?"

"Nah. Was on me way up to have a look at the ancestral home, wasn't I? But it was closed." He glanced down at his plate, seemed to realise he hadn't finished eating, and speared a few penne before shoving them into his mouth.

Kyle ate a mouthful of spaghetti while he thought about an appropriate reply to that. *Why didn't you just knock on the door?* seemed unlikely to elicit a favourable response. "You wanted to have a look around before introducing yourself?" he said at last. "You don't think it might be misconstrued?"

"What do you mean?"

"Well . . . It might look as though you're checking them out. Checking the house out, even. To see if it's worth claiming a relationship with the family."

"Oi, money's got sod all to do with it!"

"I know that. But they don't. And, well, they seem a little on the suspicious side." His face felt hot, which was ridiculous. "I went up there, a while after you'd left. To introduce myself as a neighbour."

Dev's expression was difficult to read. "You went up there. Just after I—" He broke off, and stared out of the window.

Kyle ran a hand through his hair. "Look, there's nothing sinister about it. I *am* a close neighbour. With a possible family connection."

"What did they say to that?"

Shit. "I didn't mention it, in the end. They weren't all that welcoming," Kyle added, with a defensive tone even he could hear. Ye gods. If he'd responded to questions in court with this sort of ineptitude, he'd have deserved to be disbarred.

Dev frowned. Kyle expected the interrogation as to his motives to continue, but in the end what Dev asked was, "Did you see her? Beaten Roscarrock?"

"No. Two men—brothers, although they didn't look at all alike. Bran and Jory. It was Bran who did all the talking." He paused. "I take it the family is expecting you? Or your mother is, at least?"

Dev was shaking his head. "Nah. Thought I'd surprise her, you know?"

Surprise? Shock, more like. Kyle tried to think of a tactful way to voice his misgivings. "Are you sure that's wise? Don't you think it might be a bit of a bombshell for her, if you turn up out of the blue? Have you thought about writing to her first? Seeing if she's willing to see you?"

Dev's chin went up. "Why wouldn't she want to see me? I'm her son."

Kyle could think of lots of reasons. Although probably none that Dev would want to hear. "I still think you should get in touch by phone or by letter before actually going to see her."

"I did, all right? I wrote letters and stuff. Just . . . I'm not sure if she got them. Maybe her family didn't want her to or something—I dunno."

God. This was a bloody minefield. "She's a grown woman. She must be, what, in her forties by now? Why would her family be intercepting her mail? Maybe, just plausibly, they might want to spare her the upset of receiving your letters, but how would they even know they were from you?"

Dev made an angry gesture. "Look, I've gotta see her, all right? I gotta know why she gave me away. If she regretted it, after. If she ever thought about me while I was growing up."

"And if you don't like what you hear?"

"Then I'll deal with it. I'm not a little kid."

He looked horribly young to Kyle right now. Kyle didn't mean to do it. But somehow, his hand was across the table, grasping Dev's arm in a repeat of his earlier gesture. He nodded. "I get it. I do. And, well, if you want any kind of support, or to talk about things . . ."

"Cheers, mate." Dev nodded once, then ducked his head in apparent shyness, and started forking up his pasta once more.

They split the bill more or less evenly after they'd eaten, and strolled out into warm sunshine—not a minute too soon for Kyle, who'd been starting to feel drowsiness overcome him once he'd finished his food.

He should probably thank Dev for a pleasant morning and let him get on with his holiday. Let him go find his birth mother, if that was what he really wanted to do. Despite Kyle's own misgivings over the matter.

"So what sort of bike do you ride?" he asked instead.

"Honda Hornet. Got a sweet deal on it a year or so back. It's a good ride. Not too heavy on fuel in the city, for a 600, and handles great. Looks pretty cool and all." Dev shot him a challenging glance. "Know a lot about bikes, do you?"

"Absolutely bugger all," Kyle admitted. "I've always driven cars."

"Yeah? What you got right now?"

"Ah. A Ford."

"Ranger? Mustang? Don't tell me you got a GT?"

Kyle found himself wincing. "Fiesta, actually."

"Yeah? No offence, mate, but I would not have put you down for a Fiesta driver."

Wouldn't it be more offensive if he *had*? "I, uh, downsized after I gave up work."

"Fair enough. Hey, I know you said you'd be fine to walk home, but I was thinking, yeah, do you fancy a ride on the bike anyhow? We could take the coast road, have a look at the scenery and all that? If you reckon you'd be okay on it, which, see, I been thinking. If you're all right to drive you gotta be all right to ride pillion, yeah?"

When he put it that way, it sounded like fun. "Okay. Thanks."

"No problem, mate."

Once they were through the town they turned their steps inland, towards where Dev was staying.

Dev's B&B turned out to be an old stone farmhouse on the outskirts of town. It looked a bit on the cheap and cheerful side, but at least the latter part of the description seemed as apt as the former. Instead of going to the front door, Dev led him around the side of the house to the back garden. It was modest but well-kept, with half a dozen hens scratching happily in a coop to one side. There was a weathered swing and a slide for small children that weren't presently being used, and a picnic table that was. Sitting in the shade of an umbrella advertising Foster's lager—Kyle speculated as to whether it had been liberated from a local pub—were a couple of middle-aged ladies, playing cards.

Dev greeted them with a wave. "All right, Val? Carol? This is Kyle. He's sort of a local."

"Sort of?" the more senior of the two queried in a strong Scottish accent.

Kyle shrugged, a little uncomfortable under her penetrating gaze. "I've only lived in Porthkennack for a couple of months."

"Kyle's got a house on the cliffs up over Mother Ivey's Bay," Dev told them. "You two having a quiet day in, then?"

The more feminine looking of the two nodded. "Val's hip's playing up again," she stage-whispered.

"Oh, hush," her partner scolded. "Are you stopping, now?"

"Just come to pick up me bike," Dev said. "Gonna take a ride. You ought to try it some time, you two."

Val shook her head. "My biking days are over, laddie. Well, good to meet you, Kyle." She gave him another piercing stare.

What exactly had Dev told them about him?

Dev's bike was under a lean-to at the end of a drive that went down the length of the garden. "Ain't she beautiful?" he asked, his tone endearingly proud. "Go on. Admit it, you're well jell. Right, you sure you're gonna be okay on the back? What if you get an attack?"

"I'll be fine." Impatience warred with guilt in Kyle's stomach. It was his life to risk, damn it. Even if it would probably be deeply upsetting to Dev to lose a passenger.

Dev frowned in that way Kyle was starting to recognise meant he was thinking something through. "Got an idea. You start feeling a bit iffy, you slap me twice on the leg, yeah? And I'll pull over."

That . . . was actually pretty sensible. "Okay."

Dev trundled the bike out onto the path and swung his leg over it. Kyle got on gingerly behind.

"Cool. Right, bung this on and off we go. 'S all right, put your hands round my waist. I ain't gonna take it the wrong way." Dev grinned and pulled on his helmet. They set off, slowly at first and then more speedily once they got onto the road.

The last time Kyle had been on a motorbike, he'd been in his teens, going out with a young man called Si, who'd been tattooed, multiply pierced, and whose wardrobe consisted entirely of leather and studs. If Kyle was honest, he'd been with him chiefly to shock his parents after their anticlimactic lack of reaction to his announcement he was gay. Goodness knew why Si had been with him—they'd had very little in common besides a shared love of getting into each other's pants—but it had been fun while it lasted.

It felt different riding with Dev. For one thing, Dev didn't piss about revving the engine and screeching round corners to show off. For another . . .

Well. They weren't together. Which made it feel a lot more awkward holding on to his waist, particularly as he was only wearing a T-shirt. The warmth of his skin coming through the thin cotton, coupled with the way they sat pressed together, Dev's body between his legs, made Kyle worry about inappropriate physical reactions. He considered dropping his hands to Dev's hips, which were clad in thick denim, but decided that would probably be even worse.

Still, it came back to him—the way he had to lean with the rider in front as he went round a corner. The way the wind felt, whipping at his clothes. The roar of the engine and the vibration beneath him.

The exhilaration no car ride could counterfeit. God, how long had it been since Kyle had felt so free, so alive?

He couldn't recall.

CHAPTER TWELVE

When they got off the bike outside Kyle's cottage, Dev seemed restless. Hyped up by the ride, perhaps. He parked the bike up by the wall and hung the helmets on the handlebars, then couldn't seem to stand still. Did that mean he wanted to be gone?

Should Kyle invite him in, or just let him go? He couldn't think of much worse than an awkward cup of tea with a man impatient to be out of his sight.

Oh God. Maybe Dev had noticed something during the ride. Had Kyle been gripping him too tightly? He opened his mouth to thank Dev for the ride and say a swift good-bye.

It was Dev who spoke first, however. "Hey, I've shown you mine—gonna show me yours?"

Kyle blinked. "What?"

"Your ride, mate." Dev grinned, although he still had a slight wariness about his eyes. "What did you think I meant? So where do you keep it?"

"Just down the road—that row of garages?" None of the cottages had been built with motor vehicles in mind, so the garages had been constructed at some point in the past thirty or so years. Kyle seriously doubted they'd get planning permission these days, although with their white-painted exterior and grey roofing, they blended in surprisingly well with the cottages they served.

"Come on, then," Dev urged.

Kyle raised an eyebrow. "Seriously? Are you missing your job?"

"Nah. Well, maybe a little bit. I got this thing—I like matching rides to people, yeah?"

"You think the kind of car a man drives tells you something about him? In that case I'm definitely not showing you my Fiesta."

"Go on. I'm here for three weeks, you know. Bound to catch you in it sooner or later. You might as well get it over with."

"Fine. But don't say I haven't warned you."

They strolled down to the garages, Kyle relishing the way the short walk loosened up muscles in his legs that had stiffened during the bike ride. His garage was the closest, presumably because his cottage was the farthest from the little block. Kyle took out his key and opened up the door, letting out a waft of musty air. Dust motes sparkled in the afternoon sun.

Dev waved a hand in front of his face. "Been a while since you drove anywhere, has it?"

Kyle shrugged. "It's easier to get groceries online. And I prefer to walk when I'm only going into town. With all the tourist traffic around, it's often quicker." And a badly timed sleep attack wouldn't risk bringing the one-way system to a standstill.

"Fair enough. Right, then. Let's take a look at you." Standing there with his arms folded, Dev examined the Fiesta.

Kyle tried to see it through his eyes: almost as old as Dev himself, with a dented wing, scratched paintwork, and a flourishing crop of rust . . . He winced and gave up. "You may want to keep your thoughts on what this says about me to yourself. Just saying."

Dev shook his head slowly. He even pursed his lips, although mischief danced in his eyes. "Mate. *Mate.* This is seriously fucking tragic, and I've seen some well tragic motors in my time. Is that thing even legal?"

"She passed her MOT. Last September," Kyle added apologetically.

"I can believe it, mate. Well, not that she passed, but that it was nearly a year ago. This is seriously not the sort of car I'd have seen you with."

Kyle gave him a bitter smile. "When I got diagnosed . . . they told me I was still okay to drive, you know? That I'd have enough warning of attacks to pull over. I didn't believe them."

"So you got yourself an old banger so if you pranged it, at least you wouldn't give a shit?"

"Actually, I decided to get a top-of-the-range Lexus." So he could go out in style. "I was there in the showroom, halfway to signing the papers, and then I thought it'd be a crime to waste something so beautiful. So I told the salesman no thanks, and on my way home I stopped at the first used-car place and swapped my BMW for the cheapest thing on the forecourt."

Dev's expression was so comical Kyle had to stifle a laugh. "The trader couldn't believe his luck. He was probably crossing his fingers the Fiesta's engine wouldn't fall out before I got it on the road. That was six months ago."

"Fuck me, she's kept on going that long? Looking at her now I wouldn't trust her to make it six miles."

"It's the car that won't die. I'm actually getting quite attached to her." There was that lightness again. Happiness.

"So if I told you it'd be a kindness to take her down to the scrapheap? If she makes it that far?"

"Not going to happen."

"Thought not. At least let me take a look at her, yeah?" Kyle's doubt must have shown on his face, as Dev grinned. "Trust me, I'm a professional. Got me Level 4 Certificate and everything."

"If you like." Kyle tossed his keys over. "But careful if you get in the back for any reason. There's a hole rusted right through the floor there, and it'd probably be best if it didn't get any larger."

Snatching the keys easily out of the air, Dev unlocked the driver's door and climbed in so he could pop the bonnet. "No worries, mate. I'm well up-to-date with my tetanus jabs and all."

"Is that something to do with being a mechanic?"

"Nah, it's something to do with living with Mal." Dev propped up the bonnet and leaned over the engine. He pursed his lips again.

"I'm not quite sure what to make of that statement," Kyle said cautiously. He wondered what Dev could see. Everything looked a uniform shade of oily grime to him.

Dev glanced round at him and laughed. "Sorry. He keeps rats. Always has done, since he was like five or something. Sometimes the little fuckers bite."

"God. It sounds like the stuff of nightmares."

"Nah, they're well cute, really. I mean, they ain't like wild ones. They're a lot cleaner than most people think, but, yeah, it don't hurt to keep your jabs up." Dev seemed to think about that. "Actually, yeah, it does hurt, but they last like ten years or something."

"With you both away, did he have to get a rat-sitter?"

"Nah, he took 'em round his mum's. She's used to it all. So, did you have pets when you were younger? I always wanted a dog, but, you know." He shrugged.

Kyle had a heart-breaking vision of a younger Dev, forever disappointed in his childhood hopes. "I had a Labrador. Tilly." She'd sickened while he was at university, and his parents had been forced to have her put down. He'd been equal parts devastated and guilt-stricken, although the vet had said it was cancer, not pining for her owner, that'd done for her.

"Yeah? Ever think about getting another?"

"Not recently." Kyle frowned. Why *hadn't* he? Jeffrey hadn't liked dogs—but Jeffrey was history now. "I suppose I thought it wasn't fair to get one, with my condition."

"Bollocks."

Startled, Kyle had to fight a momentary weakness in his knees. "What?"

"Why wouldn't it be fair? And they can help, right? I was reading about this girl in America. She's got a service dog, and it warns her when she's about to have an attack. And it's gotta be good, right, if you're out on your own and you go down. Like a guard dog. Stop anyone, I dunno, nicking your wallet or drawing a dick on your face while you can't stop 'em." The Fiesta, its grimy inner workings still shamefully on display, seemed to have been forgotten.

"Do you do this much research on everyone you meet?" Kyle asked, only half-joking.

Dev flashed him a cheeky grin. "Nah. Only the ones I fancy."

Kyle put a hand out to steady himself against the garage's dusty, cobwebbed, but nonetheless comfortingly solid side. He hadn't thought—hadn't expected Dev to just come out with it like that.

"Uh . . . that all right? Me saying that?" Dev looked uncertain for a moment, then seemed to rally himself. "Mate, I know you said you weren't interested. And if you want me to back off, just say the word.

But I, well, I seen you looking at me, and I reckon maybe you got a bit of a thing for greasy mechanics. Or, well, *a greasy mechanic.*"

Kyle was about to tell him no—but to hell with it. It was just sex, wasn't it? It didn't have to mean anything. And he was so bloody *tired* of not living. What could it hurt, to give in, to take a bit of physical pleasure when it was offered? What had Dev said? *Nothing here was real.* In a couple of weeks, Dev would be back in London, laughing with his mates over the weird bloke he'd slept with on holiday. And that was for the best.

The thought of it was like a knife in his chest—but then Dev stepped forward, took Kyle's face in his hands, and kissed him, and Kyle buried the pain under an avalanche of desire. Dev's lips were salty, as if he'd been drinking in the sea air. Once he'd tasted them, Kyle couldn't get enough of them.

But not here. Anyone could wander past and get an eyeful. That'd hardly endear him to his already unfriendly neighbours. Kyle broke the kiss, breathing hard. "Let's get back to the house."

Dev's face was flushed, and his chest was heaving. "Yeah. Good plan." His hands weren't quite steady as they closed the Fiesta's bonnet.

Kyle almost forgot to lock the garage. They half ran up the road back to the cottage, Dev grinning and Kyle fighting the urge to laugh. He dropped his keys on the doormat, picked them up, fumbled them into the lock, and then finally, *finally* managed to push open the door. They stumbled inside, Kyle barely able to wait until the door had swung shut behind them before he grabbed Dev once more and pulled him close. Their teeth clashed in a powerful kiss, and it was so, so good. How had he lived without this?

Kyle let out an *oof* as Dev backed him up against the living room wall, their bodies pressed together as they explored each other's mouth. God, it'd been so long. Even before they'd officially broken up, Jeffrey and he hadn't—

Kyle was damned if he was going to think about Jeffrey right now. He focussed on the hard body in his arms, the belt buckle digging into his hip. Something else starting to dig into his thigh, just below. God, he needed this. The kiss turned frantic, and Dev's hands tugged at his shirt, pulling it out of his trousers. Good idea. Kyle grabbed at

Dev's T-shirt, awkwardly pushing it up until he could get his hands underneath.

The first touch of Dev's skin seared him with heat. He wanted more. No, he needed it. One hand on Dev's chest, Kyle shoved the other down the back of his jeans and pulled their bodies even tighter together.

"Fuck me," Dev gasped, breaking off the kiss and laughing softly. "Okay, are we gonna take this somewhere horizontal? 'Cos that floor don't look too comfy and no offence, mate, but if you fall down, I'm not sure I'll get my act together in time to catch you."

Kyle's mouth was dry, and he struggled to find words. "Yes. Come on." Then he contradicted himself by pulling Dev close again and sinking back into that addictive kiss.

Oh God.

"Bed?" Dev panted into his mouth. "Or sofa?"

Kyle had just enough presence of mind left to reflect that while the bedroom seemed a million miles away, the sofa was narrow and falling off would be painful as well as embarrassing. "Bed," he said hoarsely and pulled Dev along with him. How they made it through to the dining room and up the stairs without taking a tumble, entwined as they were, was a mystery. Kyle kicked the bedroom door open, and they stumbled through to land in a heap on the bed. He still had a hand on Dev's arse, and Dev was scrabbling at his flies.

"Jesus, fuck, what bastard invented clothes," Dev was muttering, and Kyle had to tamp down on his instinct to laugh or this would all be over before it'd even begun.

The thought sobered him. Kyle forced himself to stop. To push himself up on his hands for a moment, look down into Dev's warm brown eyes and speak plainly. "Need to warn you—sex can be a trigger." His chest felt tight. Was this where Dev decided he wasn't worth the bother?

Dev just grinned. "Don't worry, mate. Gonna make it so fucking good you won't be able to fall asleep."

Which entirely missed the point, but damn it, Kyle was only human. Kneeling astride Dev, he tore his shirt off and threw it on the floor, then tugged at Dev's T-shirt until Dev took the hint and stripped it off. God, his chest was gorgeous. Darkly furred, all man, with small brown nipples that were already peaked. Kyle bent to take one in his mouth, and his cock surged with the salty taste and the feeling of it hard against his tongue.

"Fuck me," Dev gasped, and managed to get Kyle's trousers undone. Then his hand was on Kyle's cock, and his voice switched to a porn-star growl. "Oh yeah, baby. Fuck *me*."

"Don't make me laugh," Kyle begged, torn between delirium and terror. If he had an attack *now* . . . He'd almost prefer it if he never woke up again.

"Gonna do better than that. Gonna make you come." Dev jerked Kyle's cock a couple of times, his grip deliciously firm, then he wriggled his way down the bed until his face was level with Kyle's crotch.

Then he plunged his mouth over Kyle's cock.

"*God.*" It was too much. Kyle wasn't sure he could keep his body from giving up on him under the sensory overload. But damn it, it was good. He stood it for another moment, then drew away from Dev's mouth, swinging his leg over to lie down by Dev's side. "Come here," he said, tugging at Dev's shoulder as if to pull him bodily back up the bed. "And get those bloody jeans off."

Dev let out a soft laugh, undid his jeans, and pushed them off, briefs and all. Then he scrambled back up the bed and rolled over on top of Kyle. He was heavier than he looked. A solid, grounding weight. Kyle gazed down between them, impatient. He could feel Dev's hard cock pressed against his own erection, but he wanted to *see* it.

It was gorgeous. Flushed dark. Uncircumcised. Bending slightly to the left—and that was all Kyle had time to see before Dev claimed his mouth in another kiss. Both of them were hungry. Demanding. Pressed together yet still not quite close enough.

"Fuck, yeah," Dev gasped between kisses. "Knew you'd be fucking gorgeous."

Kyle reached up to bite Dev's lip and encourage him down for another kiss. He'd have used his hands, but they were wrapped around Dev's arse and he couldn't seem to make them let go. Dev was *amazing*—all taut, compact muscle. His chest hair felt fantastic rubbing against Kyle's more sparsely furred skin. And his shoulders— God, his shoulders. They should be illegal. They probably *were* illegal. He smelled like motorbikes and wild nights.

Needing to taste, Kyle lifted his head and bit Dev gently on the neck.

Dev groaned. "Oh, fuck me, this ain't gonna last."

"Don't care," Kyle gasped out in reply.

Holding his weight on one arm, muscles taut, Dev reached between them to wrap a hand around both their cocks. "Oh yeah. Gonna make you come so fucking hard."

The heat of his cock against Kyle's was incredible, and his firm grip set up a punishing pace. Sensation ratcheted up with every stroke. Damn it, how could he have lived so long without this? It was *nothing* like being on his own. Kyle felt alive. *Connected.*

"Shit, I'm gonna come." Dev's voice was a rasp, his movements becoming jerky.

"Don't stop," Kyle begged, and he crested the wave, ecstasy flooding his body with electricity. It was *glorious.*

It was . . . too much.

CHAPTER THIRTEEN

"Fuck, that was good." Fizzing all over with the aftereffects of the world's best orgasm, Dev rolled off Kyle's fucking awesome body and lay down beside him. He cuddled up to Kyle's side, but the bloke was oddly unresponsive. "Kyle?"

No answer. Dev pushed himself up onto one elbow.

Shit. Kyle was just lying there. Dev was hit with a horrible, sick, cold dread that it'd happened ten minutes ago and he'd just carried on shagging the poor sod without noticing—but no, that was bollocks. Kyle had been talking and everything. Thank fuck. Dev almost collapsed with the flood of relief.

He pressed a kiss to Kyle's cheek and lay down next to him again, wondering if he could sling an arm over Kyle's chest. Granted, Kyle wasn't in a position to give consent, but Dev was ready to go out on a limb and say he probably wouldn't mind a bit of a cuddle.

Then again, it wouldn't kill him to wait until he could ask the bloke, would it?

Well . . .

No, it wouldn't. Dev grabbed a handful of tissues from the box by the bed and wiped himself off, hesitated, then told himself *no one* would mind not being left covered in jizz. He wiped Kyle down gently, chucked the tissues in the bin across the room (he scores!), and lay down again, next to Kyle but not touching him.

It was good to get a chance just to look at him. For an ill bloke, he was well fit, with powerful shoulders. Nearly as hairy as Dev himself was, which Dev liked. He'd never seen the point of manscaping—seriously, who the hell wanted stubble burn *there*?

No tatts that Dev could see, but Kyle wasn't really the sort, was he?

It was harder than he'd thought, lying so close and not touching him. Dev grinned to himself. Just as well they'd already shagged, or it'd be even harder, pun very much intended.

Dev was dozing off himself when Kyle stirred. He blinked himself awake. "You all right, mate?"

"Yes."

He didn't sound all right. "Hey, no worries. You didn't freak me out or nothing. And I swear I didn't lay a finger on you while you were out. Didn't even grab a cuddle. Wouldn't mind one now, though," Dev added.

Kyle didn't say anything. After a minute, Dev decided it was up to him to make a move. Making it slow, he rolled over and snuggled up to Kyle's side, putting his head on Kyle's chest.

There was a horrible moment when he thought he'd got it wrong, but then Kyle's arms wrapped around him and squeezed convulsively.

"Yeah. That's better." Dev let out a slow, relieved breath.

There was silence for a while, until Dev's thoughts got too loud, and he had to voice them. "Would you have minded if I'd cuddled you while you were . . . You know. Out of things?"

"I . . . Yes. Sorry. I don't like being touched while I'm helpless. Not unless it's necessary."

Dev didn't like the sound of that. "Did . . . Did something bad happen to you one time while you were . . . uh . . . cataplexed?"

"No. I just hate the feeling of being helpless while someone else's hands are on me."

Dev's stomach lurched. "Wait, what? You can feel it? You mean you're, like, conscious while it's happening? Christ, you mean that time on the cliff, when I was faffing around trying to make sure you were still breathing and all, you were awake for that? You knew what was happening? Shit, bruv, that fucking blows." God, he'd pulled the poor bastard's *mouth* open. "Mate, I'm sorry, yeah?"

"You didn't know." Kyle's shoulder twitched. "You were trying to help."

"Why didn't you tell me, though? When you said you might have an attack when we, you know." Dev gestured down at their naked, sweaty bodies. Huh, and still streaked with spunk. He'd missed a bit. It was all dried on now. That was well gross.

"I . . ." Kyle shut his eyes, but he opened them again a moment later so he probably hadn't fallen asleep. He gave that sad, twisted smile of his. "Some people find it off-putting. To have me lying there like one of the undead."

Anger spiked in Dev's chest. Kyle sounded like he was quoting something some arse-wiping *bastard* had said to him. "They're tossers, then." Christ, he must mean that partner of his. The one who'd buggered off and left him to deal with all this on his own. "So, next time it happens, is there stuff I should do different? I mean, yeah, not touch you. Got that. But . . . do you want me to talk to you? Uh, play YouTube videos or something?"

Kyle frowned. "You don't have to do anything. I just have to wait for it to be over."

"Sure? If there's something that makes it better for you, I wanna do it, all right?" Kyle didn't say anything, but he was stroking Dev's back, so he probably wasn't pissed off with him for banging on about it. "So what else causes the attacks? Sex, yeah, and laughing—anything else?"

He'd done some reading, but it was a lot to take in all at once and anyway, the websites said everyone was different.

"Shock," Kyle said softly. "Any sudden strong emotion. Anger, sometimes, but usually it comes on gradually enough I'm okay. Trying too hard to resist falling asleep."

That made sense, then, that he'd had a nap up by the Round Hole. But— "Shit, what about last night? I didn't make you have one then, did I?" Dev was amazed Kyle was even still *talking* to him.

"No. No, not last night."

That was one thing to be thankful for, at least. Christ, how bad would Dev have felt knowing he'd left Kyle lying on his own living room floor, all because of Dev starting a stupid argument when he'd thought he knew better than Kyle did?

"Do you take stuff for it? I was reading about this drug, Zy-something? Some bloke online was saying it was brilliant—nearly stopped him having attacks altogether."

"Xyrem. No." There was a heavy pause. "The specialist wanted me to try other options first. It's . . . You do know what Xyrem is, don't you? GHB. Liquid ecstasy. *Easy Lay*."

"You're shitting me. Seriously?" Mal had got in with a crowd that was doing that crap once. He'd been sick as a dog. Dev had nearly decked him when he'd found out what he'd done—Christ, people used that shit for date rapes. "And you can get it on the NHS?"

"Not if they can help it, no."

"So what's the other options?"

"Stimulants. Antidepressants. Amphetamines." His tone was bitter. "I told her I'd let her know."

"Fuck me." Dev thought about it. "But it'd be different if you weren't, like, taking them to get high, wouldn't it?"

"Maybe." Kyle closed his eyes.

"Oi, stay with me, mate." Dev hesitated, then kissed him. Kyle's eyes sprang open, and Dev grinned. "There you go. Hey, you know what, I could bloody murder a cuppa."

"The sex wasn't enough, you have to have tea as well?" Kyle muttered, but he swung himself out of bed, treated Dev to an awesome view of his arse, back, and legs as he stretched, and then padded out of the room still naked.

Dev heard soft footsteps going down the stairs. He was half tempted to follow, but laziness won out. He lay back for a minute or two, checking out the room, but soon got bored looking at neutral-coloured walls, bland artwork, and the general lack of personality that reminded him this wasn't *really* Kyle's home.

He wondered what the place in Surrey was like. And if that git of an ex was still infesting it. That wasn't getting him anywhere, though, so he had a look at the stack of books on the bedside table. Huh. Fond of his classic murder mysteries, Kyle was. Out of the six books, only one had been published after 1945 and nearly all of them had something like *death* in the title. The other one had the word *mishap*, and Dev would've bet his bike he knew what that was a euphemism for.

Maybe Kyle was missing his job too.

About to have a nose in the drawers to see if he could find a remote for the small telly mounted on the wall, hotel-room style, Dev was interrupted by Kyle coming back, mugs in hand.

Still naked. "I love the service round here," Dev said, reaching up to take one of the mugs.

"Be sure to leave me a good review on TripAdvisor." Kyle sat down on the edge of the bed, facing him.

"Not a chance. I'm keeping this all for me, I am. Christ, that hits the spot," Dev added after he'd taken a sip of tea.

"And you were on at me for being stereotypically British, earlier. Sure you don't want a scone with that?"

"Yeah, *no*. Any more of the pasta-and-scones diet and I'll never get me jeans back on."

Kyle gave him a look that, if Dev had been the sort to blush, would definitely have done the trick. "I can think of worse things."

"Oh yeah? Bit of a chubby chaser, are you?"

"You got me. I'm only into you for the embonpoint."

"The what now?"

"The love handles. The spare tyre. The Buddha belly—" Kyle scooted back on the bed, his smile wider than Dev had ever seen it, as Dev threatened him with a pillow, and they both nearly spilled their tea.

"Oi, shut it. There ain't an ounce of fat on me." Dev worked bloody hard down the gym to keep it that way. He gave Kyle a once-over. "Course, you're not bad yourself. Runner?"

"I used to be. It's . . . more difficult these days."

"Yeah, s'pose if you're knackered anyway the last thing you wanna do is pull on your trainers and run a marathon." Dev put his mug down on the bedside table and reached for Kyle. "Course, there's other ways of burning up calories . . ."

Kyle looked at him. "Seriously? Already?"

Dev laughed. "Nah, maybe not. But I wouldn't mind a bit of a cuddle. Come here."

They snuggled up together, lying on top of the covers as their combined body heat was plenty, especially with the late-afternoon sun streaming in the window. Kyle grabbed the remote from under the bed and switched on the telly to some American tennis tournament, which Dev wasn't particularly into but was happy to watch, so long as he had Kyle's arms around him.

It'd been a bloody good day, he realised—sightseeing in the morning, a tasty lunch in a decent restaurant, and then sex and sport, in that order. Like a proper holiday.

Trouble was, once he'd thought that, he couldn't get the real reason he was here out of his head. Maybe he tensed up, or sighed, or something, as Kyle—who hadn't even dozed off or nothing, which was flattering—gave him a look. "Everything all right?"

"Yeah . . . Just, you know. Thinking about my mum."

Kyle stroked his hair. Dev could get used to that. "Are you planning to go to see her soon?"

"Yeah. Yeah, guess so. Bit daft putting it off, innit? No point going up there on my last day and saying, 'Hi, Mum, sorry, gotta go home now,' is there?" He let out a breath. "Course, that's if she's home anyway. Be just my sodding luck to pick the one time to come here when she's, I dunno, taken a month off to go trekking in the Himalayas or some shit."

"Doubt it," Kyle said, his fingers still running through Dev's hair. Soothing him. "People in their forties tend to have got all that sort of thing out of their system already. Do you know what she does for a living?" he went on.

"Yeah." It came out a bit squeaky. Dev coughed. "Yeah. Found out on the internet. She's a financial advisor. Tells rich people how to get richer. At least, the website didn't look like it was aimed at old grannies trying to make their pensions reach. It was all on about portfolios and wealth management and all that bollocks."

Kyle shrugged. Dev felt the movement more than he saw it. "It's probably intended to impress the potential customer."

"Well, it worked on me." Dev fell silent. He didn't want to say what he was thinking—what if his mum was disappointed he was just a mechanic? He hadn't even been to university.

Maybe one of the side effects of narcolepsy was being able to read minds, 'cos Kyle's arms tightened around him. He didn't say anything, though, which Dev was glad about. "They had a picture of her up on the website," he said to break the silence. "She looked nice."

She looked . . . Well. Like a successful financial advisor, he supposed. She looked too young to be his mum, but he'd checked her age out. Maybe it was an old picture. "She was just a kid when she had me. Sixteen."

"God."

"Yeah. Don't expect it, do you? Coming from a family like that."

"The middle classes aren't exempt from mistakes." He added under his breath, "God knows I've made plenty."

Dev pulled back and looked at him. "You better not be counting me as one of 'em."

"No. Of course not."

Dev would've liked it to sound a bit more heartfelt, but whatever. "Best mistake you ever made, I am," he said, snuggling back down. "Hey, if I hang around long enough, are you gonna cook me dinner?" he asked after a while, making it sound like a joke even though he was dead serious.

He didn't want to have to leave, to go and find somewhere to eat on his own. He wanted to stay here. With Kyle.

"Thought you said I didn't have to keep feeding you?"

"Yeah, but that was before you had a reason to want me to keep me strength up. So, you gonna? Promise I'll help chop stuff."

Kyle took a deep breath. "You can't stay the night."

Okay, that was direct. "Yeah. Fine. Whatever." Dev had a feeling he might not have managed to keep all the hurt out of his voice.

There was a frustrated sound from Kyle's direction. "I didn't mean . . . I don't sleep. Not well, and not for long. I get . . . dreams. A lot. Mostly nightmares. And there's the sleep paralysis. Sharing a bed with me for a whole night is not generally a pleasant experience."

"That what that ex of yours told you?"

"*Nobody* had to tell me."

Dev bit back a knee-jerk comment, 'cos assuming Kyle didn't know what he was talking about was what got him in trouble last night, wasn't it? "Got a spare room, ain'tcha?"

Kyle looked at him. "Why would you . . .?"

"So I can sneak back in here for a shag first thing, innit? *Duh*. And mate, seriously, you gotta save me from the B&B breakfast. I'm gonna be the size of a house by the end of three weeks."

Dev could *tell* the moment Kyle gave in. His face sort of softened and relaxed.

"All right, then," Kyle said. "If only to save the country's obesity statistics from getting out of hand."

"Don't forget all the hogs you're saving from being made into pudding. It's a public service." Dev stretched out in bed, then wrapped his arms back around Kyle. He felt fucking fantastic. On top of the world. Like he could do anything.

Maybe even . . .

He glanced at the clock—yeah, the time seemed about right—and took a deep breath. "Bit early, yet, to eat, though, innit? I was thinking maybe I'd go and see if my mum's in. Get it over with, yeah? I mean, if she's been working today, she'd probably be home by now, wouldn't she?" Nerves jumped in his stomach. He told them to fuck off and die.

Kyle gave him a long, steady look before speaking. "Are you sure that's a good idea?"

"Why not?" Dev didn't mean it to come out so snappy, so he tried plastering on a smile to make it better.

Kyle didn't seem convinced. "You could try contacting her by post or by email one more time. Even hand-deliver a letter to her door. Just explain that you're in the area, and you'd like to meet."

"What? Nah." Dev looked away. "I mean, yeah, I get what you're saying, but shit, I've only got three weeks. I wanna see her."

He couldn't face waiting and hoping. Not again. Not when he was so near he could almost touch her.

Kyle grasped his shoulder. "I'll come with you, if you like."

No. Christ, no. This was gonna be hard enough already, without anyone watching. And he just wanted to get on with it. *If* she was even there. "'S okay. Can I borrow your shower, though?" He didn't want his mum's first impression to be that he stank like a used jockstrap.

"Of course." Kyle paused. "And you're sure you won't want company?"

"In the shower?" Dev grinned. "You could persuade me."

"I meant, going up to Roscarrock House."

Well, that was disappointing. Although on the other hand . . . No, shower sex with someone who collapsed when he came probably wasn't the best idea Dev had ever had. "Yeah. Sure. Cheers, though." Dev jumped out of bed, way too restless to stay even a moment longer, and padded to the bathroom.

The shower helped with the nerves—or at least, it did while he was under the hot water. As soon as he'd towelled off, though, the butterflies in his stomach came back with a vengeance, and they'd met up with some mates on their travels and brought them all back for a party. Dev's hand slipped on the door handle as he came out of the bathroom, and he was glad to find Kyle was no longer there when he got back to the bedroom. He didn't want a witness for him going to pieces like this.

Dev took a few deep, steadying breaths, then hunted out his clothes and pulled them back on.

He jogged downstairs to find Kyle in the kitchen, chopping vegetables. "Oi, I said I'd do that, didn't I?"

"You've got more important things to do."

Well, there was that. Plus, if Dev tried chopping anything right now, there was a real danger he'd end the evening minus several fingers. He jammed his hands in his jeans pockets. "Right. Well, I'll see you back here, yeah? Dunno how long it'll take. Five minutes, probably, if she's not in. Well, ten, maybe. But more, yeah, if she's . . . I mean, we got a lot to catch up on, yeah? I could text you, if you want, tell you I'm on my way? Or—no. Um." By the time the words dried up, Dev's mouth had dried up too.

Kyle gave him a steady look. "Just come and tell me how it went, whenever works for you."

Dev nodded and grabbed one of Kyle's handmade mugs. Not the greatest choice, seeing as he only just about managed not to chip it on the kitchen tap as he filled it with water. At least he didn't throw any water down his front as he drank it. "Right. I'll see you."

"Good luck," sounded after him as he walked out of the cottage.

CHAPTER
FOURTEEN

Dev had drunk too much water, and it roiled in his stomach as he walked briskly up the cliff path to Roscarrock House. God, he was going to feel a right tit for getting so worked up if it turned out she wasn't there after all.

Maybe he *should* just drop a note round by hand? Maybe she hadn't answered the letters he'd sent, but it'd be different if she knew he was right here in Porthkennack? He could leave a note, and then it'd be up to her to get in touch . . .

No, 'cos that'd be even worse, waiting and hoping. Sod it. He'd come this far. He could bloody well take the final step.

She *would* want to see him, right? Despite what Kyle said. She was his *mum*. And, yeah, maybe she'd had some issues back when he was born, but that'd been twenty-four years ago. She'd been a kid herself. She was all grown-up now, and she'd got her life sorted.

She'd be *glad* to see him. She'd probably spent half her life wondering how he'd turned out. What had happened to him after she'd given him up for adoption. She'd cared enough to name him, hadn't she? Even if she couldn't keep him herself. She'd *cared*.

The skies had clouded over while he'd been inside with Kyle, and the grey stone of Roscarrock House looked even grander and more forbidding than the last time he'd seen it. Dev squared his shoulders, walked up to the front door, and knocked.

It felt like hours before the door was opened by a bloke around forty or so, with dark hair and cold eyes. He was shorter than Dev, and looked him up and down like he wouldn't trust Dev as far as he could throw him. And like if he had his way, that'd be straight off the edge of the cliff.

Shit. That was the nerves speaking, wasn't it? Like thinking everyone in the Sea Bell wanted him to piss off?

"Yes?" the bloke said.

"I, um. I'm here to see Beaten Roscarrock? I'm, um, I'm Dev Thompson?" He hadn't meant it to come out sounding like a question.

The bloke stilled. "You'd better come in."

He led Dev through a hallway filled with heavy old mirrors and posy side tables with spindly little legs, and into a living room that didn't look like anyone lived in it ever. It was all clean and tidy like a spread in *Hello*, with no magazines scattered around, no saggy spots on the sofa, and absolutely nothing that hadn't been invented a hundred years ago.

Well, maybe the electric lights. Dev was a bit hazy on when all that had happened.

He didn't sit down. It would probably have invalidated the guarantee on the furniture if anyone actually used it.

There was the muffled sound of a conversation coming from the hall. Dev couldn't make out the words or even the tone. He wiped his hands on his jeans while he waited, then didn't know what to do with them afterwards. Put them in his pockets? He didn't want to come off like some kind of yob. Fold his arms? That was supposed to look defensive, wasn't it? Put his hands behind his back? He wasn't a bloody squaddie.

Shit. Dev found he was wiping his palms again and stopped as a woman walked into the room.

Christ. This had to be his *mum*.

She was shorter than him. Dev wasn't sure why he'd expected anything different, but . . . yeah. She seemed tiny, almost fragile, and way younger than forty. That photo on the website couldn't have been more than a year old, if that.

She was wearing a business suit with a skirt, and her hair and makeup were perfect. Like, woman-on-TV perfect. Someone reading the news, maybe, or an MP getting interviewed. Someone important.

She buttoned up her jacket and gave him a cool smile. "How can I help you?"

"I'm Dev. Devan. Your son," he added desperately as her face hadn't changed.

It stayed frozen for a minute longer. "I haven't got a son."

Dev felt as though the bloke who'd let him in *had* thrown him off the cliff and into the sea. "But . . . you're Beaten Roscarrock, right? That's the name on my birth certificate . . ."

"I did give birth to you." She said it like some Tory politician admitting he'd made an election promise. "That doesn't make you my son."

Dev could only stare at her.

"I gave you up," she said impatiently. "I carried you for nine months, yes, I gave birth to you, and I arranged for you to be adopted by a decent couple. *They* are your parents."

"They died, din't they? When I was four." Dev's tongue felt thick and clumsy. He took a deep breath. Didn't want to mangle his words now. She *had* to understand. "And no one wants to adopt older kids, 'specially not mixed-race ones what no one even knows what race they're mixed with."

"What about relatives? Surely they'd—"

"I ain't bloody got any, 'ave I? 'Cept you. Mum and Dad's folks didn't want me—not blood, see? Not even the right bloody colour."

"That's unfortunate, but you're a grown man now. I'm not sure what you think I can give you, but you have to see—"

This wasn't happening. This was *not* fucking *happening*. Dev's chest was so tight it felt like a couple of ribs were about to give way. "Christ, if that's how you feel, why did you even keep me long enough to give birth? Why didn't you just take a morning-after pill and flush me down the bloody bog?"

"I really don't think that's relevant after all this time."

"Not relevant? This is my *life* we're talking about!"

She pressed her lips together, and when she spoke again she wasn't looking at Dev. "I was a very young girl when you were born. Fifteen when I fell pregnant. The decisions I made then . . . I very much doubt I'd make the same decision today." She turned back to him then, and her expression was cold. Worse than that. Empty. "I regret that you've come all this way for nothing, but I don't think either of us would benefit from trying to make something out of what was merely an accident of birth."

Dev found he'd taken a step back from her. He wasn't going to cry. He *wasn't*. "That's it? I'm your fucking *kid*, and that's all you got to say to me?" His voice came out funny, all thick and too loud.

"Please don't raise your voice at me in my own house, and don't swear. I really don't know what it is you want from me. You're not a child anymore, and you must be aware all legal obligation on my part ceased twenty-four years ago. If it's money—"

"Money— Do you even— *Christ*." Dev backed away, his heart, his fucking *soul*, all twisted up in knots inside him. "I don't want your money," he choked out, and then he couldn't stand it any longer.

He turned and, half-blinded, ran for the door.

Dev wasn't even sure how he got out of the house and back onto the cliff path. He wanted to punch something. Fucking *destroy* something.

How could she stand there and *say* all that stuff?

He meant nothing to her. *Nothing*. And she was his *mother*. Dev stumbled down the path. He couldn't see straight. That was it? That was what he'd planned all fucking *year* for, ever since he'd found out her name?

Dev came to a dead stop outside Kyle's house. Christ. He was supposed to tell Kyle how it went? Fuck that. He couldn't do it. Couldn't walk in and admit what a shit-storm it'd all turned out to be. Just like Kyle had warned him, with his *Are you sure that's wise* and all that other crap about taking it easy and not getting his hopes up.

He couldn't make his feet walk any farther either, though. Frustrated, his fists clenching so hard his hands ached, Dev screwed his eyes shut as if that could blank out the whole, shitting world.

"Dev?"

Dev opened his eyes.

Kyle was standing in his front doorway. He took a step forward, then another. "What happened?"

Dev laughed then. "Like you don't fucking *know*? It was just like you said. Happy now? She don't want nothing to do with me."

Kyle had reached him now and put a hand on his arm. "Dev, I'm so sorry—"

Dev shook it off and swung round, fists clenched. "Just leave me alone, all right? *Go take a fucking nap.*"

CHAPTER
FIFTEEN

Dev's words hit so hard Kyle's knees almost buckled. He stared at Dev's retreating figure as it stormed down the path away from him. The pain was fiercer than anything he'd felt in as long as he could remember.

Take a nap. God. He'd thought Dev *cared* about him.

No. This wasn't Dev. This was down to whatever had happened up at Roscarrock House. Kyle stared up at its blocky, grey form, damning the inhabitants for hurting Dev like that.

Should he go after Dev? Kyle's feet itched to follow him—but he couldn't see that ending well.

No. Give him time to calm down. Time to come to terms with his mother's rejection. What the hell could anyone say to make that better?

The pain receded as fury mounted. How could anyone *do* that to a young man like Dev? Would it have killed the woman to be kind to him? Whatever the circumstances of his conception and birth, she'd had twenty-four years to get over it, for God's sake.

How could *anyone* reject their own child?

Kyle grabbed a jacket and jammed his feet into his shoes almost before he'd consciously made the decision to go up there himself. He took a couple of deep breaths to calm himself—collapsing on their doorstep might be dramatic, but it would also be pointless, and likely inconvenient if not downright unpleasant. Then he headed up the cliff.

When he rang the doorbell, there was a delay between the sound of footsteps and the opening of the door. As if, say, the inhabitants had paused to make certain it wasn't Dev returning before they answered.

Kyle felt another surge of anger. It didn't abate when he looked into Bran Roscarrock's superior face.

"Can I help you?" Bran's tone was clipped, and his general demeanour carried even less warmth than he'd shown the first time they'd met.

"I want to talk to your sister."

The welcome chilled a few more degrees. "Regarding?"

"It's a personal matter." For all Kyle knew, Beaten Roscarrock might have somehow contrived to keep her brother in the dark regarding her illegitimate child, and regardless of the way he felt about her right now, he wasn't about to betray any secrets without good cause.

"Connected with the young man who just called?" Bran Roscarrock's lips were a thin line. "You can leave now, and if either of you returns we'll be calling the police. There are laws against harassment in this country."

Anger surged, and Kyle grabbed on to the doorframe for support. The man wanted to invoke the law did he? Kyle could give him chapter and bloody verse. "The law defines harassment as repeated attempts to impose unwanted communications and contact upon a victim in a manner that could be expected to cause distress or fear in any reasonable person. I'd strongly dispute whether you, or your sister, are acting in a manner a court would agree was *reasonable*."

Roscarrock's eyes narrowed. "If you're planning to test that out, you may be in for a shock. The Roscarrock family name means something in this county. I suggest you bear that in mind before you attempt any ill-advised legal action."

Ye gods. Kyle was starting to feel like he'd kicked a stone and set off an avalanche. "The only person who's mentioned legal action is you, Mr. Roscarrock. However, you'll find that as a practising barrister I'm not easily intimidated by threats of that nature."

"A practising barrister? I can't say I've noticed too much evidence of that since you moved here. In fact we were under the impression you were here for something of a *rest cure*."

The heavy emphasis on the last two words made it crystal clear what he was talking about: Kyle's supposed alcoholism. Well, he'd taken a savage enjoyment in allowing that rumour to take hold.

It was only fair it should come back to bite him now. "You've been misinformed," he snapped. "And I'd like to remind you that no one is above the law."

"I'm quite aware of that, Mr. . . . . Anthony, was it?" He said Kyle's surname as if it left a bad taste in his mouth. "However, I'd have thought, given your *previous* career, you'd also be aware that the law is, in many instances, open to interpretation. I suggest you do nothing that might lend itself to an interpretation you will come to regret. Good-bye."

He shut the door. Seething from the emphasis Roscarrock had put on *previous*—he might as well have come out and called Kyle a useless has-been, for God's sake—Kyle only just snatched his fingers away from the frame in time to keep them from being crushed.

Damn it.

On the way back down to the cottage, Kyle couldn't shake his unease. No one was above the law, true—but the law was only as good as the people who implemented it, and he had a nasty feeling Roscarrock might indeed have undue influence with the people who implemented it around here.

It was entirely possible things were about to get unpleasant, both for Kyle and for Dev. And it was all Kyle's fault for sticking his nose into something that didn't concern him. God. Dev had been right. He should have just taken a bloody nap instead of storming over to the house, all guns blazing with righteous fury. He wasn't even sure, now, if it was Roscarrock being unreasonable or Kyle himself. That unsubtle reminder that his career was now over had raised his hackles, no doubt about it.

He needed advice. From someone who'd be able to be objective about it all. And there was an obvious place to go for it.

Sujata, from chambers. She was something of a specialist in stalking cases. Standing only four foot nine in her court shoes and wig and weighing in at under seven stone, she liked to say she was a walking reminder of how fragile and vulnerable a woman could be. And then she'd laugh, and the rest of chambers would laugh with her, because there was absolutely nothing fragile or vulnerable about Sujata Das.

Nor was she very understanding of other people's frailties. Kyle's reluctance to call her was almost visceral. But this was important.

He made the call as soon as he was inside his front door. Before he could change his mind. It was late enough now that she certainly wouldn't be in court. She'd probably be at home, unless she was travelling.

She picked up on the second ring. "Kyle. *Finally.*"

"Can you talk?"

"For half an hour. Amal is cooking dinner. How are you? And when are you coming back to work?"

He ignored that. "Sujata, I need your advice. It's about a possible harassment charge."

"And who have you been harassing?"

Kyle winced at her teasing tone. "I— It's complicated." He outlined the problem with the Roscarrocks as succinctly as he could, pacing up and down his hallway. Her mention of dinner seemed to have gone straight to his blood-sugar levels, but he couldn't afford to have an attack now.

She listened. Asked a few questions. Kyle blinked back sleep and had to force himself to concentrate.

Finally she made a decisive little sound. "Well, I don't think you or your friend will go to prison. But as your legal representative, I would have to advise you both to stay away from the family in future. It's sad about your friend, but he must see that he can't force the woman to acknowledge him, or to form any kind of relationship with him." She hesitated. "Is there no chance you will get back together with Jeffrey? I can't help thinking your relationship with this young man—"

"*Don't* finish that sentence. Not if you want us to stay friends."

"And is a friend not allowed to be concerned?" She sighed. "I was hoping your call meant you'd finally come to your senses."

Kyle's hackles rose. "What's that supposed to mean?"

"When are you coming back to work, Kyle?"

Damn it. "I *can't* work, you know that." He was so bloody tired. Food was getting to be a priority. Kyle walked through to the dining room and sat at the table. Maybe it'd fool his body into waiting for the energy recharge instead of crashing.

"That's not true. I've read up on your illness. There are treatments. Drugs you can take. As long as you—"

Anger flared. "You've *read up on it*? Can you even hear yourself? What, you managed to find the NHS website and now you're a bloody expert on *my* condition? You've no idea what it's like living with narcolepsy. I can't appear in court—I certainly can't risk travelling on a daily basis. What if I have an attack halfway through a trial? Do you know how bloody hard it is to travel by train without falling asleep? And God, just the sheer exhaustion . . ."

"Kyle." It was the tone she used on her four-year-old, damn it. "You wouldn't have to work full-time. I'm sure we'd be able to work something out at chambers."

"You're not even listening to me. I. Can't. Work." Kyle slammed his hand on the tabletop and stood up, his palm stinging.

"You know what your problem is?" Sujata went on. "You give up too easily."

Outraged, Kyle drew in a breath, but she cut him off before he could get a word out.

"No, you listen to me. Plenty of narcoleptics manage to carry on working. You haven't tried—as soon as you were diagnosed you cut yourself off from everything and everyone. It isn't healthy."

"*I'm* not healthy," he snapped.

"No, but you're not dead yet, either. So stop acting as if you are. You talk as if your life is over. You know, I've changed my mind. I think your Dev is a good thing if he stops you wallowing in your depression."

"I'm not depressed. And he's not my Dev."

"Then perhaps he should be. Kyle, I have to go now. But I'll call you tomorrow or the next day. And this time, you answer me. Oh, and call your ex-boyfriend too."

"Jeffrey?" Kyle grabbed on to the back of the chair.

"How many boyfriends have you had lately? He rang chambers the other day, and said you weren't returning his calls either."

"That would be because I don't want to speak to him." Kyle tried to keep his voice even. This wasn't Sujata's fault.

"He said he was worried about you."

"Too little, too late."

"So will you call him?"

Oh, absolutely. Just as soon as the seas froze over in Mother Ivey's Bay, and the ghost of Mother Ivey herself came dancing out of the icy waves. "I'll think about it," Kyle lied.

"Good. Now I must go, or Amal will divorce me." She said it with the light, carefree tone of the happily married. "Be careful, Kyle."

They hung up, Kyle with mixed feelings. He was relieved to find his own judgement of the case had been sound—but uncomfortably reminded why he hadn't called her back any of the times she'd tried to get in touch since he'd left Surrey. He liked Sujata, but she wasn't afraid to say what she thought—and she never stopped pushing.

She'd never liked Jeffrey, either, he recalled suddenly. She'd thought him unambitious, content to plod along managing the art gallery and relying on his inheritance to keep up their joint standard of living. Kyle would never have imagined she'd think a relationship with a motor mechanic was a *good* thing. Which was absurd, when he thought about it. Dev had worked hard to make up for unpromising beginnings . . .

And it was all completely beside the point, because they weren't in a relationship and never would be, even if by some miracle Dev ever spoke to him again. Kyle wouldn't do that to him. He deserved someone he could live a full life with.

More to the point, if Kyle forced himself to admit the bitter truth, one day Dev would realise that for himself and tell Kyle it was over.

Kyle knew he couldn't face that. Not again.

All at once, the thought of getting up and making something to eat seemed utterly overwhelming. Kyle sank his head down onto his arms and let sleep overtake him.

CHAPTER SIXTEEN

Dev stomped into the Sea Bell and slapped a twenty-pound note on the bar. "Vodka. Double. Don't bother with the Coke."

"Ice and a slice?" Jago's voice was mocking.

Dev could have decked him. Maybe it showed, 'cos the bastard just looked at him a long moment, then turned to pour his drink.

Dev tossed it straight down. The burn on his throat felt fucking awesome. "'Nother."

The git gave him that stare again.

"You got a problem with that? Thought you was in the business of selling drinks."

Jago poured the second double measure without a word. But when he turned round again, he put it on the bar and didn't let go. "Had some bad news?"

"Like you give a fucking monkey's."

The hand on the glass didn't move. "Try me."

"Me mum's dead. Happy?"

Another long stare. Jesus, what was fucking *with* this bastard?

Jago spoke at last, his voice low. "Sorry to hear that, lad. But do you think she'd want you getting drunk?"

Dev almost laughed. "Don't matter, do it? She ain't just dead, she never . . . she never even fucking *existed*. So are you gonna give me my fucking drink or what?"

The bastard took his hand away, but he didn't stop staring at Dev as he downed his vodka.

This one didn't go down so easy, and Dev choked a bit, ending up wiping his mouth on his sleeve. "What?" he demanded, daring the git to say something.

Jago didn't speak, just took down a pint glass from a shelf and filled it with water from the tap. He handed it to Dev.

"What the fuck?"

"No more alcohol until you drink that. Got it?"

Dev was so fucking *done* with this. He wanted to chuck the water in the bastard's stupid face. He'd have done it too, if the wanker hadn't turned away to serve someone else.

Like Dev didn't fucking exist.

Shit.

Dev's eyes were stinging again. He *wasn't* going to cry.

He wasn't gonna let someone make him drink a pint of water like some stupid teenager after his first binge, neither. Dev slipped off the stool, steadying himself with one hand on the bar, and headed for the door.

Trouble was, he had nowhere he wanted to go. Dev leaned on the wall outside the pub and tried to think of anywhere he could face heading right now. Not back to the B&B. He couldn't stand Val and Carol going all motherly on him. Maybe the offie. He could get a bottle of something and take it up by the Round Hole, and if he was really lucky, the ground fucking well *would* open up and swallow him.

He pushed away from the wall and set off down the path, weaving a bit from two double vodkas on an empty stomach. Christ. He was turning into Mal's uncle. Next thing he knew it'd be whisky for breakfast and liver disease before he was forty.

Sod the offie. And sod Jago, Kyle . . . *her* and the whole bloody lot of them. He was heading down the chippie.

Dev felt a lot better once he had a warm parcel of fish and chips open on his lap and half of it already in his stomach. He'd taken his food down to the seafront, which could have been a dodgy move. Luckily there were some kids a bit farther down the prom throwing bread for the seagulls, right next to the big sign telling people not to feed them. Which, yeah, in principle Dev agreed with, 'cos anyone could see it'd only encourage them, but he wasn't gonna argue right now with anything that stopped him getting mugged by the greedy, screeching bastards.

Well, physically he felt better. More solid. Not like he was about to fall over any minute in a bad impersonation of Kyle having an attack . . .

Ah shit. He'd promised himself he wasn't gonna think about Kyle. Or his . . . *her*, or anyone else he'd totally fucked things up with lately. Mal. He was gonna think about Mal. Lying on a beach in Portugal, probably turning as pink as the walls in the Spindrift B&B 'cos he was well white, Mal was. Not ginger, but he still freckled when the sun came out.

Dev shoved a couple of chips in his mouth, wiped his hand on the paper, and got his phone out of his pocket. There weren't any texts—well, none from actual people. Dev scrolled down his contacts and sent Mal a quick text that just said, *Miss you, mate.*

He didn't get a reply, but it made him feel better anyway. Just reaching out. And Mal would be back soon. Well, ish. They'd gone for a fortnight.

Christ, what was Dev gonna do for the rest of his three weeks off? Nope. Not gonna think about it. Not tonight.

Maybe he could get a flight out to Portugal and kip on Mal's floor? Or in his bed, even?

Dev knew he wouldn't do it. At least, not without trying to make things right with Kyle first. If the bloke would ever talk to him again.

The anger—that first rush of rage against *her*, against Kyle for being right, against the whole fucking world—had died down, drowned in vodka and buried under a mountain of greasy comfort food. But the hurt was still there, like a knife in his chest. How could she . . . ?

Nope. Not going there. She wasn't worth it.

Dev dived back into his fish and chips, although his appetite seemed to have buggered off back to London without him. He ate anyway. It wasn't like he had anything else to do.

He was just finishing up when he heard an earsplitting scream that hadn't come from a seagull.

"Oi! Dev!"

Dev looked around to see Chantal-from-Birmingham and her mate, waving wildly from the other side of the road. They tottered across on sky-high heels to join him on the prom.

Great. Just what he needed right now.

"What you doing all on your own again?" Chantal asked, then carried on talking without waiting for an answer. "Want to come for a drink with us? We're going down Piskies again later, but we wanna get tanked up first." She giggled, making Dev wonder how much tanking up she'd done already. "It were bostin' last night. Susie met a fella, but she went for a pee and he got off with some other tart."

The mate—Susie—looked narked, and not just at last night's bloke.

"Cheers, love, but I'm not in the mood."

"What, that girl from the caff giving you grief? Come with us. We'll cheer you right up." Again, she giggled.

For a moment, Dev was tempted. Just to spend some time with someone who actually wanted him there, even if all she wanted was a bit of holiday romance.

Then a text pinged through on his phone. Dev checked it— unknown number. It said *Sup? Ceri.*

He smiled. "Sorry, ladies. That's her now. Gotta go." He gave them his best under-the-thumb impersonation, based on Masood at the garage when his missus called, 'cos they all knew who wore the trousers in that relationship, and stood up. "Maybe we'll see you around, yeah?"

If Chantal bothered with an answer, he didn't hear it as he walked away, already calling Ceri back.

She answered with, "You all right?" It sounded properly worried, not just like she was saying hello.

Well, he should have expected that, maybe. "Peachy. Your Uncle Jago been telling tales, then?"

"He told Dad. I got it out of him. What's this about your mum?"

"She ain't my mum." Dev heaved a sigh. He didn't want to talk about it. But he didn't want to be on his own anymore either. "Wanna come for a drink?"

There was a pause. "You pissed? Jago said you was chucking vodka down like water."

"Yeah, well, I ain't had any more since then." The alcohol must still be in his system, but Dev couldn't feel it. Maybe it was the sea air blowing on his face as he walked along the prom. Clearing his head. He had to remind himself that getting the Hornet out for a spin would be a shit-stupid idea.

Ah, sod it. He'd left it at Kyle's, hadn't he? He'd forgotten all about the Hornet, what with everything else.

Well, if that didn't stop him trying to ride it tonight, nothing would.

"Could meet you at the Sea Bell."

Dev snorted. "What, so your uncle can tell me to piss off? He already cut me off once tonight."

"He won't. Not if you're with me."

"We could get a bottle and take it somewhere. Like up the cliff or something," he tried, although to be honest there was already a drop of drizzle in that sea air, and he wasn't exactly dressed for sitting out in the rain.

"No." It sounded final. Maybe she didn't like the look of the weather either.

"Ain't there any other pubs round here?" The Slug and Lettuce would have done for him right now, but she'd already said she hated it.

"I don't want to go nowhere else."

It made sense, he supposed. It was the one place she was safe from that crowd that had it in for her, for whatever reason. "Fine. Sea Bell it is. But if he chucks me out, you'll be on your own there."

Dev glanced up at the darkening sky as he set off through town. The clouds had thickened, and it looked like he'd be lucky to escape a drenching tonight whatever he did.

Well, he'd survived worse.

It helped, too, to know that every step he took nearer the Sea Bell took him farther away from Roscarrock House. Not as the crow flew, maybe—without his map in front of him Dev was hazy on the geography, but he was pretty sure there was a two-sides-of-a-triangle thing going on. But he didn't reckon there was any danger of running into *her* slumming it at the Sea Bell.

It still hurt.

He managed to reach the pub before the rain really started and found Ceri waiting outside, leaning on the wall. "Took your time," she said by way of hello.

"Who d'you think I am, Mo Farah? You all right?" God, it was good to see her. He fought down the urge to give her a hug. She'd think he'd totally lost it if he did that.

"Yeah." She looked all right, anyhow. Not exactly happy, but not sad, neither. "You?"

Dev shrugged. "We going in or what?"

She pushed herself off the wall and opened the door. "Yeah. It's gonna piss it down in a minute. I'll buy."

"Suits me. I'll have—"

She'd already gone. Dev watched her for a mo, then gave a wary nod to Jago behind the bar. He got an *I'm watching you, lad* glare in return.

Fair enough. He found them a free table in the corner where they'd sat before. The pub was busy tonight—not heaving, exactly, but most of the tables were occupied and there was the usual row of men on stools at the bar. Not bad for a Monday night. A couple of the locals turned to give him a wary nod.

Ceri came back with what looked like the usual for her and a pint glass of something dark for him. He sipped cautiously. Yep, neat Coke. "Cheers," he said sarcastically.

"You can have something proper in the next one, all right? So what's happened with your mum?"

"Fuck, you don't mess about, do you?"

"Are you going to tell me or what? Uncle Jago was that worried about you, after you were in earlier."

Dev huffed. "Fine. I'm adopted, right? Me mum gave me away when I was born. And I came here to meet her. So I went round her house today. Waste of time. She told me to piss off."

Saying it out loud made his chest ache again. He took a gulp of Coke, wishing he had a real drink.

Ceri frowned. "What, she changed her mind about seeing you?"

"Nah, it wasn't like it was arranged or nothing. I just went to see her." He gave a bitter laugh. "Thought it'd be a surprise. Got that right, didn't I?"

"A surprise?" She was staring at him like he'd grown another head and it was a dead ringer for the Beast of Bodmin. "A fucking *surprise*? Jesus, did you even *think* what it must have been like for *her*? To have you showing up in her *house* after all this time?"

Dev... Dev hadn't been expecting that. "What else was I supposed to do? She never answered my letters."

"So you *knew* she didn't want to see you, and you still went? You fucking selfish *bastard*." She turned away from him and stood up all in one awkward motion that almost had her chair toppling over.

"Oi, that's not—" Dev stood too and grabbed her shoulder, pulled her round to make her face him. Christ, if anyone was going to be on his side, he'd thought Ceri would be. How could she—

She was crying. Dev dropped her shoulder like it'd burned him. He could only watch, stunned, as she scrubbed angrily at her face, then practically ran out of the pub.

The sound of the door slamming behind her brought him back to his senses, and he ran after her, expecting all the time to get his collar felt by Jago. Christ, the bloke must think Dev was a total waste of space by now. Well, he could join the fucking club.

He caught up with Ceri outside. She was standing by the wall in the rain, like she didn't know where to go now.

"Ceri? Babe, what's up?" Dev made his voice soft.

She rounded on him, her face red and tear-streaked. "You ever even *think* how it might've happened? Maybe she never wanted to sleep with whoever your dad was? Maybe he was some stranger who got hold of her on her way home from school? Or... or maybe she liked him, and she thought he liked her, so she goes out drinking with him, but all he wants is to get his bloody leg over, and he don't give a toss whether she wants to let him or not? You ever think of that?"

Dev's chest felt hollow. "Ceri..."

"Maybe it was the worst night of her *life*, when she got pregnant with you. Maybe that one night ruined her whole life, and she can't take being reminded of it, and all you can do is stand there all *Oh, poor me, my mummy doesn't want me.*"

Christ, it hurt. It hurt like being ripped in two. "I didn't—"

"No. You never fucking *do*, do you? You men. It's just... nothing to you, innit? It's all about you. You got any idea what it's like, when some bastard... and everyone says you was asking for it, and you led him on, and you're a bitch for calling the police, because you'll ruin his life, and it's *all about him.*"

She was sobbing now, her face contorted. Dev stared at her. What she'd said . . . It wasn't *fair*, and it'd fucking nearly killed him to have her scream at him like that, when he was already raw and bleeding.

But Christ. It'd hurt her even worse.

Dev would've put his arm around her, but he was scared to touch her. Scared for her, because he didn't reckon she'd take too kindly to a bloke hugging her right now. And scared for himself, because he just couldn't take any more.

He did the only thing he could think of. "Give me your phone," he said roughly.

She thrust it at him, arm outstretched, without even looking at him, and Dev scrolled through her contacts, hunching over to stop the rain spattering the screen, until he found *Dad*. He hit Dial.

The answer came quicker than he was ready for and sounded concerned. "All right, love?"

"Uh, it's not Ceri. It's me. Dev. Could you maybe come and get her? She's a bit . . . upset. We're at the Sea Bell."

"On my way," Ceri's dad said curtly, and hung up.

Dev tried to give the phone back to Ceri, but she still wouldn't look at him. Christ, what a fuckup.

Next thing he knew the pub door opened again, and Jago stormed out, his sleeves rolled up, heading straight for Dev.

Christ on a crutch. Dev backed away, holding up his hands. "Oi, it ain't what it looks like, all right?" Which, yeah, maybe wasn't exactly true, but sod it, he hadn't *meant* to upset her.

Jago folded his arms, which, Dev couldn't help noticing, were pretty cut for an old bloke who worked behind a bar. He wasn't exactly small, either. "Looks to me like you've got Ceri's phone there."

"Uh, yeah." Dev had all but forgotten it was still in his hand. He held it out warily to Jago. "I called her dad. You, uh, you wanna look after it for her?"

Ceri snatched it out of his hand. "You shit," she said, her voice cracking. She looked a mess, her hair hanging down around her face in rats' tails and her eyes red and swollen, her cheeks blotchy.

"I'm sorry, all right?" Dev said desperately. "I didn't mean to . . ."

To bring up the worst memories of your life, which was what he was pretty sure he'd done. But he couldn't say that now, could he? It'd only make it worse. "I'm sorry," he said again.

"Ceri?" Jago's voice softened. "Can you tell me what's happened?"

"No."

"Was it anything like . . ."

"*No.*" She practically screamed it this time. "Why can't you all just leave me alone?"

Jago turned to Dev. "Time you were off, lad."

"Yeah. Fine." Dev hesitated. "You'll look after her till her dad gets here, yeah?"

Jago raised an eyebrow.

"Right. Fine." Dev cast one more glance at Ceri, and walked off, rain running through his hair and dripping down his face and neck.

He turned to look back when he was about to go round a corner. Jago had his arms around Ceri now, and she had her head on his chest, probably sobbing her heart out. Jago's old-man cotton shirt had plastered itself to his shoulders and back, but he didn't seem to care. She was so fucking tiny next to him, a stick figure in skinny jeans.

She'd be all right. Wouldn't she?

Dev still couldn't face going back to the B&B. If Val and Carol asked him what was wrong, he'd probably end up blubbing like a baby himself. And no way was he going to try apologising to Kyle tonight. The way he was feeling right now, one more rejection and he'd bloody top himself. Take a short step off a high cliff. Throw himself into the Round Hole and let the tide take him out to sea.

Some poor bastard would probably still end up having to scrape him off the rocks, but it wasn't like he had a mum to get upset over him, was it?

He took the path around the headland, in the opposite direction from . . . from *that place.* It was getting dark, although at least the rain had blown over before he got very far. Every now and then the clouds shifted in the sky to show a pale, full moon, but the stars couldn't seem to be arsed coming out tonight. Dev shivered in his wet clothes. Christ, he was such a fuckup. He veered off the road, over the short, scrubby grass towards the cliffs. He knew he wasn't gonna jump—fuck that shit—but it made him feel better, in some screwed-up way, to play with the idea he just might.

He should have stayed in London. Or better, gone to Portugal with Mal and the lads.

He hadn't *thought*. He'd known his mum was just a kid when she had him, and he'd assumed that was the reason she'd given him up. 'Cos she didn't feel old enough to look after a kid, and maybe her family had been on at her not to waste her life, that sort of crap. It'd never occurred to him that maybe the reason she didn't want him was 'cos she'd never wanted his dad, neither.

Dev had reached the edge of the cliff now, and he sat down on the grass looking over the sea. It was damp from the rain earlier, but how much wetter was he going to get? There was no beach below him around this side of the headland, just charcoal-grey waves breaking against the dim white cliffs. The breeze was cold and heavy with the scent of salt and seaweed.

It hurt, thinking about it. Fuck, who wanted to hear they'd got fifty percent of their DNA from a fucking raping bastard? But Christ, how could he have been so fucking *stupid*? He knew what went on in some families. It'd happened to Tasha, hadn't it? How could he have been so sodding blind when it came to his own parents?

It wasn't like this on the telly, when they showed reunions and stuff. Mums finding the kids they'd been forced to give up for adoption decades ago, or people meeting brothers and sisters they'd never known they had. It was all happy tears, and *Oh my God you look just like your grandad*. Not *Piss off and never come here again*.

Dev blinked into the wind. Kyle had tried to warn him, hadn't he? Dev hadn't wanted to listen. He wished . . .

Sod it. Wishing never got anyone anywhere. Dev stood up, dusted his jeans off, and headed back to the B&B. At least he'd be warm and dry there.

CHAPTER SEVENTEEN

Dev was up late the next morning and only just made it down in time for breakfast. Val tapped her watch, Carol tutted at him fondly, and then they were on their way out for the day already. Dev thanked Christ he wouldn't have to make conversation while he ate. He felt like he hadn't slept at all, but he knew that was bollocks because nobody had dreams that crap while they were awake. Nasty, unsettling stuff he didn't want to think about.

Maybe the conversation wouldn't have been so bad after all. There were a few tourist leaflets in a stand on the windowsill, and Dev grabbed a couple to take his mind off his own thoughts while he picked at his food. God knew what he was going to do today. He scanned the leaflet on the naval museum but couldn't muster up a lot of interest in old ships and stuff.

Should he call Ceri? See how she was getting on? Dev wanted to, but maybe she didn't want to hear from him? Fuck it. This whole shit-storm was making him paranoid.

But maybe he should leave it a day or two anyway. Dev picked up the leaflet on the caves that connected with the Round Hole. They looked more interesting than a dusty old museum. Trouble was, they also reminded him of Kyle.

Sod it. He should go and see Kyle. Try and make things right. Apologise.

Mrs. Quick came into the breakfast room, probably keen for Dev to shift his arse so she could get on with her day. "Well, someone had an appetite today," she said, sounding like she approved.

Dev glanced at his plate and was a bit surprised to see he'd cleaned it. "Uh, yeah. Cheers. That was great."

"Busy day planned for today?" she asked as she took away his plate.

"Uh, yeah. Gonna go see a mate."

"That's nice."

She probably would've said the same thing whatever he'd told her. Well, maybe not if he'd said he was going to jump off a cliff. "Cheers," Dev said, and left her to it.

He thought about swinging past the Square Peg to see if Ceri was working today—but no, that'd be like stalking, wouldn't it? Even if he just wanted to see if she was all right. He made himself take a route that avoided the café.

Walking past the tourist shops, Dev wondered if he should get Kyle something. Like, a present. To show he really was sorry about being such a cock. Flowers, maybe? Nah, that was a crap idea. Kyle had plenty of them in his garden. Something else. Something stupid and tacky, maybe, that'd make him laugh? Or, well, maybe not laugh. That wasn't such a great idea. But smile, definitely.

Yeah, that would do it. And if you couldn't find tacky in a seaside souvenir shop, where could you? Dev almost smiled to himself as he pushed open the door of the Treasure Chest.

He hadn't been wrong about what he'd find there. He could have bought half a dozen things in the first five minutes of looking around. There was a little model of the mosque, made out of wonky matchwood with a load of badly glued-on shells, which, if you'd scaled them up with the model, would've housed some seriously scary shellfish. Then there was the knock-off Cornish pottery, with *Made in China* stamped on the bottom. Even a classic *My other car is a Porsche* bumper sticker. He thought about the Cornish phrasebook, but decided it was too serious. And it didn't have *cat's fart* in it. Dev had checked.

Then he saw it. The perfect thing. It was naff, and totally inauthentic, and so badly made it'd probably fall to pieces if you looked at it funny. Dev paid his money, took the brown paper bag, and set off up to Kyle's house before he could talk himself out of it, his nerves mounting with every step.

CHAPTER EIGHTEEN

Kyle's sleep was even more troubled than usual that night. Napping so late the previous day and eating late as well had messed up his sleep pattern, such as it was. When he finally got to bed, the dreams were at their worst, and he was heartily glad he didn't remember them all clearly when he woke up. The ones he could recall were bad enough. They all featured Dev, who by turns laughed at him as he collapsed, assaulted him while he was incapable of moving, and in an impressive mash-up from Kyle's subconscious, actually became the knife-wielding mugger who'd accosted Kyle in London some years previously.

He felt sick and exhausted when he finally hauled himself out of bed. Breakfast helped—a very little. A cup of decaffeinated coffee just left him craving the real thing.

Would it really be so bad to take some stimulants during the day? His doctor had wanted him to try them and see how he went, but Kyle had been repulsed by the idea of taking drugs regularly. Now, though, he was starting to think he'd been an idiot to refuse the treatment. Tired as he was, the thought of going back to bed filled him with horror.

Maybe he should make another appointment? He'd have to go to London for that, though. Kyle had no idea what the doctors were like around here, and he certainly hadn't registered with one. There hadn't seemed much point, as his Epsom GP had simply referred him on to the London specialist. But perhaps this far from London there were other options. Perhaps he should have made more effort to get to know his neighbours, so he'd have someone to ask about these things. Then again, he'd assumed the rest of the cottages were on short-term lets too. He was fairly sure next door, at least, had had more than one change of occupants since he'd been living in Mother Ivey's Boudoir.

Kyle sighed. It was a shame the Roscarrocks had turned out so hostile. They probably knew everything there was to know about Porthkennack, its amenities and inhabitants.

A knock on the door interrupted his sluggish thoughts. Rising to answer it, Kyle half expected to be confronted with a process server delivering a summons on behalf of the Roscarrock family.

He blinked in surprise at the man on the doorstep.

"Dev?" Kyle took a deep breath, the pain in his chest as sharp as it was unexpected, and reminded himself Dev had been newly hurt when he'd said . . . what he'd said. "Do you want to come in?"

"You want me to?" There was no belligerence in his tone. He looked . . . miserable. And nervous. But mostly miserable.

Kyle nodded and stepped aside to let him in.

Dev hovered on the doormat, holding up a large, brown paper bag. "I bought you a . . . It's daft. You won't even want it. I mean, it's supposed to be funny, but it's probably just sad."

"What?" Kyle eyed the bag. Dev hesitated, then handed it over with visible reluctance.

Some of his wariness seemed to transfer to Kyle, who opened up the bag with the irrational fear that whatever was inside might actually bite. Then he frowned, drawing out a strange contraption of balsa wood, string, and an exuberance of feathers. It took a moment for recognition to hit. Then he smiled. "A dream catcher?"

Dev shoved his hands in his jeans pockets. "I got it in that souvenir shop down by the beach. You know, you were saying you dream a lot, so I thought you'd want something that'd make 'em be good ones . . . I said it was stupid."

"No. That's . . . Thank you." Kyle took a deep breath, and held up the dream catcher to the light. Brightly coloured nylon cord webbed a hoop about a foot in diameter, from which large, fluffy feathers dangled, garishly dyed to match. One of them shed a bit of fluff as he looked at it.

Was it ridiculous to be so touched by a cheap bit of tourist rubbish? Probably. Kyle didn't care. "It's perfect. Thank you." He realised he was repeating himself. "Come on in and sit down. I'll make some coffee."

There was a hook on the kitchen wall, which Kyle had assumed had been knocked in to hold a calendar at one time. He hung the dream catcher on it for now—although come to think of it, he was almost as likely to sleep in here as anywhere else—and busied himself filling the kettle, setting it to boil, and getting out mugs and coffee.

Avoiding talking to Dev. The trouble was, he wasn't sure what to say. He was still wondering when he handed Dev a mug of decaff.

Dev flashed him a nervous half smile. "Cheers. Uh. So, yeah, last night. I was a dick, all right?"

The rush of fondness that swept through Kyle was almost worrying in its intensity. "Don't worry about it."

"Yeah, but . . . It's not on. I shouldn't've talked to you like that." He hunched around his mug. "Sorry."

"I mean it. Forget about it." Kyle paused. "Do you want to talk about what happened up at . . . at the house?" He shied away from saying *Roscarrock*.

That name had never brought them anything but trouble.

"'S what I told you. Basically." Dev leaned back on the kitchen counter and stared at the opposite wall. "She said . . . She said she didn't want nothing to do with me. She said she wished she'd had an abortion." His voice cracked.

"Oh God." Kyle's arms were around Dev before he'd even realised he'd moved. His chest ached. God, how must Dev feel? "I'm so sorry. You . . . You do know that isn't what I wanted for you?"

"Yeah. Yeah, I know that. Now. Sorry I was such a fucking dick yesterday. Shit. I was a right twat." He pulled back from Kyle to stare him in the eye. "You know I didn't mean it, yeah? It just did my head in for a bit. Seeing . . . Seeing *her*."

"I don't blame you."

"No? You're the only one, then." Dev ducked his head.

Kyle took hold of his chin and gently drew it back upward. The rasping tickle of Dev's stubble against his fingers was more arousing than it should have been, given the topic of conversation. "The way she acted, the way she feels, is not your fault, and it's no reflection on you. You shouldn't take it personally."

He felt like an idiot saying it. Who *wouldn't* take it personally if they found out their mother wished they were dead? God.

But Dev was nodding. "Yeah." He cleared his throat. "Yeah. I know that. 'S just . . . I don't feel it, yeah? Not inside."

"Any reasonable person would be proud to have you as their child. Would want to get to know you. *I'm* glad I've got to know you." It was true. Whatever happened, however soon they parted, Kyle would always be grateful for the memory of someone who seemed happy to be with him despite all his problems. Who'd cared enough to read up on an obscure illness that generally provoked more laughter than sympathy.

God. A chill ran through him. Dev could be leaving much sooner than he'd thought, because what was there to keep him in Porthkennack now? Kyle felt suddenly hollow, and his hand on Dev's arm clenched tighter without him willing it to.

Dev looked him in the eye then. "Me too. You know that, right?"

Kyle was still trying to work out what he meant when Dev kissed him.

It turned hungry fast. God knew, Kyle was desperate to take this chance—maybe his last chance—to be with Dev, and Dev, well . . .

Maybe he just wanted some human comfort. Stubble rasped against Kyle's beard, and he pressed against Dev, body heat mingling through their clothes. He was hard already, and Dev was too. He *needed* this.

Kyle pushed up Dev's T-shirt, craving the feel of skin on skin. When he got it, the contact was like completing a circuit as electricity fizzed through every nerve. Impatient hands were pulling up Kyle's shirt, no doubt crumpling it beyond salvage. He didn't care. More than that, he wanted it—wanted Dev to leave his mark, somehow, so that when he was gone—

No. Kyle wasn't going to think about that. He fumbled at the fastenings of Dev's jeans, his fingers clumsy because he was too busy kissing Dev to watch what he was doing. Dev's hands tightened jerkily on Kyle's bare torso as he finally got the button undone and made short work of the zip. Dev's briefs were damp to the touch, a wet patch spreading from the tip of his hard cock. He moaned as Kyle cupped him, too desperate with need to be gentle.

"We should—"

Kyle never found out what Dev thought they should do. Too impatient to listen, he cut off Dev's words with another hungry kiss, then dropped to his knees on the hard kitchen floor.

"Mate, are you—" Had it looked like a cataplexy attack? Amusement fighting a losing battle with arousal, Kyle set about proving he was still very much awake and in control of himself by pulling down Dev's jeans and briefs and letting his cock spring free. Then Kyle plunged his mouth over the head and took in as much as he could.

The sounds Dev made were loud, inarticulate, and wonderful. Kyle sucked hard, then drew back to run his tongue over Dev's cockhead. His own arousal was starting to become painful, so he pressed a hand to it until the worst of the ache subsided. He could wait. Dev's cock tasted glorious, salty and musky, and he wanted to have his full attention on it.

Especially as he couldn't afford to come first and was dangerously turned on as it was.

He used his hand, rolling Dev's balls and teasing his perineum with a finger, all the while sucking and licking Dev by turns.

Dev couldn't seem to keep quiet. "Fuck, you're killing me . . . Yeah. Yeah, *that*. Oh, fuck, don't stop . . ." He gave a long groan, and then he was coming, filling Kyle's mouth with hot, bitter spurts. Kyle swallowed eagerly, sucking him through it.

"Fuck me," Dev breathed—then dropped down to the floor beside Kyle. "Fucking *awesome*." He kicked off his jeans and briefs from where they'd tangled around his ankles, then sat back against the kitchen unit, his legs splayed. "Fuck me, them tiles are hard. Come here. No—with your back to me. Yeah, that's it."

Kyle ended up in the V of Dev's legs, his back against Dev's chest, its rise and fall erotic and heavy from the force of Dev's orgasm. Strong arms wrapped around him, going straight to the fastenings of his trousers. *Oh.*

Yes, that would do nicely, Kyle thought wildly, as a calloused hand slid into his underwear and wrapped around his hard cock. Dev's touch was different from his own—gentler, and seeming all the more so from the way he'd subconsciously expected it to be more rough and ready. Slower than he usually preferred, which was almost frustrating until he realised it really, really wasn't—and then he was coming, his climax shooting out of him almost lazily and spattering onto the kitchen floor between his legs.

It was heaven, the high staying with him even after the last spasms had finished. For the first time in months, bone-deep relaxation spread through Kyle's whole body, without the usual struggle to stay awake. He felt refreshed, as if he'd just woken from a good night's sleep—he couldn't remember the last time that had happened. "Thank you," he said, because he couldn't imagine trying to convey how he actually felt.

"Anytime, and you can hold me to that. Hey, you didn't—you know. Have an attack." Dev's tone changed abruptly. "Shit, does that mean it wasn't any good?"

Kyle had to smile. "It was great. I just didn't get triggered this time, that's all."

"You're sure it was okay? You'd tell me if I was shit, right?"

"Trust me. You've got no worries on that score." Kyle pressed a kiss to Dev's muscular upper arm, just below the sleeve of his T-shirt. He couldn't believe how many clothes they still had on. Well, mostly on. Or, for that matter, how comfortable he was sitting on the kitchen floor with Dev's arms around him. They'd have to move soon, though. Probably. "That was great," he said, in case Dev still had any doubts.

"Yeah? Buy you tourist tat every day if this is what it gets me, then." Dev kissed his neck. He chuckled softly, his breath teasing Kyle's ear. "If anyone had tried to tell me this was how we'd end up this morning, I'd've told them they was barking. After the way I fucked up last night."

"You didn't fuck up."

"Yeah, I did. That was a bastard of a thing to say to you." Dev was silent for a moment, and his arms went stiff around Kyle's shoulders. "I fucked up with Ceri too."

Kyle reminded himself firmly it was ridiculous, in the circumstances, for him to feel a stab of jealousy. Dev wasn't his to keep, and never would be.

"What do you mean?" he said, his voice stupidly hoarse. He could kill for a glass of water. But that would mean moving from Dev's arms, and it wasn't like he was going to have many more opportunities to enjoy them.

"I told her about my mum, and, well. She went right off on me. Started banging on about me being selfish and not thinking about it from her point of view. My mum's, I mean. She, um . . . Nah. I can't— I wanna tell you, but it's not right. Not fair on her."

Kyle frowned, struggling to work out what Dev was saying. "She was angry with you for going to see your mother?"

"Nah . . . Well, yeah, she was, but she was upset too, you know? I mean, really upset. I—I know why—least, I think I do—but I can't say it. Shit." He took a couple of deep breaths. "You were trying to get me not to go, weren't you? I should've listened, maybe. I dunno. But do you think—I mean, you never said—I wasn't being a dick, was I? Going to see her?"

"No." Because he knew how much it had meant to Dev. Kyle shifted on the hard floor, twisting so he could look Dev in the eye. "*No.* I don't think your actions were unreasonable. Impetuous, perhaps, but not unreasonable. She was the unreasonable one. She should have answered your letters. Even if it was to tell you she didn't want to see you."

Even as he said it, Kyle wondered if that would have stopped Dev from visiting her. Would it have stopped him, in Dev's position? Impossible to know. He couldn't imagine it—this burning need to know where he'd come from.

And Beaten Roscarrock was only half of the story, at that. "Did she say anything about your father? Or . . . do you already know who he is too?"

"No. That bit's just blank on my birth certificate. And I didn't get a right lot of chance to ask her any questions, did I? She just wanted me out of there. 'Sides, I wasn't really thinking straight, with her being like that." Dev gazed past Kyle at the wall beyond, and his Adam's apple bobbed as he swallowed. "I think Ceri reckons he raped her. My mum, I mean."

Kyle stilled in shock. "Why does she think that?"

"I don't . . . It'd fit, though, yeah? Why she gave me away, and she don't wanna see me now."

"Dev, it's all supposition. There could be any number of other reasons. Perhaps she loved him, and he left her. Or died, even. And seeing you brought back painful memories. You don't *know* anything." He wrapped his arms tightly around Dev, as if he could squeeze in the certainty.

"Yeah. I know. It's doing my head in, though. So, I was thinking, yeah, I ought to give it another go. I mean, it's like you said, right? It was all a bit of a shock for her, me turning up out of the blue like that. So I thought, maybe I'll go round again. Take her a bunch of flowers or something."

The ache in Kyle's chest was back. "Dev, you can't."

"Why the hell not?"

"Continually visiting someone after they've told you they don't want you to is harassment. She could have you arrested."

"Yeah, but she'd never . . ." Dev's eyes narrowed. "What?"

Oh God. Kyle rubbed his face. "I'm sorry, Dev. After you'd gone, yesterday, I went up to talk to her."

"You *what*? What did she say? Fuck, what did you say to her?"

"I didn't see her. Her brother Bran opened the door, and basically told me to get lost or he'd call the police. He doesn't want you going back there, either."

"Yeah, but that's him, innit? I don't give a shit about him. What about her?"

"We have to assume she feels the same. No, wait, Dev—this is serious. Do you really want to get arrested?"

"Just for knocking on their fucking door?" Dev broke free from Kyle's embrace and stood up before angrily snatching his discarded clothes and pulling them on.

Kyle followed suit, a little more slowly. "He implied—actually, he more or less stated—that the family has a lot of influence around here. Things could be made quite unpleasant for you." And for Kyle too, for that matter, but that was his problem, not Dev's.

"That's crazy. I ain't threatening them or nothing. What the fucking hell's their problem?"

"I don't know. God knows I think they're being totally unreasonable. But the law's on their side. Literally, around here, it seems."

"There's gotta be a way around it." Dev's tone was mulish. He leaned against the kitchen counter with his hands in his jeans pockets, staring at the floor. "I ain't going home until I've seen her again."

Now it was Kyle's turn to be totally unreasonable—at least, he'd have been hard put to justify in moral terms the surge of happiness that swept through him. Dev was staying, at least for a while. "You have to leave it a few days though," he found himself saying. "Give her a chance to get over the shock." And give Kyle more time with Dev, God help him.

Dev was nodding. "Yeah, I can do that."

"Maybe think about your approach a bit. She may feel less threatened if you don't go to her home." He gave a wry smile. "And we wouldn't have to deal with big brother again." Kyle held his breath—had Dev noticed his use of *we*?

It seemed not. "Yeah. Yeah, that's a good plan. Wish I'd thought of it before. I just thought she'd want to keep it all private, you know?"

"It was a reasonable assumption to make. You couldn't have known what would happen."

"Not what Ceri said."

Ceri should keep her big mouth shut about matters that didn't concern her, Kyle thought uncharitably. "She didn't have any right to get angry with you. It's nothing to do with her."

"Not her fault. She was upset."

"Why?"

"Look, just leave it, yeah? It don't matter." Dev gave him an obviously forced smile. "I gotta go, yeah? Wanna check she's okay."

"Of course," Kyle said, and matched the smile with one of his own.

CHAPTER NINETEEN

Wheeling the Hornet from Kyle's cottage over to the road, Dev wasn't sure why he'd said all that crap about checking up on Ceri.

Well, yeah, he knew why he'd done it, but he wasn't sure *why* he'd done it.

Ah, shit. This was making his head hurt. But he'd had to get out of there, or Kyle was gonna keep pushing him about why Ceri had got upset, and Dev didn't want to go there. Not fair on her. 'Specially after what she'd said about people judging her for it, the smug, two-faced bastards.

Kyle wouldn't have been like that, though, would he? Except . . . Well, he was a lawyer, wasn't he? That had to make a bloke cynical about what people said. He must see people lying their arses off every day—had used to, anyway. And Dev knew Ceri was telling the truth: all anyone had to do was look at her face to know that, but that wasn't easy to explain to someone who didn't know her, was it? *Exhibit A: artist's impression of the victim's expression.* Yeah, right.

Maybe he should check up on her, at that. Not by getting in her face, though. Dev kicked the stand on the bike, pulled out his phone, and texted off a quick *K?*

Just as he'd got it back in his pocket, an answer buzzed through. *K. U?*

Dev gave it a proper answer this time. *I'm good. U working?*
No.
Meet up? Ill buy you and icecream.
U cant afford me.

Dev stared at his screen and cursed. *An*icecream. Then he smiled. She wouldn't have texted that if she was still mad at him, right? *Meet on prom in half an hour?*

Maybe.

"I'm still mad at you," was the first thing she said when she turned up on the prom forty minutes later.

Dev stood up from his perch on the railings. "Yeah, listen, about last night. I'm sorry, okay? Didn't mean to, like, upset you or nothing."

She looked at her feet. "'S okay. Dad reckoned I shouldn't have gone off on you like that. You didn't know."

Relieved, Dev gave her a winning smile. "Hug and make up?"

She didn't look exactly won. "Not a kiss?"

"Fuck, no. You're a girl. That'd be well gross." He gave her a slo-mo, one-armed cuddle she could easily duck out of if she wanted to, and felt some of the tension leave her. "Wanna talk about it?"

"No."

"Fair enough. Ice cream's this way." He pointed to the nearest kiosk.

"Not that one. It's shite. Shaving foam tourist crap." She led him up a side street to a little pocket-sized café with like fifty different flavours on display and proper sugar cones, not those cardboard-flavoured soggy wafer ones you got most places.

It was three times the price of most places and all, Dev realised ruefully as he pulled out his wallet to pay for a double pistachio for her and a mint choc chip for him. No wonder the middle-aged blonde behind the counter was looking so flippin' cheerful. Ceri got in first though and paid for the both of them, which either meant she was feeling militantly feminist today or she really had forgiven him for last night.

And he had to admit, when he tried his ice cream, it was totally worth the price. Proper creamy stuff that didn't taste fake, with the chips made out of real chocolate or a bloody good imitation.

"You pulling a sickie?" he asked as Ceri licked the side of an ice cream almost as big as she was. "I mean, we gotta steer clear of the caff?" They were heading down to the prom again to finish their ice creams by the sea, but it'd be good to know for later.

"No. 'S all right. You make up with that bloke of yours, then?"

Dev cricked his neck turning to look at her. "What?"

"Mrs. Hammet said he came to the café. Yesterday."

Christ, had it really been only yesterday? Heh, they'd shagged twice since then. Dev couldn't help grinning. "Yeah, we made up."

"You gonna keep seeing him after you go home?"

Dev opened his mouth, about to say, *Course I am.* Then he shut it again. "Early days yet. I got another two weeks to go here. More than."

"It's just a holiday thing, then?"

Dev's shoulders hunched. "I dunno, do I? Just gonna go with the flow." Except it felt wrong, saying that. Like he was lying to her and cheating on Kyle. Which made zero sense, 'cos he wasn't, but that was what it felt like. "Ah shit." Mint choc chip had dribbled all down his hand. Dev licked it up as best he could without actually dropping the rest of the ice cream out of the cone. "We ain't talked about it or nothing."

She snorted. Maybe Dev was reading too much into a snort, but it seemed to say all kinds of stuff like *Men,* and *Too busy getting your end away, were you?*

Shit. Was that what Kyle had thought when Dev pissed off straight after sex this morning? Like that was all he was after? "Gonna go round again tonight," Dev said, deciding on the spot. He couldn't take him another present to say sorry, 'cos that'd be well naff, but he could . . . What? Cook for him? *Oi, mate, budge over, need to borrow your kitchen. Beans on toast all right?* Nah, maybe not. Takeaway?

Ceri was giving him a look. And now, *now* Dev was getting really paranoid, because all he could see in her expression was, *Ain't you worried it's gonna drop off if you keep wearing it out?*

"I like him, all right? But we only met a couple of days ago. It ain't like I'm gonna propose to him or nothing."

"And it don't bother you, him being sick?"

"He ain't sick. It's a condition. And it ain't his fault." Yeah, it was a pain sometimes, but there was so much of life Kyle could still have. Dev wanted to show him that.

Wanted to share it with him.

Dev stared out over the beach to the sea. The tide was out, pretty much as far as it ever got, he reckoned, and there was an endless stretch of sand in front of them. Close by, it was dotted with families, with towels laid out, cool boxes in easy reach and umbrellas jammed in the sand so the kiddies could get some shade. Down by the water, lads in shorts and girls in bikinis were mucking about, some with surf boards—the serious surfers were all off to one side, not doing a right lot because the wind had dropped. The smell of the sea was almost overpowered by the scent of cheap suntan lotion. It was the sort of scene Dev was used to from his holidays abroad—but suddenly, he wished he was over the other side of the headland, down by Mother Ivey's Bay. It was quieter there, and wilder.

And Kyle was there.

"You got ice cream dripping on your jeans," Ceri said, and broke the spell.

CHAPTER TWENTY

Kyle watched Dev go with an uneasy feeling in his gut. What was it about this Ceri girl? Things had been going so well with him and Dev—and then suddenly they weren't. He'd practically run out of the house.

Maybe Kyle was imagining it.

Or maybe Dev had just got what he'd come for and hadn't seen any point in staying.

Yes. That was probably it. After all, what were holiday flings for?

Sex, that was what. And Kyle was an idiot if he expected anything else.

Why the bloody hell hadn't he thought to make arrangements to see Dev again before he'd left? Kyle loathed the ridiculous mathematics of working out the optimum interval before calling. Surely none of the normal rules applied when one party was only in the area for three weeks? Shouldn't they be spending as much time together as possible? If this was all they'd ever have?

The thought left him with a hollow feeling in his chest.

He jumped when his phone rang. Kyle's heart rose briefly—then sank again as he saw who it was. Not Dev. Mum.

It must be late afternoon in Perth, so hopefully this wasn't an emergency, although he struggled to think why else his mum would be calling so soon after they'd last spoken. Maybe she wanted to remind him one of the kids' birthdays was coming up? "Hello, Mum, everything all right?"

She didn't bother with *hello*. "Jeffrey rang me."

Oh hell.

"He said you hadn't been answering his calls, and he was worried about you. And when I said, oh, yes, you seemed fine, although a little down about the breakup, he asked me if there was 'any better news on the health front.' So of course I asked him what he meant by that." She finally paused for breath. "Kyle, what haven't you been telling me? I've been worried half to death. Is it cancer? Darling, why didn't you *tell* me?"

"I . . ." Kyle wasn't sure which question to answer first. None of them, for preference. "He didn't tell you?"

"Of course he didn't! That's why I've been so frightened. He just said I should talk to you about it, but not to worry too much. As if I could *not worry*. Darling, what's wrong?"

Kyle closed his eyes. "It's narcolepsy."

There was a pause. "Narcolepsy? Is that the one where people get sleepy all the time?"

"Yes." It was the path of least resistance.

"Oh, thank heavens." There was laughter in her tone. "And here I was getting so worked up. Well, thank goodness it's nothing serious."

The overwhelming rush of hurt and betrayal that swept over him was irrational. Kyle knew that. Mum didn't know what she was saying. Why should she? He hadn't known the first thing about narcolepsy either, until he'd started to suffer from it. And it was fine. He hadn't wanted her to worry about him, and now she wasn't.

"Yes," he forced himself to say. "Nothing serious."

"Have you been to the doctor? I'm sure they can give you something for it. And there's all these drinks with caffeine in nowadays, although they're probably not very healthy to drink too much of. I know Lily, that's my friend from church, she gets some pills when she's flying. To help with the jetlag, of course. Now, what were they? Oh, yes. Melatonin, which I always thought was something to do with getting a suntan but apparently not. She says they work wonders for her. I'm sure you'd be able to get them over the counter at Boots. You can get all sorts of alternative remedies there these days."

Kyle let her talk, and tried to listen to her voice, not the words. He'd heard them all before. She meant well. Just like all his former colleagues and friends who seemed to think narcolepsy was something you could cure with a couple of cups of coffee and a vitamin pill. God, if only it were that simple.

"And make sure you don't work too hard," she finished with. Just to remind Kyle he was still lying to her about more than just his illness.

Later that day, he went for a walk along the edge of the cliff overlooking the beach. It was still too early to take the path down and walk along the sand—there were families there, and a few couples, seeking more quiet and privacy than was afforded by the more commercial beach on the other side of the headland. Kyle envied them. *"I have heard the mermaids singing, each to each. I do not think that they will sing for me."* He'd never been much of one for poetry, preferring visual art forms to stark words, but the long-ago-read lines crept into his head all the same.

Kyle stood and gazed out across the endless blue water, sparkles of sunlight dancing across the waves. *"I should have been a pair of ragged claws, scuttling across the floors of silent seas."*

Was it over? Kyle wasn't even sure what *it* was—him and Dev? Life itself?—but something inside him rebelled at the thought. No.

It wasn't over.

At least, not yet.

He should have brought his sketchbook with him. There was a wealth of beauty out here waiting to be captured. Next time he'd think of that. There was one thing he could do right now, however.

Kyle took one last look at the sea, then turned towards the pottery with a newly confident tread to ask about using their facilities.

Kyle woke up on the sofa. The sun was low in the sky, casting a rich orange glow into his living room, and there was the sound of banging. He blinked at Dev through the living room window, which was presumably what had been taking a beating. Dev raised his eyebrows and made a complicated gesture Kyle would have struggled to interpret if it hadn't been pretty obvious from the situation that he was asking to be let in.

A shame the builders of the cottage hadn't installed French windows, Kyle thought as he opened the front door and waited for Dev to walk round from the back.

"For future reference, there's a key under the stone," he said when Dev appeared.

"Yeah? Cheers, mate." Dev looked happier about it than it seemed to merit.

"Were you waiting long?" Kyle stood back to let Dev in the door.

Dev kicked off his trainers and padded over to the sofa. He sat on it with such an expectant look on his face that Kyle sat beside him almost without deciding to do so. "Nah, just ten minutes or so. Was it all right, waking you up? I'd have left you, but I thought it was probably a bit late for you to be napping, so . . ."

"No, you're right." It was also a little late for Dev to be calling on him for any other reason than because he intended to stay the night. Desire surged even as he felt an irrational sense of hurt at the apparent confirmation that this was all he was useful for to Dev. "Busy day?" he asked, almost entirely certain he'd kept his tone mild and even.

"Nah, just lazed around with Ceri. She went home for tea, and I went back to the B&B for a bit to put me feet up in the garden." Dev grinned suddenly, the picture of relaxation with one foot resting on the opposite knee. "Fell asleep, didn't I? I blame you being a bad influence. Lucky I was in the shade or I'd have got well burned. You ever done that?"

"Only once." So far. "Have you eaten? I've got some leftovers from tea, if not." He'd cooked extra just in case. More fool him.

"Nah, I'm good, ta. Grabbed a burger on the way." Dev hesitated. "You all right? You seem a bit . . . I dunno. Not up for company tonight? I mean, I know it's late . . ."

"It's fine," Kyle said quickly.

"I'd have come round earlier but like I said . . ."

"You fell asleep." The irony of Dev's excuse wasn't lost on Kyle. "Well, I suppose it makes a change for me to be on this end of it."

"Yeah. I felt like a right twat when I woke up. At least you've got a good excuse."

"For being a twat?"

"No, you cock." Still smiling, Dev glanced pointedly at the six inches of sofa between them. "You coming over here or what?"

"We could go straight upstairs." Even as he said it, Kyle was sliding over to close the gap, but it felt awkward, somehow. As if he were following stage directions rather than acting of his own volition.

There was a beat of silence. "In a hurry, are you?"

"No, I just thought—"

Dev gave him a serious look. "I didn't just come here to get my leg over. I mean, don't get me wrong . . . Just, no hurry, is there?"

"Oh. Okay. Would you like a drink?"

"Glass of water would be good. Tell you what, I'll get 'em." Dev jumped up and headed into the kitchen.

Kyle took a deep breath. Why were things so strained between them? Was it him? Was he subconsciously resenting Dev's abrupt disappearance this morning?

He tried to force himself to relax as Dev returned with the drinks.

"So what did you get up to today?" Dev asked, sitting back down close beside him.

Kyle couldn't help feeling a frisson of an entirely different type of tension where their legs pressed up against each other. "I finally got around to going into the pottery."

"Yeah? So are they cool with you using their stuff?"

He nodded, smiling at the memory. "I didn't have anything with me, but they seemed quite interested when I showed some photographs of the kind of things I've made. They're happy for me to go along there in the evenings, after they close." The timing wasn't ideal for his alertness, but if he made sure he got his naps, he'd manage.

"That's great." Dev gave a worried frown. "Uh, were you planning to go there tonight? 'Cos I can piss off if you want."

"No, it's fine. I spent over an hour there this afternoon, and I don't want to wear out my welcome." Kyle paused. "Oh, and I told Mum about my narcolepsy." He didn't confess he'd been more or less forced into it.

Dev looked, predictably, pleased. "Yeah? Good on you, mate. How did she take it?"

She laughed it off. "Very well. She didn't seem too worried."

"Uh, seriously? What exactly did you tell her?"

This conversation was not going the way Kyle had hoped it would. "Just that I have it."

"Uh-huh. So she basically ain't got a clue how bad it is?"

"She's the other side of the world. What would be the point in upsetting her?"

"Yeah, but mate . . ." Dev trailed off, shaking his head. "Nah, she's your mum."

There was a slight emphasis on *your*. Kyle wasn't entirely certain what Dev was getting at, but he was more than willing to leave it if Dev was. "Are you sure you don't want something to eat?" he asked instead.

"Don't come here just for meals, either." Dev grinned. "Hey, can I see some of those pottery pics? I've only seen your mugs so far."

Kyle dutifully got out his phone and showed a few of the bowls and vases he'd constructed, flicking quickly past the ones that hadn't turned out so well.

"You still got all these?"

"I'd have enough to open a small shop by now if I did. No, mostly I give them away. Generally my colleagues at chambers bear the brunt."

"Heh, that's one perk of being a lawyer I wouldn't have expected. Hey, have you got any pics of you in the full legal getup?"

Kyle frowned. "I don't . . . Yes, actually, now I think about it." He got up and fetched his laptop from the dining room. "Let me find it . . . Here. This is Sujata Das, my colleague, and me, just after a trial we worked on together." It was odd, staring at this former version of himself. He was clean-shaven and radiated smug confidence.

Dev laughed. "Bloody hell, the wig's bigger than she is. But you're looking good, mate. Very good. Gotta say though, I like you with the beard and all." He turned to stroke Kyle's now hirsute cheek, then pulled him in for a kiss.

Finally, *finally* something felt right. Kyle sank into the kiss, tasting Dev's familiar mild spice, this time with a hint of ketchup. He shifted to get closer—and almost dropped the laptop. "Bugger."

"Hey, don't put it away yet. I wanna see some more photos."

"I don't think I've got any more of me in court dress on here. Sorry."

"What, not even on your website? I mean, you got a website, right? Or, well, this firm you and Sujata work for?"

"Almshouse Chambers. That's what it's called. But I'm afraid we're in plain clothes there." Kyle quickly typed the URL into his browser, and navigated to his own personal page within the site.

Dev read aloud. "Year of call, Inner Temple . . . Jesus, it's like you're a priest or something."

Kyle stifled a laugh. "Hardly. The call is the call to the bar, meaning I got through my Bar Professional Training Course and qualifying sessions. And Inner Temple is just the name of the professional organisation I joined. It's one of the Inns of Court. It's been around since the twelfth century, in some form."

"Yeah, and let me guess, they ain't changed a thing since then?"

"More than you'd think. The Knights Templar were the original founders, and sorry if this comes as a disappointment, but I haven't actually got an arsenal of weapons and a suit of armour stashed away back in Surrey."

"Probably just as well. Weren't they the ones that went round killing people who looked like me?" Dev's smile was definitely on the grim side. "So what, you get this call and then you're a barrister?"

"No, *then* you have to do your pupillage. But that's only another year."

"And then you get to wear the wig?"

"And then you get to wear the wig. You know, you seem to have something of a wig fixation. Are you perhaps a drag queen in your spare time?"

"Nah. Sorry if *that* comes as a disappointment. But if I was, I'd be *fabulous*, darling." Dev fluttered his eyelashes and blew Kyle an exaggerated kiss.

It was back—the lightness Kyle was used to feeling in Dev's company. He could tell he was smiling helplessly, so he closed up the laptop and put it to one side. Then he slipped an arm around Dev and kissed him.

CHAPTER TWENTY-ONE

Dev kissed Kyle back, openmouthed but no tongue, just easy, relaxed kisses, sprawling over the sofa. He wanted to take it slow this time. Show Kyle it wasn't just about getting his end away.

Trouble was . . . Ah, sod it. Kyle was a fucking awesome kisser, and Dev was only human. He couldn't help it if his body wanted Kyle's body, could he? And, okay, maybe it was his fault he ended up half on top of the bloke, grinding his hard-on against Kyle's belly, but it was definitely Kyle who started shoving at clothes first.

The first touch of skin on skin, and Dev was a goner. He broke the kiss, breathing hard. "Bed?"

"Bed," Kyle said. He looked as far gone as Dev felt, hair all mussed and his lips red and swollen from kissing.

He was fucking gorgeous. Dev got to his feet and held out his hand. "You coming?"

Kyle laughed softly. "Do I really have to make the innuendo?"

"Nah. I prefer actions over words any day." Kyle's hand in Dev's felt like it *meant* something, somehow. Like a promise. Dev pulled him up gently, and they hit the stairs, both of them with big, soppy grins on their faces.

Best high ever.

Except it wasn't, 'cos when they got in the bedroom and started taking their kit off, it got even better. Dev could hardly wait for them both to get naked before he was on Kyle again, pressing their bodies together, their skin searing hot where they touched.

Kyle drew him down into a fierce kiss, and this time, it was no-holds-barred. Dev thrust his tongue into Kyle's mouth, loving the taste of him.

Fuck, he wanted more. He wanted it *all*.

He pulled back, took a breath, and forced his voice to be steady. "Hey, look, you can say no if you wanna, no pressure, but I really fucking wanna get inside you. Is that okay? Tell me if it's not okay. We can do anything you want."

Christ, Kyle's *face* . . . Like Dev had offered him the world, all wrapped up with a fancy bow and a cherry on top. He didn't say anything—just nodded sharply, looking a bit overwhelmed.

"You lie back, yeah?" Dev tried to make it sound reassuring. "I'll do everything. Just let me do everything."

And Kyle did just that, no hesitation, no questions asked. He put himself in Dev's hands and fuck, the *trust* he was showing almost did Dev in.

Made him want to be worthy.

He went as gently as he could, lubing Kyle up and stretching him out even though it nearly killed him, holding off for so long. And when he finally gloved up and pushed in, Kyle's hips raised up on a pillow and one of those long legs over Dev's shoulder . . .

God.

Kyle let out a moan, but it didn't sound like pain.

"It's all right, I got you, gonna make you feel so fucking good," Dev gasped anyhow, desperate to go in all the way but holding back because Christ, he'd rather chop his own dick off than hurt Kyle.

"It's okay, it's good . . ." Kyle's voice was breathless, and his eyes were dark as a Cornish night sky. Dev couldn't stop himself pushing in further. Kyle opened up to him like a fucking flower, and then he was in, all the way, as close as it was possible for two people to get, and it felt *amazing*. Like it was more than just skin on skin. Like it was pure electricity zapping between them.

"Yeah, that's it, that's it," Dev heard himself saying, and then Kyle grabbed hold of his arse and drew him in even *tighter*, and that was it, Dev was off. He pulled out just far enough so he could thrust back in hard, again and again, barely aware of Kyle's muttered, "Yes, yes!"

Dev knew he wasn't going to last, even before his balls tightened up and his breath caught in his throat. "'M close," he breathed—and then ecstasy surged through him like a lightning strike from the world's most bad-ass thunderstorm. "Jesus . . ."

His orgasm seemed to last forever, wave after wave of pleasure washing over him and through him. Still fizzing with the aftershocks, he made a grab for Kyle's dick, but he'd barely touched it before Kyle let out a huge groan and spurted all over his stomach in thick ropes of spunk.

And then he went limp.

Ah shit. Cataplexy attack. Dev felt a massive surge of fond protectiveness rise up in his chest. Kyle looked so bloody vulnerable lying there. What kind of guts must it take to put himself in that kind of position? Especially after . . . Fuck, if Dev ever met that bastard ex of Kyle's. Nope. Not going to think about that git. Not here, not now. He pulled out, eased Kyle's leg down carefully, and grabbed a handful of tissues from the box by the bed. One went to wrap up the condom, and he used the rest to gently clean Kyle up. Then he lay beside him to wait it out, careful not to touch. "That was fucking magic, mate," he breathed into Kyle's ear and then felt like a dick because what they'd just had? Trying to put it into words was like . . . like trying to build a Lamborghini out of Lego.

Lying next to Kyle, even if he couldn't touch him, was seriously Dev's new favourite place to be. He couldn't help thinking how much he didn't want to get up, get dressed, and go back to the B&B.

Fuck it. It was worth a try.

He waited until Kyle was moving again before he spoke. "Hey, you okay?"

Kyle smiled. "More than. Sorry about the—"

"Fuck that. You think I care? Gave me a chance to catch my breath, didn't it?" Okay, it wasn't strictly true—he *did* care, because Kyle cared—but hopefully that was going to change with time. "Some blokes'd take it as a compliment, you know. Like I made you come so hard you passed out." He grinned to show he was only joking, then reached out to stroke Kyle's face, the beard soft and springy under his fingers. "Look, I know you said you don't want me to stay the night, but could we just give it a go? I can kip in the spare room or on the sofa, whatever. I just wanna be here in the morning, you know?"

Kyle blinked a couple of times and didn't answer straight off. Dev braced himself for a refusal.

What he actually got was, "If you want, we can give it a go."

Dev stared, his chest tight, hardly daring to believe it. "Seriously?"

"Yes." Kyle reached out to pull him close. "Stay with me."

CHAPTER TWENTY-TWO

Sleep was slow to come. Kyle had been expecting the sleep paralysis, but he hadn't expected to feel so at ease with Dev lying beside him. He *trusted* him, beyond sense, beyond reason. Perversely, it unnerved him, kept him wakeful.

Or maybe it was the memory of having Dev inside him that made it impossible to quieten his thoughts. The sex tonight had been different from the previous occasions. Less urgent. Less like scratching a desperate, mutual itch.

More like making love.

Dev had been so gentle, so careful not to hurt as he'd stretched Kyle, readied him to take his cock. All the while he'd murmured filthy endearments, and Kyle had floated on a sea of *Fuck, yeah, so tight, so fucking gorgeous, can't wait to have you.*

And when Dev entered him . . . It had been almost too much. Too close, too intimate. Kyle had felt enveloped by him, surrounded by Dev's scent, his heat. When he finally bottomed out, it was as if they really had become one, as if Kyle had been *made* to take him. And afterwards, he'd shown so much consideration for Kyle's feelings, as he lay there paralysed.

A knife twisted in his chest. It was going to hurt *so much* when Dev left.

This couldn't go on.

But Kyle knew he wouldn't be able to stop it. Not until Dev, inevitably, did.

It was almost comforting to wake some time later from a familiar nightmare.

"Y'orright?" Dev muttered, still half-asleep.

"I'm fine. Go back to sleep." Dev did so with enviable ease. Kyle kissed him and got out of bed to go and watch TV in the living room with the sound turned down.

Kyle woke up on the sofa to find Dev had sat down next to him and was kissing him on the cheek. "Is it morning?" he asked, and felt like an idiot when he registered the light streaming in through the thin living room curtains. God, he must look a sight, sprawled on the sofa and rumpled from sleep. He only hoped he hadn't drooled.

Dev gave him a smile to match the sunshine outside. "Eight o'clock. You sleep all right? Sorry. Shit question. See any good telly last night?"

Kyle slid his arm around Dev and pulled him in tight. "You really need an answer to that?"

"Hey, I seen some good documentaries when I've got home too pissed to go to bed, sometimes. There's this woman, Mary something, she does all this Roman stuff. Really gets into it, and she's not all posy and pretentious like some of the blokes are. You know what they're like." Dev put on a heavy, ponderous voice: "'And it was *on* that day that the *fate* of the *Otto*man Empire was *sealed.*' That sort of stuff. Bores the crap out of me. 'S what gives history a bad name. If Mary What'sherface had been my history teacher, I'd definitely have passed my GCSE."

Kyle was arrested by the idea of Dev watching history documentaries. He really should learn not to judge by appearances. "Sorry. All I've got here is Freeview. I have to make do with teleshopping and *Heir Hunters.*"

Dev grimaced. "You wanna set up iPlayer before you go to bed. Or get in some DVDs. I mean, if you know you're gonna wake up a lot, it's gotta be worth it, right?"

Kyle wasn't sure. It felt like giving in to it. "Breakfast?" he said instead of starting a debate he really wasn't awake enough for.

"Fuck, yeah. Need to keep me energy levels up, don't I?"

He seemed to have plenty of energy already. Kyle followed wearily as Dev fairly bounced into the kitchen and opened the fridge.

"Great—you got bacon. Want eggs? Or bacon butties—uh, you got bread, right?"

Dev didn't wait for an answer, just opened the correct cupboard without hesitating and pulled out the half loaf of wholemeal Kyle had stored there. "Brill. This'll do." He switched on the grill and started laying out bacon slices in a careful top-to-toe pattern.

"Bit OCD, that, isn't it?" Kyle teased.

"Maximum crispiness, man. Very important." Dev looked up and grinned. There was something endearingly puppyish about him this morning.

Kyle should make the most of it while it lasted, shouldn't he? It was a bitter thought. He turned to get out plates and cutlery, not wanting Dev to read his expression. There was no point spoiling both their moods.

"Hey, you got ketchup?"

"Ketchup? In bacon sandwiches? Philistine." Kyle got out ketchup for Dev, and brown sauce for himself.

"Ain't my fault. I had a deprived childhood. Sometimes ketchup was the best bit of the meal."

Was it a straight line for a joke? Was Kyle supposed to say, *Ketchup? You had ketchup? I used to dream of ketchup?* But given how different their childhoods had been, the words stuck in his throat.

Dev didn't seem to notice his silence. "Right, you want butter on your bread? Me mate Mal's got this idea bacon butties should only have bread and bacon in 'em, but I like a bit of butter."

It wasn't really butter, just low-cholesterol spread from the fridge that Kyle had bought in a fit of self-loathing, but Dev didn't seem to mind. He spread it on the bread in a slapdash fashion at odds with his precision with the bacon.

Feeling something of a spare part, Kyle was relieved to see the bacon needed turning over.

"Cheers, mate," Dev threw over his shoulder, as if he were the host and not Kyle.

If he hadn't already known about Dev's childhood, Kyle would have been willing to believe it deprived just from the amount of ketchup Dev squeezed onto his bacon once the sandwiches were prepared. Was he still, at twenty-four, making up for years of never quite getting as much as he wanted?

Dev noticed him watching, and held up the sandwich. "Fancy a bite? Go on. You'll love it."

"I wouldn't want to deprive you of the pleasure," Kyle said politely. "And there's ketchup dripping on your sleeve."

"Ah shit. Not my day for that. Don't s'pose you know where there's a launderette round here?"

"A launderette? You're standing three feet away from a washing machine."

"Yeah, but I didn't want to, you know, assume or nothing. That all right, then, if I bring my stuff round? This is my only clean pair of jeans and all." Dev looked down. "Ah shit. Was."

Kyle *didn't* laugh at the red splodge that had appeared on Dev's jeans leg. He wanted to eat his bacon butty while it was hot, not succumb to a cataplexy attack and drop it on the floor. "I doubt any of my jeans would fit you." Or that Dev would be seen dead in them, for that matter. He favoured the sort of ultra-skinny jeans that Kyle would have felt ridiculously self-conscious wearing. "But I could lend you some jogging bottoms and a T-shirt if you like. Let's go eat for now."

They sat at the dining table, looking out over the sea as they ate. The bacon really did seem exceptionally crispy this morning, and the sun was glinting off water as blue as Kyle had ever seen it. Porthkennack was beginning to feel like home, Kyle realised. It was an odd feeling, and a little troubling.

"I gotta bring Tasha here someday," Dev said out of nowhere. "Don't think she's ever been anywhere like this."

He didn't know? Then again, he hadn't known her all her life, had he? Not like Kyle and his sister. It must be so strange, to go and live with people as if they were your family, when you didn't know them at all. But it seemed to have worked out well—at least, for Dev and Tasha's relationship. Kyle hesitated. "You told me Tasha's your foster sister, but you never talk about your foster parents."

Dev shrugged. "Not a lot to tell. They fostered a lot of kids. Think they were glad to see the back of me and Tasha when we turned eighteen."

That was . . . horrifying. "They just left you to fend for yourselves after that? Is that how it works?" When Kyle had been eighteen he'd only left home to go to university. He'd still brought his washing home every other weekend, for God's sake. And his mum had never let him go back there without a food parcel.

"Varies. I mean, some families, if they like you, they stay in touch and that. Mine never liked me being into blokes—it was all, 'You can do what you like when you leave here, but while you live in this house, you play it straight.' And Tasha . . . She took a while to get her head on properly after the last place she'd been. Don't think they knew how to handle her. She was always pushing, you know? Testing the limits."

"Breaking the rules, staying out too late?"

"Sort of."

Kyle gave him a questioning look.

Dev sighed. "Ah, shit. There was this bloke where she used to live, he messed around with her, all right? You know. Like that. So she used to do stuff. Like, flirt. Come downstairs in just a towel, or just a T-shirt and knickers. Sit really close to Andy—that was our foster dad. See if he was gonna be like that too. He didn't know how to handle it. He used to get really mad at her, 'specially when he'd had a few." Dev looked Kyle right in the eye. "It was just a test, all right? She wasn't asking for it. She *never* asked for it."

Kyle nodded, a bad taste in his mouth. "Inappropriately sexualised behaviour. I've read about it." There had been an article about it in one of the Sunday papers. He'd found it psychologically interesting, if rather appalling, and he'd been glad he'd never had to deal with a case involving child abuse.

It was a lot more appalling when the victim was connected to someone he cared about. "Didn't she get any help, after it happened?"

"Dunno. She never wanted to talk about it, much. I wasn't gonna ask." Dev stared out of the window. "She just came out with it, one day. I mean, I asked her why she was pissing Andy about, and she just said something like, 'It's what they all want, innit?' Then she said that was why she liked me. 'Cos she felt safe with me."

"Because you're gay?" As he said it, Kyle realised it was the first time he'd asked if Dev was gay or bi, and held his breath for the answer.

He got a twisted smile. "Nah, it's just my natural trustworthiness, innit? Hey, you wanna head out for a bit? Could do with blowing away a few cobwebs and all that."

Discussion over, then. Kyle matched Dev's crooked smile with one of his own. "Fine. Where do you want to go?"

Dev shrugged. "I dunno. Into town, maybe? I still ain't seen that mosque yet. That's s'posed to be a thing, innit?"

"A thing?"

"You know. One of the things you come and see while you're here. Me mate Jamal was saying it's, like, historically important? First purpose-built mosque in England? Or Cornwall, maybe. Something like that. Hey, do they do that call to prayer thing here?"

"If they do, I've never heard it." Kyle heard the St. Ia's church bells sometimes on a Sunday morning, or a Saturday when there was a wedding, if the wind was blowing from the west.

"Shame. S'pose not, though. Jamal gets his prayer times from the Balham one by text message."

"Even deities have to move with the times, I suppose."

"Yeah, sorry to break it to you, mate, but it's a messaging service that sends them, not Allah."

"Oh, ye of little faith." Kyle realised as he said it that it could possibly be seen as offensive. "Um, are you Muslim?" Lack of adherence to dietary rules didn't necessarily mean anything.

"Me? Not really anything, to tell the truth. You?"

Kyle shook his head, then felt a vague sense of guilt, leftover from confirmation classes at age twelve, that prompted him to say, "Church of England, I suppose. But not exactly practising. My parents are very involved in their local church, though."

"Yeah? They all right about you being gay?" Dev gave him a sharp look, as if wondering whether this was the reason Kyle hadn't been more open with them about his illness.

No. He had no excuse. "It honestly couldn't have been less of an issue. Mum was already volunteering with an LGBT charity, and Dad's never exactly been the old-fashioned sort. You know what they argued about the evening after I'd come out to them, after they thought I'd gone to bed? Dad was ranting about how absurd it was, in this day and age, that any child should feel the *need* to come out to their parents, and Mum was defending my right to make a statement of my identity if that was what I wanted to do." The guilt returned. "I suppose it was rather different for you."

Dev shrugged. "Yeah, well, I never really came out to my foster parents. They just sort of found out. So, we going to see this mosque, then?" He stretched, showing his midriff, then got up.

Kyle could take a hint. He stood up as well. "I'll put the plates in the dishwasher and then we can go."

The mosque, when they got there, seemed to fascinate Dev, with its walls inlaid with shells in intricate patterns. It was tiny, for a place of worship, and reminded Kyle strongly of fishermen's churches he'd seen around the world, although their shape and religion were different. He mentioned this to Dev, who shrugged.

"S'pose they'd want a bit of extra prayer power when they were about to go out to sea on some rickety wooden boat, right?"

"And the sense of community for people who were far away from the land they were born in," Kyle added, thinking of his parents.

"Yeah. S'pose so." Dev's voice was quiet.

Had that been part of what he'd been looking for, coming to find his birth mother in Porthkennack? That sense of belonging somewhere? Kyle wanted to put his arms around him.

It seemed a little disrespectful, though, while they were visiting a mosque. And once they were out in the sunshine again, Dev's mood seemed to pick up instantly. "Want to head down to the prom? Think there's s'posed to be something on today."

There *was* some kind of event going on down on the seafront. There was bunting up—or rather, even more bunting than usual; Kyle wasn't sure he'd ever seen the place entirely bunting-free. Folksy music played fuzzily from large speakers set up next to a small marquee. Kyle cast a wary eye around, but there didn't appear to be any Morris dancers lurking in the vicinity. Lines of tables had been placed along the street, laden with handicrafts of varying sorts for sale, and several food stalls were filling the air with appetising aromas.

A banner informed them they were at the PEBBLE Fayre, and helpfully explained that PEBBLE stood for Porthkennack Enterprise and Business Benefiting the Local Environment.

"Fuck me, backronym much?" Dev muttered in a tone of disgust, making Kyle smile.

"Someone was probably paid a fortune to come up with that," he murmured back.

There did, in fact, seem to be a certain amount of emphasis on recycling among the stalls on offer, so at least the organisation was making some attempt to live up to its last three letters. A slender, heavily tattooed man was selling tables, cupboards, and other pieces made from repurposed wood, his disreputable appearance at odds with his eco-friendly wares. He met Kyle's gaze with a frank look that seemed to ask, *Like what you see?* For a moment, Kyle wasn't sure if the man meant his wares or himself—then he was joined behind the stall by a striking redheaded woman who grabbed him by the arm with casual intimacy. Kyle shook his head at himself, amused, and quickened his pace over to a stall offering driftwood sculptures that had caught Dev's attention. Dev was running his hands over the sea-smoothed surface of the wood of one of them, which had the vague form of a seal.

"Kinda like this one, but I'd never get it home on the bike in one piece," he said as Kyle joined him, then turned over the price tag and gave a low whistle. "'Specially not at that price. Guess I'll have to make do with a pet rock." He nodded at the next stall along, while Kyle wondered if he could somehow manage to buy the thing without Dev noticing, and get it delivered.

Some chance. He didn't even know Dev's London address. It was a sobering thought.

A whistle of feedback made everyone turn to the small dais at one end of the Fayre, with an open-fronted tent set up to shield it from any inclement weather. An overweight man with a forgettable, if slightly red, face was standing there with a microphone, his business suit looking uncomfortable and out of place among all the shorts-clad holidaymakers. "I'd like to welcome everyone to this year's PEBBLE Fayre. As I'm sure you're all aware, PEBBLE was set up three years ago to promote local enterprise, and since then it's gone from strength to strength . . ."

Kyle stopped listening. If the man couldn't avoid a cliché in his opening words, there was little hope for the rest of the speech.

His attention was drawn back when a petite, pretty, dark-haired woman stepped up to join the man at the microphone. It was hard to judge her age—midthirties? Early forties? Surely no older than that—and for some reason, she looked familiar.

"And now, a few words from the chairwoman of PEBBLE, Bea Roscarrock."

The name sank in even as he heard Dev whisper, "Fucking hell." Kyle grasped his arm, not knowing what to say. Should he ask if Dev was all right? How *could* he be all right? But Kyle had to say something.

Dev beat him to it. "That's her," he said, his voice wrecked. "That's my mum."

CHAPTER TWENTY-THREE

Dev stared at his mum, and wondered why, with all his attention on her, he still hadn't got a bloody clue what she was talking about. He had to speak to her again. He *had* to. It was, like, fate or karma or something, wasn't it? Her turning up on stage right when he'd got here. He was *meant* to talk to her.

"Dev . . ." Kyle's tone made him turn. The expression that greeted him wasn't what Dev would call encouraging. "If you're planning to go and speak to her . . . Harassment charges, remember?"

"Fuck that." It came out a bit harsh, so Dev softened his tone. This wasn't Kyle's fault. "I got to, yeah? And it's perfect, right? Out in the open. It's not like I'm camping out on her doorstep or nothing." He had to make Kyle understand he wasn't just being a dick. "Look, if she tells me to piss off, I'll leave her alone. But it's like you said, yeah? I gave her a shock last time. Maybe she's had second thoughts about it all. Maybe she wishes she'd, I dunno, told me a bit more about it all. Why she did what she did."

Kyle squeezed his arm. "Do you want me to come with you? As a witness?"

"Nah. Don't wanna crowd her." And if she *did* tell Dev to piss off again, he wasn't sure he could take having Kyle there to see it. "I'll see you back here, yeah?"

"You're going to wait until she steps down from the dais?"

"Course I'm gonna wait." Shit, did Kyle really think he was planning on causing a scene?

"All right." It sounded more like, *If you must.*

"And you're gonna be okay, yeah? Not have an attack or anything?"

"I'll be fine."

"Cheers, mate." Dev flashed him a wobbly smile.

"Better go now, then. Before she leaves."

Shit. Dev hadn't realised she'd stopped speaking and stepped down from the stage. He legged it over there. He had to step over a fair few cables when he got to the stage, and a couple of people gave him funny looks, but nobody actually came out and said, *Oi, you can't go back there.*

It was quiet behind the stage. In the lack-of-people sense, at least. Dev was fairly sure the volume of noise couldn't actually have dropped noticeably due to him moving a couple of yards, but it definitely felt like it had. Everyone was out front, gawping at the displays and browsing the stalls.

She was standing alone to one side, checking her phone.

Dev took a deep breath and approached, being careful not to block her in.

"Uh, Miss Roscarrock?" It felt weird, calling her that, but what the fuck else could he call her? They weren't on first-name terms, and anything else . . . There wasn't anything else.

She froze, but just for a moment. So short that once it'd finished, Dev was left wondering if he'd only imagined it. Then she spoke, her voice even. "I've said all I have to say to you." She turned and walked away.

Dev ran after her. "Look, I'm sorry about, you know, earlier. Coming to your house. It must've been a shock. I get that now, all right? But I just wanna talk to you for a minute, yeah? Please? Seriously. One minute. And then I'll leave you alone. Promise."

She stopped. "Except that's never how it works, is it?" Her voice was soft. Almost kind, maybe? Not cruel, at least.

Dev seized on it, which probably proved her point. "I just . . . You're the only one who can tell me about my dad. Did he . . . Did he treat you bad? Is that why you don't want nothing to do with me?"

She looked startled for a moment—but then it was gone, and her face was as expressionless as before. "It's not . . . He was just a boy. Here on holiday. We met, and . . ." She shrugged, a faint hint of a blush on her cheek.

"Was he Indian?" Dev urged.

"British. But of Indian ancestry."

"Was it him who named me?"

She made a breathy sound through her nose. Like Dev had said something a bit funny. But only a bit. "No."

"Did he . . . Did he know about me?"

"No."

"Why not?"

She gazed at him steadily. "There was no point. His family were traditional, and they'd already picked out a bride for him."

"And you didn't . . . Christ." Dev's head was spinning. "Can you tell me his name? Where he used to live?"

"He won't welcome you, you know," Bea said. "He'll have a family of his own. He won't want—forgive me—a half-caste bastard turning up to embarrass him."

"You mean, like you didn't." The hollow feeling inside threatened to swallow him up entirely, the casual racism just one more slap in the face. So this was what his family was like? Then fuck them. Fuck them all.

Who needed a family anyhow? They were a bunch of self-centred wankers. He was nothing more than a bit of wasted sperm to them, and he didn't give a *shit*, all right?

"Cheers," he managed, his throat almost too tight to talk. He turned away. She wouldn't give a toss if he said good-bye or not, so why waste his breath?

"Wait," she said, louder than he'd heard her speak so far.

Dev spun, more out of surprise than anything else.

For the first time, she wasn't looking so closed off, so certain she was doing the right thing. "I'll send you all the information I have about him. Your father. But you shouldn't go to see him. It won't end well."

"Why? He gonna set the law on me and all?"

Her colour deepened. "You mustn't blame my brother for being protective of me. We're twins. He took . . . what happened . . . personally."

"So why didn't your bruv set the law on *him*?" Dev demanded, his voice thick.

"It wasn't . . . I was young, that was all." Meaning *he'd* been older. "I wasn't used to drinking."

Fucking *shit*. "And he . . ."

"It wasn't what you're thinking."

"Like *fuck* it wasn't." Fucking hell, she was tiny now. What must she have been like at fifteen? How many drinks had it even taken before that bastard had been able to do whatever the fuck he wanted with her?

She blinked a few times, quickly, then took a deep breath. "It *wasn't*. Yes, I was underage. But there was no coercion involved. And it was all a long time ago, in any case. I'm not interested in raking things up now."

"I don't wanna rake stuff." Dev hugged himself. Tried not to look threatening. "Just . . . Can I keep in touch?"

"I don't think that's a good idea." She met his gaze steadily, but Dev reckoned it took an effort. "You look a lot like him."

"I'm sorry," he managed, his throat tight.

She didn't say, *It's not your fault*. She just nodded and walked away.

Dev watched her go, then made his way back out into the crowd.

He found Kyle standing by a stall, his posture tense and uncomfortable. A wary expression flashed across his face as Dev joined him. "How did it go?" Kyle asked softly.

Dev cleared his throat before he spoke, but his voice still came out sounding funny. "Can we go somewhere?"

"Where?" Kyle's expression had turned sad.

Dev couldn't look him in the eye. "Dunno. Not back to yours. Anywhere. Long as there's no people."

"This is Cornwall in the summer. Could be a tall order." Kyle gripped Dev's hand. "Let's try this way."

He led Dev out of town, the crowds thinning as they walked. Were they going to the Round Hole again? That was a no, as Kyle took him on past. They didn't stop at the castle, either, just kept going. A small white lighthouse poked its head up over the rise as they went on, getting taller as they got nearer. Dev could see the grey roofs of cottages around it when they reached the edge of the cliff. He glanced down. There was no beach here, just waves crashing against craggy cliffs like they were fucking furious at them and trying to knock the bastards down, raising angry white clouds of spray.

There was a stiff breeze blowing in from the sea, and the gulls' screams seemed harsher here. Dev looked around. There was no one else in sight. No one at all. Something seemed to lift inside him.

"Okay here?" Kyle asked. He had to raise his voice against the sound of the sea.

Dev nodded. It was a good place. He sat down on the rough, springy grass. Kyle arranged himself behind him, legs spread wide so Dev could lean back into his chest, Kyle's arms wrapped around his shoulders, warming him and keeping the world at bay. They sat there for a long while, gazing out across the water. There was a lump of jagged rock a short way out to sea, standing alone as if it was all that was left of a previous cliff face that'd lost the battle with the waves. Gulls swooped around it. Fuck knew why, 'cos there was no one there to chuck bits of half-eaten sandwich for them.

Kyle didn't ask him any questions.

"Don't you wanna know what happened?" Dev said in the end.

"Only if you want to tell me. *When* you want to tell me."

Dev gripped one of the arms guarding him. He didn't have the words for what that meant, right now. "This place got a name?" he asked instead, after a while.

Kyle breathed a laugh into his neck. "Stinking Cove."

"Shut up. Seriously?"

"Seriously. And you see that rock out there? That's the Giant's Midden."

"That the same giant what fell in love with the Round Hole girl?"

"That's the one. Legend has it that he used to come out here and try to write love poems to her beauty. But he could never get them right, and so he'd wrap them around the remains of his lunch and toss them out to sea in disgust. When he died, the heap turned to stone and formed that stack out there."

"You're shitting me."

"Actually, yes."

Dev twisted round to stare at him. "What?"

"I made it up. Sorry. Although this place really is called Stinking Cove."

Huh. If you'd asked him five minutes ago, Dev wouldn't have thought he could dredge up a smile for anything. Seemed he'd been wrong.

Wrong about a lot of stuff. The heaviness in his heart returned. "Dev?"

"Tell me some more. Real stuff, made-up shit, I don't give a monkey's, all right? Just tell me stuff."

Kyle was silent for a moment. "You see the lighthouse?"

Its white walls were almost blinding in the sunlight now breaking through the cloud. "Can't bloody miss it, can you? S'pose that's the point."

"There's a legend about that too. One of the keepers had previously been stationed at a lighthouse that could only be reached by sea, and he'd been all on his own for months after the only other keeper took ill and died. He was driven half-mad by the loneliness and the stress of constantly keeping the lamp lit all by himself—no electricity in those days—and when they finally relieved him, he was a shadow of the man he'd been. He was sent here as a softer posting, so he could recover. He lived in the lighthouse on his own, but he could go into town anytime he wanted, and he kept a pet for company, a sleek black cat called Jenny. All went well for a few months, although the townsfolk noticed he came into town less and less, and walked more slowly when he did. People began to say he should retire and let a younger man take over, but he was determined he could manage." Kyle stopped.

"And then what?"

"There was a great storm one night. Dozens of ships were wrecked, but many more were saved by the light which kept burning all night long. When morning came, the grateful fishermen went to thank the lighthouse keeper for his part in saving lives." Kyle paused. "They found him stiff and cold in his bed, clearly dead for several days, apparently of a heart attack. But the cat was strutting proudly around the lamp room. The townsfolk couldn't decide what had happened. Had the keeper's ghost kept the light burning? Or was Jenny the cat a witch?"

"So what—they exorcise him and burn her at the stake?"

"Nope. He was buried in the local churchyard, and Jenny received free fish for life. After all, there was no proof she was a witch—but if she was, best to keep on her good side. And ever since then, there's been a cat kept at Porthkennack Lighthouse that's a direct descendant of Jenny. And the light's never gone out."

Dev smiled. "That's bollocks, innit? You just made all that up. Nah, don't tell me." He sat there a while longer, enjoying the warmth of Kyle's arms and the weight of his head on Dev's shoulder.

Then he took a deep breath. Enough wallowing. Kyle probably needed to eat or have a nap or something by now. "Wanna head back to yours?" He shifted in Kyle's arms, and they fell limply from him. "Kyle?"

There was no answer. Carefully, so the bloke's head wouldn't fall off his shoulder, Dev wrapped Kyle's arms around him once more and held them in place.

CHAPTER TWENTY-FOUR

Kyle woke up with a stiff neck, a numb arse, and a foot that had gone to sleep. He was still wrapped around Dev, though, which made up for a hell of a lot. "Dev? Sorry."

He shifted back and rolled his shoulders. Bloody hell, when had the ground got so hard?

Dev turned. "What for?" He was smiling, which made Kyle's heart clench painfully in his chest. God, he was so young.

Kyle felt about a hundred and three. "I'd better head home," he said. "Get some lunch." He didn't want to go back into town and brave the crowds, and thankfully Dev didn't suggest it. Nor did he say a word as Kyle staggered to his feet on stiffened limbs, although he did offer him a hand.

Kyle took it. Who needed pride anyway?

"You got food at home, or do we need to pick something up on the way?" Dev asked.

Apparently he was coming home too. Kyle felt better already. "There are the eggs we didn't eat this morning. I can probably rustle up some omelettes. Or there's always takeaway." He couldn't face shopping right now.

"Yeah, whatevs, I'm easy. Long as you got what you need."

What Kyle needed? He wasn't sure what that was. He knew what Dev needed. To get away from Porthkennack. Back to his life in London, with his friends and what family he had. Away from Kyle.

Kyle tried not to let his pain at the thought show. Pointless. He'd always known this was coming. "I suppose you'll be going back to London now?" It was as good a way as any of confirming what had happened with Bea Roscarrock.

"Wait, what? No. I still got two weeks. Told you."

"You're going to keep trying with her?" If that was the case, Kyle would definitely need to brush up on harassment law.

"No. That's all done and dusted." Dev sent a dark look out towards where the sun was setting.

"Then what's keeping you here? Ceri?"

Dev huffed. It was almost a laugh. "No, you prick. She's got her family, ain't she? They seem to be looking after her all right" He gave Kyle a look that was half-fond, half-exasperated. "You. I'm staying for you, you tosser."

"What?" Kyle recoiled.

"Jeez, someone did a right number on your ego, didn't they? Yeah, you. And I was thinking, right, I know long-distance is crap and all, but you never said you were definitely gonna stay here after the summer, and Surrey's like next door to South London. And even if you don't go back there, maybe we could work something out? Split the difference or something? I mean, I like London, but I ain't got to live there, you know what I'm saying?"

This was all too much. Too fast. Too *wrong*. "Dev, this isn't— That's not what this is about." Dev deserved so much better than a useless invalid, old before his time.

"What do you mean?" Dev's tone was painfully sharp.

Oh God. Could Kyle's timing have been any worse? Dev had just had a huge disappointment. A huge rejection, for God's sake. If he was happier pretending Kyle and he had a future, then Kyle should bloody well let him pretend for now. "Nothing. Sorry. I just meant, how long are you planning to stay in the area?"

Dev frowned. "No, you didn't. I said I wanna keep seeing you, and *you* said that ain't what this is about. So what *is* it about, eh?"

God, why did Dev have to choose *this* issue to push him on? "We can talk about it later."

"Or we can talk about it now." Dev folded his arms and stopped dead in the middle of the lane.

Fine. Absolutely bloody *fine*. "This isn't a long-term thing, Dev. You have to see that."

Dev's hurt look stabbed him in the gut. "What, 'cos I don't talk with the right accent and I didn't go to the right school and I work in greasy overalls instead of a posh suit and a fucking wig?"

"That's got nothing to do with *anything*. I don't care about your bloody job." Oh God. That wasn't well put. "I mean—"

"I know what you mean all right. Bollocks. Just 'cos I never went to uni and I don't get paid a hundred grand for wearing fancy dress and knowing a few words of Latin—"

"Well, thank you for reducing all my years of study and work to a bloody costume party." *Damn* it. Why were they even arguing about this?

Dev drew breath—and then they both jumped as his phone rang. Dev looked conflicted—then he screwed up his face, already reaching into his jeans pocket. "I gotta— It's Tasha."

Kyle took a few deep breaths of his own, and tried to be glad of the interruption, which might just help them calm down a little. Getting mad that Dev had chosen to answer the phone rather than talk to him any longer was counterproductive, unfair, and immature.

And if he kept telling himself that, maybe one day he'd believe it.

Dev had turned away, but Kyle could hear him loud enough as he spoke with his sister. "Tasha. *Tasha.* Calm down, all right? I can't understand a bloody word. Take it slow, yeah?"

Oh God. There was something wrong. Kyle's anger was gone so suddenly he half expected to find himself on the ground.

There was a short silence, punctuated by a couple of sharp intakes of breath from Dev, as if he was about to say something but held himself back. His face darkened as he listened to what Tasha was apparently telling him, his posture becoming more hunched.

Kyle ached to touch him. To reassure him.

"That fucking *tosser*. I'll fucking kill him." Kyle's blood chilled. God, what had happened to her?

"You've told 'em you're diabetic, right? You got your insulin? You gotta make sure they know you— Yeah, I know, all right, but you gotta— Oi, just *listen*, will you? They got you a brief yet?" There was a pause. "Course they're saying that. It ain't to make *your* life easier. You gotta tell 'em you want legal advice. And you don't say nothing until you get it, and then you do what they tell you. Don't give the bastards a reason to throw the book at you. Just keep your head down. And I'm coming back, yeah? I'll see you soon as I can."

There was another silence.

"I'll sort it out, babe. Trust me." Dev hung up, shoved his phone in his pocket, then scrubbed his face with both hands. "*Christ,*" he muttered.

Kyle reached out warily to grasp his shoulder and found himself suddenly with an armful of Dev.

Thank *God.* And then Kyle felt like a complete bastard for being glad Tasha's problem, whatever it was, had helped them reconcile.

"Fuck. How the hell am I gonna..." His face twisted. "It's my sister. Tasha. She's sharing a house with a few people, yeah? She woke up this morning to a fucking *police raid.* Turns out one of her housemates is a dealer, the stupid fucking tosser. Not only that, but 'cos him and her had a bit of a thing going, on and off, the bastard hid part of his stash in her room, and now they're saying she knew all about it. She's shit scared she's gonna get done for intent to supply."

Kyle blinked. This, at least, was something he knew. "She's still in police custody? Or has she been remanded yet?"

Dev looked up, his expression unreadable. "Police. She ain't been charged yet, but she reckons they're gonna. She's fucking terrified."

"Good. That gives us some time."

"Us?"

"Do you *want* her case to be handled by some overworked duty solicitor who hasn't got the time or the energy to care about one more teenager in trouble?"

"No, but . . . What are you saying?"

Kyle felt more awake, more *alive* than he had in months. This was what he *did.* What he was good at. "She's in London, yes?"

Dev nodded. "Lavender Hill nick."

"Then one of the solicitors I usually work with will be fine. I'll give them a call . . ." He trailed off, thinking. Saltash & Kopeck might be too busy to take the case, but Tom Saltash owed him a favour. He'd start there. Kyle pulled out his phone and dialled.

Tom answered immediately, thank God. He was probably still on his lunch break.

"Anthony, long time, no hear. How are you?"

Kyle took a deep breath and forced himself not to rush through the pleasantries too obviously. "I'm fine, thanks. You?"

"Oh, can't complain. Although I frequently do, of course. So what can I do for you? Is this a business call?"

"Pretty much. I've got a friend who needs a good solicitor in a hurry." Kyle outlined Tasha's situation.

"First offence?"

Kyle looked at Dev and repeated the question. He nodded. "Yes."

"Well, that's something to work with. If it does go to court, will you be taking the brief?"

"Yes." Kyle said it before he'd even thought about it. Was that a mistake? But her first hearing would in any case be a short one, just to decide on bail, which she should get for a first offence. He could see how that went—perhaps ask Sujata if she could be on standby, in case of emergency—and take it from there.

"Good. Glad to hear it. We've missed you, you know. When are you planning on getting back to work properly?"

"I'll . . . I'll let you know. But thanks for taking this one."

"No problem. I'll call you after I've seen her."

Kyle thanked him again and hung up. Dev still looked worried. "I dunno if I can pay—"

"That's not an issue." Obviously Tom, unlike Kyle, would expect to be paid, but damn it, what was the point in having money in the bank if he didn't use it to help out people he cared about? "Tom's going to go down to the police station, and he'll keep us informed."

Dev nodded, grim-faced. "I'd better get on me bike."

Oh. Oh, of course, he'd want to be there. "It's up to you," Kyle said slowly, "but it might be better to wait until we hear back from Tom. It'll take you, what, a good five hours to get back to South London by road, and it may be he'll be able to get it all straightened out before you're even halfway there."

Dev shook his head, a rough motion. "I can't . . . I can't just wait. And I *know* they probably won't even let me see Tasha when I get there, and yeah, all right, I'd be no bloody help even if they did. But at least I'll be there for her."

And who'd be there for him? "You know it's only an hour to London on the plane from Newquay," Kyle found himself saying. "And there's a direct train from Gatwick Airport to Clapham Junction."

"I dunno . . ."

Kyle guessed why he was hesitating. "It's not that expensive. And this way I can come with you. I think we both know that tearing up the motorway with me on the back of your bike isn't a great idea, and if we took my car, we're likely to get held up in traffic. You know what it's like in Cornwall in the summer. It could literally take all day to get there."

Dev gave a weak smile. "If we tried taking your car all that way, I reckon we'd be the ones causing a jam while we wait for the tow truck. Are you sure you wanna come with me? This ain't on you."

"Because I have so many other demands on my time? Besides, it'll be good to see Tom again, and, well, if the matter does go any further, at least I'll be on the spot."

He could tell he'd won. Dev took a deep breath, shoved his hands in his jeans pockets, and nodded. "Right. Uh . . ."

"You go back to the B&B, tell them you've had to go home for a day or two for a family emergency, and pick up anything you need to take. I'll book the plane tickets and see you at my house."

CHAPTER TWENTY-FIVE

Dev grabbed his rucksack and chucked in his toiletries bag. Then he frowned and pulled it all out again. He had plenty of all this crap back in the flat. He picked up his phone charger and his jacket and headed out, glancing at his watch. Past one o'clock. And they still hadn't eaten. Shame they hadn't checked out those food stalls down by the seafront. He hoped Kyle would think to make himself a sandwich while he was waiting for Dev to get there. Dev wasn't sure he could stomach anything right now.

God, were the cops feeding Tasha regular? Were they checking on her to make sure she hadn't gone into a hypo? They wouldn't let her die in custody, would they?

No. No, shit, he was worrying about nothing. She'd *said* she'd told them all about her medical issues. They had to know how to treat people with diabetes. It wasn't *that* uncommon.

It wasn't just Tasha's situation that was doing his head in, though. Kyle had been so *different* once he'd got on the phone to that solicitor mate of his. Before, even. He'd looked more ... Shit. More *awake* than Dev had ever seen him. It was like he'd flicked a switch and gone into legal-eagle mode.

Dev had thought ... Well, he'd thought he knew the bloke, that was all. And now he wasn't sure.

Christ. Was this what he'd meant about them not being long-term?

Fuck it. Tasha was all that mattered right now. Dev got on the Hornet and headed off to Kyle's.

Against all odds, the Fiesta made it to the airport in Newquay. Dev wouldn't have trusted her, but Kyle had promised if she broke down they'd leave her by the side of the road and get a taxi the rest of the way.

Getting on a plane to go somewhere in the same country felt well weird, like cheating or something, but Kyle seemed to take it in stride. "You do this a lot?" Dev asked.

"Hmm?" Kyle was staring out of the window at the runway as the plane started to taxi. Dev wondered what he'd been thinking about.

"Fly across country. For work and that."

"Oh, no. Trains, usually. They're better for working on."

"Yeah? Mal hates travelling by train." Christ, why had he even said that?

"Travel sickness?"

"Nah, it's . . . he's a Tube driver. Don't like riding on a train if he ain't driving it."

Kyle put a hand on his arm. "Are you okay with flying? I should have asked earlier."

"What? No. I mean, yeah, I'm fine." Shit, he had been acting weird, hadn't he? "Just worried about Tasha, you know? Sorry. I'll shut up. You probably wanna get some rest."

"I don't have to—"

"Nah, but you oughtta, right? Gonna be a while before you get another chance." And it'd stop Dev making such an arse of himself and all.

Kyle squeezed his arm and was asleep almost before the plane's wheels left the tarmac.

Dev leafed through the in-flight magazine, briefly amused himself wondering what the pale, flaky stain on page seventeen was— baby milk, if he had to guess—then spent the rest of the short flight worrying.

Mostly about Tasha. But every now and then he managed to convince himself she'd be okay, and then, like rust creeping through a chassis, doubts about him and Kyle would seep in and corrode his confidence. Dev tried to tell himself it was stupid—for fuck's sake, the bloke was flying across the country to help him out. That had to mean something, right?

But then he'd remember Kyle's words. *"That's not what this is about."*

So what the fuck *was* it about for Kyle? Just a bit of rough for a couple of weeks?

No. He couldn't think like that.

Kyle tried ringing Tasha's solicitor almost as soon as they'd got off the plane, but it went to voice mail. They managed to get on a train down to Clapham with barely a moment to spare, and he tried again with the same result.

Which was good, probably, because it meant the bloke was busy sorting Tasha out, didn't it? Whatever that involved. Just being there while they questioned her? Or telling her what to say when she made a statement? Shit. Dev ought to know this stuff, didn't he? Bloody fantastic big brother he was turning out to be. He ought to know about solicitors and stuff, not just trust legal aid to sort it all out, because it wasn't like the care system had done either of them any favours, was it? Why should the legal system be any better?

The next time Kyle tried, his mate answered, and he was off, asking all kinds of questions Dev wouldn't even have thought of. Dev sat there on the train feeling more and more useless by the minute.

And of *course* it was great that Kyle had taken charge, and everything just might turn out all right. But Christ . . . What the fucking hell had Dev been thinking, getting involved with someone like that? Kyle—*this* Kyle—wasn't the sort of bloke who ended up with a sodding motor mechanic from a shit area of London. This Kyle was the sort of bloke who, yeah, had a nice house in fucking *Surrey* with a partner as professional as he was. They probably spent their weekends playing tennis and golf and buying antiques and walking the Queen's corgis, for all Dev knew. Not vegging out in front of the telly or going down the pub with a bunch of working-class lads like Dev and his mates.

How the fuck had Dev ever managed to convince himself they had a chance together?

When he hung up, Kyle looked tired but, maybe, pleased? "She's being released."

If he hadn't been sitting down, Dev might have had his own little cataplexy episode right then. "Oh thank fuck."

A woman in a business suit sitting opposite gave him a dirty look. Dev didn't care.

"Don't get too excited," Kyle warned. "It's on police bail, which means the investigation is ongoing. She might yet get charged with an offence."

"Shit." Yep, dirty look number two, right on time.

"Don't worry. With luck, it won't happen. It seems this flatmate—boyfriend, did you say?—of hers is quite well-known to the police in relation to drugs offences. And if, in the worst-case scenario, it goes to trial, I'm confident we'll be able to get the court on our side."

"Yeah. Yeah, I guess." Dev scrubbed his face with his hands. "Don't know what I'd have done without you."

Kyle was smiling at him. "Just glad I could help. It's a bit of a novel feeling these days."

"Bollocks. What about all them meals you cooked me?"

"They were hardly cordon bleu."

"Ate 'em, didn't I? Didn't even complain."

"No? I suppose I must have dreamed that comment about poorly cooked pasta, then."

"Yeah, well, it's the narcolepsy, innit? Bad dreams go with the territory. It ain't your fault." They were both grinning like idiots, and Dev's heart clenched. They had to have a chance, right? Him and Kyle. So what if they came from different backgrounds? All that mattered was having a good time together, wasn't it?

Fuck, he hoped so.

They got a taxi from Clapham Junction down to Lavender Hill Police Station. The cabbie seemed to want to be nosy, but Kyle shut him up quick, just saying it was a business matter. And then they were there, anyway. Dev hadn't realised it was so close to the railway station.

Tasha and the solicitor were waiting for them outside the nick. She ran up and hugged Dev so tight he could hardly breathe, then backed off and gave Kyle a wary look. "This is Kyle, yeah?"

"Good to meet you." Kyle held out his hand. Dev was well proud when she shook it and didn't even laugh. "I'm sure Tom's told you this already, but we'll be doing all we can to get you out of this unfortunate situation."

Tasha beamed. "He's been brilliant, Tom has. Told them coppers where to stick it."

"In so many words?" Kyle asked. Dev was glad he was watching Kyle's face right then, because his expression was a classic.

"Hardly," the solicitor said. He was smiling pretty broad and all. He was a white bloke around Kyle's age, not so good-looking but sharp-edged, somehow. Dev wasn't sure he liked him. Maybe it was the suit, which looked well expensive and fitted him like the sort of glove they sold in Harrods.

Or maybe it wasn't. The very next thing the bloke said to Kyle was, "How's the . . ." and then he mimed sleeping, his head pillowed on folded hands, and let out a fake snore. If he hadn't just got Tasha out of jail, Dev would have had a right go at him.

"Much as it was," was all Kyle said, as Tasha gave them both baffled looks. "Tom, I can't thank you enough. This is Dev, by the way. Tasha's brother. Dev, this is Tom Saltash."

Dev and the solicitor exchanged nods. He was glad the bloke didn't hold out his hand, because Dev didn't want to shake it.

Ah, fuck it. He was being a dick. "Cheers, mate. We owe you, me and Tasha. I mean it. Don't know what we'd have done without you."

"Think nothing of it. I could hardly stand by and leave such a lovely young lady in distress, now could I?"

Dev forced himself not to make a barf face, but seriously, what the fuck was this dude on?

Kyle brought it all back to business. "What are the bail conditions?"

"Pretty lenient. Tasha just has to present herself at the police station in three weeks' time. No restrictions on place of abode." Tom smiled, like that meant something.

Maybe it did. Kyle was smiling too. "Excellent. Does she have to surrender her passport?"

"She would, if she had one. That's a routine requirement," Tom added, turning to Tasha. "No reflection on your character or their perception thereof."

Who even talked like that? "Right, well, cheers, mate. Guess we'll take it from here."

"Hang about," Tasha threw in. "Tom's gonna come out with us and celebrate, yeah?" She grabbed his arm. "You're gonna come, aren't you?"

"Ah . . . That's very kind, but I'm afraid I'll need to get back to the office." Tom gently got out of her hold. "And after that, my wife's expecting me."

Tasha pouted, but she didn't push it.

Tom said his good-byes, getting Kyle to promise they'd catch up sometime over lunch, as if the bloke had forgotten Kyle had moved to Cornwall. Course, maybe Kyle had decided to move back? Dev had thought he'd feel happy about that. Now he wasn't so sure.

"So what are we doing to celebrate?" Tasha asked, breaking into his thoughts.

Dev gave her a look. "You ain't out of the woods yet, you know. Police bail ain't the same as *case dropped*."

She folded her arms. "Fine. Bloody killjoy. S'pose I'll go home, then."

"You ain't going back to that house. Not to stay. What if they let that bastard out and all? You can pack your stuff, and you're coming to mine." She'd be a lot safer where he could keep an eye on her. And keep her away from the druggie boyfriend. "You can have Mal's room till he's back from holiday."

"Are you gonna be there? I don't wanna stay there on my own. And what about him?" She jerked her head at Kyle. He'd waved Tom off and was standing politely a few yards away, giving them some privacy.

"Course I— Ah, shit . . . wasn't thinking. We were planning to go back to Cornwall." Except what did Dev really have to go back for? That business with his mum was finished now. File closed. Game over. If Kyle didn't want him . . . Dev's gut twisted. "Hey, why don't you come down to Cornwall with me? There's another bed in my room at the B&B. It'll be great. We can have a holiday together."

"What about my job?"

"It's a shit job. You *know* it's a shit job. Ring 'em tomorrow and ask for time off, and if they don't give it, tell 'em to sod off. There's always more shit jobs. And, well, you need a break, don't you? After today and all. Change of scene. It'll do you good." He knew he was laying it on way too thick, but he couldn't seem to stop himself.

"Fair enough. They've probably sacked me already for not turning up today. You sure it's all right, though?"

"Course it's all right. Ain't like you're leaving the country, is it? You'll be back here before your three-weeks thing."

"I didn't mean the police." She lowered her voice. "I meant with your bloke."

"What, Kyle? He's got his own house down there."

"Yeah, but he ain't gonna want me tagging along all the time, is he?"

"You're family. He'll understand." At least, Dev hoped he would. If he didn't . . . Well, maybe he'd been right about them not being a long-term thing, then.

Tasha leaned close and whispered, "You sure? You said he was a wanker."

"What? No, I didn't." Had he? Shit, maybe he had, at that. Like, several million years ago. Dev's gaze snapped guiltily to Kyle. He was tapping at his phone and didn't seem to have heard, thank fuck. "Well, he ain't, okay?"

Tasha gave him a look, then shrugged. "So are we all going back to mine, now? If we're not going for a drink, I want a shower and some clothes that don't smell like prison." She shuddered.

Dev put his arm around her. "Ah, babe. Was it really bad?"

She looked at her feet. "I'm okay." Her face was hidden by the great cloud of loose, curly hair falling around it, but she didn't sound okay. Not really.

"Sure?"

"Yeah." Tasha squared her shoulders and pasted on a smile. "So, we're going back to my house to get my stuff now, yeah? Where's your bike? Or did your bloke bring a car?"

"Nah, we flew."

"What, from Cornwall? Get *you*. Daddy's got his own private jet, has he?"

"*No*. And it was quicker, wasn't it? If we'd come by car we'd probably still be sitting on the M5 in a traffic jam right now." Dev looked at his watch. Only just past five o'clock. Crazy to think he'd still been in Cornwall a couple of hours ago. He raised his voice. "Kyle, you ready to go? We're going to Tasha's to pick up her stuff, then back to mine. We'll have to get a taxi."

Kyle nodded and shoved his phone back in his pocket. "We'd better walk up towards the station. There's a rank there."

He looked tired, Dev realised. "Maybe we should get something to eat first."

Tasha groaned. "De-ev. Stop fussing. I can wait another hour or so."

Dev was about to tell her it wasn't about her, but he wasn't sure Kyle would want him spreading it around about the narcolepsy. After the way he'd let everyone just think he was an alcy . . . No. Dev wasn't gonna do that to him. Tom had mentioned it, sort of—but he hadn't actually come out and *said* it. "Uh, Kyle? What do you think?"

"Fine."

"You sure you don't—"

"I'm *fine.*"

"Right, okay." They set off along the street. Kyle flagged down a taxi before they'd got far—did they have lessons on doing that in posh schools? Dev never managed to get one anything like that quick—and Tasha gave the driver her address. Her *old* address, if Dev had anything to do with it.

Dev kept an eye on Kyle, and sure enough he started nodding off within minutes. Dev gave him a gentle nudge with his elbow, then couldn't help glancing at Tasha, who was on the fold-down seat opposite, to see if she'd noticed.

She grinned. "More sleep, less bed, that's what you need."

Kyle let out what was hopefully an amused huff but didn't fall off the seat, thank God. "If only you knew. This place we're going to—I take it you're on a month's notice there?"

"Yeah. And that's my deposit, so." She shrugged. "Feel bad about walking out on Jase and Ana, but after what Matt done to me . . ."

Dev frowned. "Think they knew he was dealing?"

"They better not of. They knew me and him was . . . what we was." She looked sad.

"Ah, babe. You really liked him?" She was too far away for a hug, so Dev leaned forward and put a hand on her knee.

"No, but . . . I slept with him, didn't I? And he was a laugh. When he wasn't halfway up his own arse. And I thought . . ."

"You're better off without him," Kyle interrupted firmly. "Anyone who could put you at risk like that isn't worth wasting regret over."

"Yeah, you got that right."

Was it Dev's imagination, or was Tasha giving Kyle a funny look?

They'd reached Tasha's house, though, so Dev shoved it to the back of his mind. Which was easy enough, 'cos now he had new worries.

He'd known Tasha's place was pretty shitty, but somehow he hadn't realised just how bad it was. Not until he had to show it to Kyle. The tiny front garden was a junkyard of rusting appliances and kebab wrappers chucked in by people on their way home from the pub. One of the downstairs windows had been broken and boarded up with chipboard. It wouldn't last five minutes against anyone who wanted to get in, but one look at the place told you no one who lived here was likely to have anything worth nicking.

Shame no one had broken in and nicked Matt's stash before the police caught up with him and Tasha.

Christ, what must Kyle think of him, letting his sister live here? Dev just hoped Kyle would realise there was no "letting" about it. Tasha did what she wanted and always had. Dev had never worked out how to do anything more than stand by and wait for the car crash.

"You wanna stay in the cab and wait for us to grab Tasha's stuff?" Dev couldn't face Kyle seeing the inside of the place as well. And he looked like he needed a rest.

"Ain't that gonna cost a fortune?" Tasha demanded before Kyle could reply.

"No, 'cos we're gonna be quick. That all right?"

Kyle nodded. "Fine." He cast a glance at the driver, but seemed okay with it, so Dev got out after Tasha and shut the door behind him.

There was no one in the house—Matt presumably still in a cell somewhere, the skank, and the other two probably at work. Or out dealing, whatever. Tasha was never coming back here again, that was for certain. "Pack as much as you can," he told her. "Make sure you bring everything that's worth anything."

Once her clothes and bedding had been swept into bin-bags, and her makeup and stuff shoved in her backpack, there wasn't a right lot left. Tasha was like him—she'd never been that into stuff. It only meant more hassle when you had to move on. They hit the kitchen to grab the few decent pans she had and her favourite mug, all stuff he'd given her, and then they were out the door and heading back to the taxi.

Dev made sure he got in first so he could nudge Kyle awake. The cabbie was busy with his phone, so either he hadn't noticed he'd had a sleeping passenger or he didn't care. "All right?" Dev asked.

Kyle blinked. "Fine. Is that everything?"

Dev looked at the collection of bags on the taxi floor. It looked like the sort of stuff people chucked in the Oxfam shop doorway 'cos they couldn't be arsed to wait until the place opened and donate it properly. Or were too embarrassed about the state of it, maybe. "Yeah. All the stuff she wants to keep."

"You gonna have room for all this at your place?" Tasha asked, climbing over bags and into the fold-down seat again.

"We'll manage."

Shit.

Kyle probably had no clue how crappy Dev's place was compared to his sunny cottage in Cornwall. And they hadn't actually talked about it, but Kyle must be expecting to stay in Dev's flat tonight, mustn't he? Unless he was planning on flying back this evening? There was a flight at just gone nine that was doable, if they could get seats on it. He'd have to let Tasha dump her stuff at the flat first, though, and give her time to pack a bag properly for going away. Which might take a while, seeing as all her stuff was now bundled up in bin bags.

Why the hell hadn't they thought of that back at her place?

If Kyle had to see the flat, Dev did *not* want him to see it in the state they'd left it in before going away, what with him and Mal a bit on the outs over Mal going to Portugal. Neither of them had felt much like tidying up after the other. Or themselves, if he was honest.

Was there any way he could stop Kyle going there? Short of just breaking up with the poor bastard and telling him to piss off?

Sod it. Even by the time they'd got to his flat, which meant Kyle had already seen what a shitty street he lived on, Dev was all out of ideas. Looked like he'd have to go with the truth. "Hey, I just remembered I left the flat in a bit of a state. I'll, uh, take the bags in and tidy up a bit, and you and Kyle can go and grab something to eat, yeah? There's plenty of places in walking distance."

"What about you?" Kyle asked, frowning.

"Not hungry," Dev lied. He gave Tasha a significant look.

She just looked baffled, but she took Kyle's arm anyway with a smile. "What kind of food we going for, then?"

CHAPTER TWENTY-SIX

Kyle supposed he should be flattered that Dev trusted him with the little sister he was so clearly protective of. But after the adrenaline of the day and an inadequate nap in the back of the cab, all he wanted to do was crash.

Still, food would help. And at least there were plenty of restaurants within walking distance from Dev's flat. He'd been dreading getting back in a taxi, certain he wouldn't be able to stay awake this time. He should go afterwards, though. He wasn't sure he could make it to the last flight back tonight, particularly while travelling alone and running the risk of sleeping past his stop on the train, but he could stay in an airport hotel and get off first thing in the morning. He hadn't really thought it through, before, but of course Dev would want to be with his sister.

He'd been so quiet during the taxi ride back from Tasha's house. Probably desperately trying to think of a polite way of getting rid of the unwanted outsider. After all, what help had Kyle actually been? Tom had done all the work.

Dev would have to come back to Porthkennack at some point to collect his motorbike and his luggage, and maybe Kyle would see him then. And perhaps they'd meet again if Tasha's case went to trial, but Tom had seemed fairly confident it wouldn't come to that.

It all felt very . . . over. And he hadn't been prepared for it. Not yet.

Dev was distancing himself already. He hadn't seemed comfortable with Kyle since they'd got to London. Since they'd met up with Tom and Tasha. Had he taken a dislike to Tom? Was it a pride thing? Did he resent having needed Kyle's help?

At least it couldn't be that he didn't want Kyle to be around his sister. Else why send them off on their own?

God, he was going round in circles.

Tasha seemed to know the area, and after he confessed his indifference as to what they ate, led him to a small, independent pizza place. It was early enough that the ready availability of a table didn't ring alarm bells as to the quality of the food, and Kyle slid into a seat by the window with relief.

The waiter handed them menus. Tasha gave hers only a cursory glance before tossing it back on the table and looking him in the eye. "You're a bit trusting, ain'tcha?"

"I'm not sure I know what you're—"

"Ain't you wondering if it's all bollocks, what I told Dev about Matt stitching me up? I mean, it's just me saying that, innit? For all you know, it coulda been me dealing all along, and I'm just putting it all on him."

Kyle blinked at her. "Is it? Bollocks?"

"No. But why would you believe me? You never even met me before today."

"Dev trusts you."

"Maybe. Or maybe he's in on it too, you think of that?"

Anger surged briefly. "Throw doubt on your own character all you like, but please don't denigrate Dev."

"That posh for diss?"

"If you like."

"What are you even doing with Dev? I mean, I know he's good-looking, but ain't you embarrassed having your mate Tom know you're with him?"

"Why would I be?" Kyle leaned forwards. "Yes, we have different backgrounds. But it doesn't matter to me. And going back to your original question: I trust Dev. And while his judgement may well be less than impartial when it comes to you, I prefer to give you the benefit of the doubt. Now, can we please order before I collapse over the table?"

She giggled, then clapped her hand to her mouth and took a moment to straighten her expression. "All right." She waved unselfconsciously at the waiter, who came straight over, not having too many other customers to occupy his time.

"I'll have the margherita pizza, ta. And a Foster's."

Not feeling adventurous, Kyle ordered the same but exchanged the beer for a salad and a jug of water.

"But it's me who's gonna collapse if anyone does," Tasha went on once the waiter had left. "Didn't Dev tell you about the diabetes?"

"He did." Kyle took a deep breath. Dev had meant well, no doubt, but in the not-wholly-unlikely event that he had an attack here, he'd prefer not to have a hysterical teenager to wake up to. "He seems to have forgotten to mention the narcolepsy, however."

"Shit! You got that? For real?"

"For real."

"So, like, if you fall asleep at work, you've got the perfect excuse? That is *so cool*."

Kyle almost laughed. "It's really not."

She gave him a look that was startling in its understanding, and far too mature for a nineteen-year-old. "Nothing ever is, is it? So is there stuff you can take for it?"

"I ... Yes, but I've been reluctant to try it." Kyle felt uncomfortable under her gaze, and hurried to explain. "It feels like giving in."

He realised even as he said it how stupid it would sound to her.

From her expression, he wasn't wrong. "Huh. If I'd said that about insulin I'd be dead now."

"Narcolepsy isn't life-threatening."

"What, so that means it ain't worth bothering about?" She shrugged. "It's your life."

Kyle stared at her, waiting for a corollary that never came.

Tasha frowned. "What?"

"Nothing. Just ... Have you got any idea how many people have said that to me, since I got ill? *It's your life.* The answer's none. Not one. Everyone's so bloody sure they know what I should be doing."

"Yeah, well, that's people for you. Fuck 'em." She grinned, and Kyle couldn't help smiling back at her.

The drinks arrived, swiftly followed by the food—Kyle supposed they'd hardly taxed the skills of the kitchen staff with their order.

Tasha tucked in to her pizza with surprising daintiness for someone who hadn't bothered to cover her mouth when the beer made her belch. Kyle wondered which was the real her, or if they both were.

"It was horrible," she said suddenly, not looking up from her plate. "In the nick, not knowing if they were gonna bring me food when I needed it. I mean, I told them I needed to eat when I needed to, and have my insulin, but what was I gonna do if they decided not to give a shit? So, you know, cheers."

"Don't mention it. I was glad to help you out."

"Just . . . It's like you're in there, and you can't do nothing, yeah? Like there's nothing *to* do, and you just sit there and worry about what's gonna happen to you." Tasha busied herself cutting up her pizza, then looked up at Kyle with a grin. "Course, if Dev had been the sort of brother what got in trouble all the time, he'd of been able to warn me about that, wouldn't he?" She cocked her head. "Surprise you? You know, him being mixed race and growing up in care and all? He's never been in trouble with the police. Not once."

She seemed to be daring him to say something, but what, Kyle wasn't sure. He shrugged awkwardly. "Well, he's one up on me, then."

"You're shitting me. You've been arrested? How come they still let you be a lawyer? What you done?"

"I was drinking with a group of friends back when I was seventeen—yes, underage—and apparently some of us were acting *too gay* for the taste of some of the other men in the pub. The fight had barely started before the police arrived and arrested everyone concerned. It was probably just as well. No one was seriously hurt and nobody was charged, in the end. But it did make for an anxious few hours in police custody." Explaining it to his parents—because of course he'd panicked and called them for help—hadn't been exactly the most fun he'd ever had, either.

"That why you went into law?"

Kyle nodded and gave her a wry smile. "I was fuelled by righteous indignation. I hadn't thrown a single punch, and there I was being fingerprinted, searched, and locked in a cell like a criminal. It's a while ago now, but I believe I was planning to end all miscarriages of justice."

"How'd that go for you?"

"How do you think?" Kyle forked up some more salad, wishing it was better dressed.

"Got me out of jail, didn't you?"

"That was all Tom."

"Yeah, but if it goes to court, it'll be you, won't it?" It seemed important to her.

Kyle couldn't bring himself to let her down. "Yes. It'll be me."

"Good." She took a swig of beer. "So what's this Porthwhatsit place like? Think I'll like it?"

"Porthkennack? You're coming?"

"You really weren't listening to me and Dev, were you? Yeah, I'm coming down. Gonna stay in the B&B with Dev."

Somehow, Kyle felt a lot less tired than he had a moment ago. "That's great. I'm sure you'll like it." Was he? Yes, he was. Who didn't like the seaside? And there were definitely nightclubs there of some sort or another.

God, any moment now he was going to ask her something like, *And what do you young people like nowadays?* And then he'd have to kill himself. It was strange, though. The five years between her and Dev's ages seemed in some ways a much larger gap than the nine between Dev and Kyle.

They were just finishing their meals when Tasha's phone rang. She answered it with an "All right, bruv?" and then listened for a short while before hanging up and turning to Kyle. "That was Dev. He says we gotta eat up and get straight back."

"Did he say why?"

She just shrugged. "You got a plane to catch?"

"I . . . have no idea. I mean, there is one, but I thought . . ." Kyle shook his head. "Never mind. I'll get the bill and we can go."

CHAPTER
TWENTY-SEVEN

After he'd waved Kyle and Tasha off for their meal, Dev had walked in his front door and stopped dead on the doormat.

Mal was sitting on the sofa with a mug of tea in one hand and the TV remote in the other.

They stared at each other. "What are you doing here?" Mal asked literally moments before Dev could ask him the exact same thing.

"Tasha had a bit of bother. What are *you* doing here?"

"Came home, didn't I? I was gonna go down to Cornwall to join you tomorrow. Wanted to surprise you."

"You did that all right," Dev said feelingly. "But . . . why? Why didn't you stay in Portugal with the lads?"

Mal looked sheepish as he put his mug down on the floor. "I felt bad, didn't I, mate? Blowing you off like that. And then I got your text, so."

Dev was touched. And guilt-stricken, seeing as he couldn't even remember sending a text, let alone what he'd said in it. "You didn't have to cut your holiday short though. What about all that sun, sea, and sex?"

"Nah, it weren't all that great there anyhow. Nav's girlfriend caught him snogging some Scottish bird on the beach and went off with one of the local lads to piss him off, so they ain't been speaking to each other 'cept for the screaming matches over the pool. And on the beach. And in the bar. And you know Josh? Turns out he can't pull to save his life, so he's just been getting shit-faced all the time. I was up till five one night with him crying on me, then the next morning he accuses me of trying to turn him gay, like I'd wanna get off with a snot-nosed miserable git like that. And Pete ain't speaking to anyone 'cos he got the hump when Nav and Josh locked him out the first night for a laugh. I just thought, two weeks of this shite and I'll end up going postal on the whole bloody lot of 'em. So I got 'em to change me flight and came here." He stood up and beamed at Dev. "So, did you really miss me or were you pissed when you texted?"

Dev had to laugh. "You tosser. Ah, come here, mate. It's good to see you." He folded Mal into a hug and even kissed the top of his head. Christ, he was going soft in his old age.

But, yeah, it was good to see Mal again. Dev knew where he stood with Mal.

"So go on, have you met your mum yet?"

"She ain't my mum." Dev's good mood evaporated like spilled petrol, and he sat down heavily on the sofa. "Don't want nothing to do with me, and the feeling's fucking mutual."

"Ah, mate, no. Seriously?"

"Yeah." Dev's voice didn't crack. He was proud of that.

"Shit, mate. I'm so fucking sorry. I should've been there for you. Christ, I'm a fucking twat. I thought it'd be all, you know, like on the telly and stuff, and I'd be a spare part hanging around getting in the way. She really don't want to know you?"

"Yeah. Can we leave it now?" *Please?* Dev added it in his head, but Christ knew, he'd say it out loud if he had to.

Mal sat down next to him and hugged him again. "You don't need her. Got me now, ain't you?" He paused. "Wanna shag?"

God, Dev had missed him. "Cheers, mate, but no."

"Sure? It'll make you feel better."

"Seriously. No." Dev hesitated, but why the hell not? "Sort of met someone, didn't I?"

"What, local, is he? Is he all 'Oo-arr, moi loverrrr, oi'll 'ave 'ee in't 'aystack wiv moi mangel-wurrrzel'?"

Dev found himself laughing again. "*What* accent was that supposed to be? Mate, leave off the impressions. And never enter *Britain's Got Talent*. Trust me, it wouldn't end well. No, he ain't, all right? He's from Surrey."

"Yeah? Posh twat, is he?"

Dev grimaced. "Yeah, bit. Used to be a barrister." Course, as of today there hadn't seemed to be so much *used to* about it, had there?

"Used to be? What, is he retired or something? Check him out of the local old folks' home, did you?"

"Oi, he's young. In his thirties. He had to give it up. Or, well, take a break."

"Took a bung, did he?"

"Jesus, bruv, where did you get your shining faith in human nature? No. He got ill. Narcolepsy." Should he have kept it a secret? But at least Kyle wasn't here to be embarrassed to his face.

"Narco what now? That some drugs thing?"

"No. Narcolepsy. He keeps falling asleep. And oi, no jokes. It ain't funny. And no saying nothing to him about it."

"I ain't said a word, mate." Mal was wide-eyed and serious. Then he grinned. "Be a bit awkward if he fell asleep mid-shag, yeah?"

Dev groaned.

"What, he never? Really?"

Great. Now he was going to have to spend half the night explaining what narcolepsy was actually like to his mate and trying not to deck him if—no, *when*—he laughed.

Funny, though. Dev couldn't really bring himself to mind too much. Then again, there was other stuff that needed doing. "Tell you about it all later. We got stuff to do . . . Ah, shit. Tasha was gonna have your bed tonight."

"Oh yeah? So what's this bother she's in? She's okay, right? You sorted it?"

"Kind of. Maybe." Dev gave Mal a quick rundown of it all.

Mal's eyes got wider and wider. "And he's here, your bloke? He came all the way over from Cornwall to help out?"

Dev couldn't help smiling, but there was an uneasy feeling in his chest. "Yeah. But it's what he does, innit? So we gotta get this place sorted before they get back from dinner. I ain't having him thinking I live in a bloody pigsty."

"He sprung for flights, didn't he? Get him to shell out for a posh hotel."

"What? No fucking way. This ain't *Pretty Woman*."

"Yeah, you sure as shit ain't Julia Roberts, bruv." Mal grinned. "She's lovely, she is. What I couldn't do with a mouth like that."

"You realise she's the same age as your mum, right?"

"Nah, she'll always be twenty-three to me. So what's the plan after tonight, anyhow?"

"Taking Tasha down to Cornwall— Ah, shit."

"Lemme guess, she was gonna have my bed there and all? You know, a bloke could start thinking you were wishing he'd stayed in Portugal."

"No, course not, mate." Dev hugged him to be on the safe side. "I just got to think it all out again, that's all."

"Nah, you don't wanna strain nothing. I got it all sorted. Your old mate Mal to the rescue." He gave Dev that smug look that was all Mal. "You and posh bloke go back on the plane tonight, or if there ain't no flights you get a hotel at the airport and have a shagfest, you lucky bastard, and Tasha stays here. In *your* bed. Then me and her drive down and join you tomoz. It's perfect, innit? Everyone's happy, and no need to get the industrial hoovers out."

Dev ignored the bit about the shagfest. Mostly because he wasn't sure that was ever going to happen, and the thought left a pain in his chest he didn't want to think about. "Oi, hang on a mo, where's Tasha gonna sleep when you get there? We've only got a two-bed room at the B&B. This you volunteering to take the floor?" And Christ knew what Mrs. Quick would say about that anyhow.

"Nah, you're gonna be off shagging the rich bloke, ain'tcha? So me and Tasha'll have the B&B to ourselves."

"I can't just invite myself to stay at his house."

"Maybe he'll offer? You know, if you tell him I've turned up to bollocks up your cunning plans? Tell you what—worst comes to worst, I'll sleep in the car till I can get a room somewhere. Done it before, ain't I?"

"You're a mate, Mal."

"I know I am. And seeing as it's only Tasha who's gonna be staying here, and she don't give a shit, we don't have to tidy up. Like I said, mate. Perfect."

Yeah. Yeah, it was. Because no amount of tidying up was going to shift the patches of damp on the ceiling, or change the fact that it wasn't so much a flat as a shoebox with two rooms just big enough to bung a bed in, or stop the screaming rows from the couple next door coming right through the thin walls. Or the noisy makeup sex that always happened afterwards, come to that.

"Why do we live here?" Dev asked.

Mal frowned. "Where else we gonna live? Chelsea?"

"I don't mean Balham." Although maybe he did, a bit. "I mean . . . this flat. I mean, it's shit, innit?"

"So? It was all we could afford, wasn't it?"

"Yeah, but that was years ago, before you got your job driving on the Tube. You're earning good money now, and I'm doing okay, so . . . Why do we still live here?"

"Well, it's home, innit?" Mal looked around. "See that sofa? Perfectly shaped to fit our arses through years of slobbing about on it. That mould round the window, that's practically a pet, that is. And there's that patch on the carpet where Hermione got out of her cage and had her babies. It's, like, our lives. In furniture and stuff."

Dev had to laugh. "Yeah, but it's shit stuff. We could afford something better, you know we could. So why ain't we ever moved?"

Mal stared at him like he'd grown an extra head, and it didn't look any brighter than his normal one. "Seriously? It's obvious, innit? We're lazy sods."

God, Dev had missed him. The tightness in his chest eased, just a bit. Yeah, spending some time with Tasha, with Mal nearby, that was what he needed.

Maybe Kyle would offer Dev house room, at that. But with the way he'd been before they heard about Tasha, and shit, the way meeting Tom fucking Saltash, flying solicitor, had rubbed in how bloody little they really had in common, especially looking at where they came from . . .

Dev wasn't going to be laying any bets on this thing between them working out.

By the time Kyle and Tasha got back from dinner, Dev had it all sorted. He'd booked him and Kyle onto the last flight back to Newquay, called Tasha so they wouldn't hang about at the restaurant, and even looked into getting a cab to take them direct to the airport.

That idea got thrown out sharpish when he realised it'd take twice as long as the train. He'd also finally managed to grab something to eat, thanks to Mal nipping down the road to get some fresh bread and milk in.

Then he stood outside the flat and leaned on the wall trying to relax until they turned up. "Change of plan," he greeted them, trying to ignore the way Kyle was looking at him warily. "Mal's home, so he's gonna explain it to you," he told Tasha, then turned back to Kyle. "Me and you got a plane to catch."

"Mal!" Tasha squealed in the general direction of the flat, then flung her arms around Dev. "I'm gonna see you soon, right?"

"Tomorrow," he promised. "Gotta run now, though."

There was only one thing Dev hadn't thought of, which was that when they got out of Newquay airport, having made the last flight by the skin of their teeth, it was getting on for eleven o'clock and Kyle looked anything but in a fit state to drive them back to Porthkennack. He'd napped a couple of times, on the train and the plane, but it didn't seem to have done him a right lot of good.

Dev wondered how to tactfully bring up the subject, but it was Kyle who mentioned it first. "Do you mind driving back? I'm not sure I'm safe to do it."

"No problem," Dev said, relieved. He was even more relieved when the ancient Fiesta started first try and made the half-hour drive with hardly a grumble. No wonder Kyle was so keen on the old girl. Dev was starting to feel fond of her himself.

Not that he'd better get too attached. It wasn't like this was going to be a long-term thing, was it? Dev's heart ached, remembering Kyle's words.

He had to wake Kyle up again when they got back to his cottage. Kyle didn't exactly invite Dev in—he didn't say much at all, in fact—and Dev felt a bit awkward about assuming he'd be welcome. Especially seeing as he'd practically forced the bloke onto a plane without stopping to think if it was what Kyle really wanted.

Dev had told him about Mal and Tasha driving down tomorrow, but hadn't said anything about where everyone was supposed to sleep, and Kyle hadn't asked.

So Dev just said good night and headed back to the B&B, hoping Mrs. Quick wouldn't have locked up and gone to bed already, seeing as she wasn't expecting him back tonight.

That'd be the icing on the fucking cake, that would.

CHAPTER TWENTY-EIGHT

Kyle woke up—in his bed, for a change—to the sound of his phone ringing, and fumbled for it blindly on the bedside table. It was Mum, he realised when he finally managed to turn the alarm off and blink the screen into focus. And it was only eight o'clock in the morning. Which meant she'd probably been waiting hours for it to be a "suitable" hour to call. God, what had happened?

"Mum?" he managed, struggling to wake up enough to take in whatever she was about to tell him.

"Why didn't you *tell* me?" She sounded on the verge of tears.

"Tell you what?"

"About your condition. When I said . . . I had no *idea.*"

Oh God. "You've been looking up narcolepsy?"

"Of course I have. Why didn't you tell me how bad it was? How many attacks do you have a day?"

"I . . . Mum, it's—"

"And I spoke to Jeffrey again, because I was cross with him for making me worry, and he said you'd given up *work* and moved *house* . . . Why didn't you *say* anything?"

"Apparently I didn't need to," Kyle snapped, feeling pretty furious with Jeffrey himself right now.

"Kyle!"

"Sorry, Mum. Look, I've literally just woken up. This isn't a good time to talk."

"Fine. Well, we'll talk when I get there. Assuming you're actually going to tell me where you're living now?"

"I— What?" *Get there?* "Mum, no. You don't need to come halfway around the world. I'm fine. I'm just . . . taking a break."

He thought as quickly as his sluggish brain would let him. "In fact I was in London yesterday on a legal matter."

"But Jeffrey—"

"Jeffrey hasn't seen me in months, Mum. He hasn't got a clue how I am right now or what I'm doing. And that was *his* choice." His confidence surged. "And I've met someone else. His name's Dev. He's a motor mechanic," he added, because his great-grandfather had been in the motor trade and Mum still had a soft spot for that kind of thing.

Mum was silent for a moment. "And he knows about your illness? You haven't kept it a secret from him?" There was a definite emphasis on the last word in that sentence. Maybe it was something that developed in pregnancy: this unerring instinct to tug on the guilt strings.

"Believe me, Mum, he knows." After all the times Kyle had collapsed in front of, on top of, or underneath him . . .

And he'd taken it all in his stride. Kyle hadn't given him enough credit.

That was going to change, starting today.

"Are you sure you're all right? You don't need me?"

"No. I'm fine, really." He was, Kyle realised. Yesterday had proved it. He'd been an idiot, berating himself for not having done anything to help in London. The point was, if he *had* been needed, he could have stepped in.

And Dev pulling away . . . Well, maybe that was Kyle's fault. After what he'd said, just before Tasha's call, no wonder Dev was wary.

What Kyle needed to do was convince Dev to give him another chance.

The first thing he did, after getting dressed and having breakfast—and, all right, having a sleep attack, but that was neither here nor there—was arrange an appointment with his specialist. It'd mean another trip up to London, but, well, he'd proved he could handle that, hadn't he? And it was way past time he explored the treatments available to him. Tasha had been right. Life was too short not to live it to the fullest. If the side effects of the drugs were intolerable, well, he'd just stop taking them and try something different. No more living in fear and dressing it up as a virtue, priding himself on refusing to *give in* to his condition. God, what he'd been doing so far, *that* was the real giving in.

Accepting help would be the first step towards . . . Not beating it, maybe.

But refusing to let it beat him.

With that in mind, he looked back over the emails Sujata had sent him over the weeks—months—since he'd given up work. Or taken a sabbatical, as she liked to put it.

They were full of advice, which was why he'd mostly ignored them, before. A lot of it was, as he'd suspected, useless. He hit Delete with a particularly vicious stab when he read the one about cognitive behavioural therapy, for instance. But the advice that related solely to the profession and how to make a working day less strenuous, yes, some of that was worth rereading.

She'd copied him in on all sorts of articles she'd found online about people with disabilities in the legal profession. One of them in particular struck him: a wheelchair user talked about going into commercial law because it would mean far less time in court—where steps were numerous and ramps practically nonexistent—and far more drafting legal documents. He grabbed a pen and notebook and started to make notes.

God, if only he'd read this months ago . . . No. Months ago, he'd probably have just deleted it, feeling if he had to give up criminal law, then he might as well give up, full stop. Now, the prospect of less travel, less advocacy, and far more flexible hours seemed a lot more appealing. Perhaps he could set up on his own, here in Porthkennack? Buy the cottage, sell the house in Surrey, get Dev to move in with him . . .

Kyle blinked awake and winced when he saw the gobbledegook he'd sleep-scribbled into his notebook. As wake-up calls went, it was nothing if not ironic.

He stood up, and walked into the kitchen to put the kettle on. Going back to Almshouse Chambers was the only sensible option, at least in the short term. Even if he abandoned the idea of setting up on his own and tried instead to get a tenancy locally, all while reestablishing himself in a new specialisation and unable to work full-time . . . Well, it just wasn't going to happen. He'd need to start slowly, in a supportive environment, where he wouldn't feel the need to prove himself.

Kyle turned to stare out of the window at the sea. God, he'd miss living here. He felt it in his chest, an almost physical tug. Then again, wasn't at least part of that the knowledge that if he went back to Surrey he'd have to deal with Jeffrey? Which was way overdue. For heaven's sake, he was still paying half the mortgage on their house, which was absurd when he wasn't earning.

It wasn't simply Porthkennack itself that he'd grown to love. It was the retreat it had become for him. But it was time to get back into the real world.

If nothing else, he'd be a lot closer to London. And Dev, because asking him to move in with Kyle after only a week's acquaintance was probably not the most sensible plan, despite what Dev had hinted . . . God, was it only yesterday? Back when Kyle had been too far up his own arse to listen properly.

Would Dev still want him there, though? After the way he'd railroaded Kyle away from his flat—and his flatmate—Kyle was no longer sure about that.

But he had to try.

The annoying thing about doubts was that once they started to creep into his head, they had a tendency to invite all their friends over for a self-pity party. What if going back to work didn't end up being feasible? Kyle knew only too well that a large part of this new determination to get his life back was down to wanting to prove to Dev—and himself—that he was worth loving. If he couldn't work, if he was forced to live on his savings until they dwindled away, was he still worth Dev's time, let alone his love?

Kyle didn't know. But one thing he was certain of: he couldn't let Dev go without trying to sort things out between them.

Right now, though . . . Maybe Dev needed some space and some time with his sister and flatmate when they arrived in Cornwall. Kyle could give him that. In the meantime, he took a cup of coffee back to his laptop, and set about identifying courses he could take to bring him up to speed on commercial law.

Then he shook his head at himself for procrastinating *again*. No. He was going to do this properly, which meant committing himself.

He called Sujata. "I want to come back to work."

"Good morning to you too. And yes, finally!"

"But I'm not sure how soon."

"You raise my hopes, only to dash them again. Kyle, you are a terrible man."

"Sorry. But I need to do some reading first, maybe take some courses."

"You're changing your specialisation?"

"Yes. To commercial law. It'll be easier to manage—more flexible hours, less travelling."

"But Kyle, you love criminal law. Are you sure you want to give it up?"

Kyle reminded himself firmly that she meant well. "Yes. It's simply not viable anymore."

"Well, I suppose commercial is where the money is. I'll tell everyone the good news. And it *is* good news. We've all missed you, you know."

"Sujata, I don't deserve you."

"Nobody does, Kyle. Now, get off the phone. We all have work to do."

CHAPTER
TWENTY-NINE

Seeing as he'd told Mrs. Quick he was going to be away, Dev wasn't surprised to get a double take when he went down to breakfast the next morning, especially as he made it only just before the end of serving time. Luckily for him, he also got fed—he'd been half afraid she'd tell him she hadn't got enough food in. Course, with the hens out the back she'd never be short of eggs, thank God.

Then he had to tell her about Tasha coming down. Luckily she was fine about it, although that might have been because Dev didn't mention the whole getting-arrested-in-a-drugs-raid thing. He just said his little sister had had some trouble with the people she was sharing a house with, and left it at that.

He didn't mention Mal. Mostly because he hadn't quite worked out what to do about all that. The one thing he wasn't going to do, though, was ask Kyle if he could stay. That wouldn't be fair on the bloke. Kyle had already proved he'd go way above and beyond to help out. And maybe some of that had just been him wanting to get back to doing what he was good at, but still.

Dev didn't want to stay with him if helping out was all it was.

Now his head wasn't busy being worried sick about Tasha, all Dev could think about was him and Kyle. Christ, what future could he have with the bloke when he couldn't even bear to let him see the place where he lived? He'd even started thinking about finding a new place, a better place, just so's Kyle wouldn't be so horrified if he saw it, and that was well fucked up, wasn't it?

Should he go and see Kyle this morning? He hadn't even thanked the bloke properly for what he'd done for Tasha. They'd both been too knackered to talk much by the time they'd got back to Porthkennack.

Dev checked the time on his phone. It wasn't exactly early—but that meant sod all as far as Kyle maybe being asleep was concerned. Perhaps he should let the poor bastard get some more rest before he went round and bothered him.

And yeah, like that was the only reason he didn't want to go there. Dev hugged himself. Thanking Kyle for helping them out—yeah, he could do that, no problem. Trouble was, once he'd done that, they were going to have to talk about what Kyle had said. About them not being a long-term thing.

It fucking hurt just thinking about it. What if he couldn't talk Kyle out of it? Persuade him what they had was worth more than just a fling? That'd be it, then. The end. 'Cos no way could he carry on in a relationship with a sell-by date. Not with Kyle. That'd be like handing the bloke a fucking great knife and then pasting a sign on his chest that said, *Insert here.*

Call him a coward—Christ knew he was calling himself one—but Dev just wasn't ready to go there. Not yet. Maybe when he had his best mate and his sister with him. Maybe then he could cope with it. But not right now.

It didn't help that he had hours to wait until Mal and Tasha got here, and sod all to do but worry. Then again . . . He texted Ceri: *U working today?*

She rang him back almost immediately. "No. Got a day off."

"Wanna meet up?"

"Okay. Sea Bell? We'll have to wait till it opens at eleven, mind."

"Nah. Think your Uncle Jago's gonna string me up by me balls if he sees me again."

She laughed. It was a weird, short sound like it'd been startled out of her. Made him think of Kyle, laughing and then crumpling up at the knees . . . "Where then?" she asked, bringing him back to the present and the weirdness that was a happy Ceri.

"Beach? I'll bring a blanket." Dev suddenly realised how that might have sounded. "Uh, to sit on, right? I ain't planning to, like, seduce you or nothing."

"You could give it a go. I like a good laugh." Her tone turned businesslike. "Not the one by the prom. By the lifeboat station in half an hour."

"Right. See ya."

"Wouldn't wanna be ya."

Dev smiled as he hung up. He could get used to Ceri being in a good mood. Right. Better get a shift on, then he could swing by the supermarket and get some drinks and stuff. He grabbed the thick, fleecy bedspread off his bed—Ceri was gonna piss herself laughing at him for turning up with something so bloody pink—and bundled it up in his backpack. Then he headed out.

The lifeboat station in Mother Ivey's Bay was basically just a big, funny-shaped hut on tall stilts, with a ramp down to the sea for the boats to go down. It had its own little bay, cut off from the rest of the beach by a curving outcrop of cliff. Ceri was waiting for him when he got there, sitting on the sand.

There was nobody else around at all.

"Quiet round here, innit?"

Ceri shrugged. She was wearing denim cutoffs, and her skinny white legs gleamed in the sun. "Most people go over the other side. Round by the surf schools. Closer to town. Or if they're over this side, they stay on the main beach 'cos this one disappears at high tide."

"That why you like it here?"

"What do you think?"

Dev grinned. "Yeah, I like it here too." He couldn't help glancing up at the cliff, though. Somewhere up there was Kyle's cottage. Was he home, right now? Longing twisted inside him . . . but it was stupid.

"You broke up with your bloke, then?"

She was too sharp for her own good. Well, Dev's good, anyhow. "Nah—well, I dunno. I mean . . . We had this row, right? And then, *then* he goes and helps me out, like, big time. Flies up to London with me and everything. I mean, Christ, if he hadn't stepped in . . . And now I ain't got a clue *what's* going on."

"Come over here."

For a moment he thought she was offering him a hug, which just went to prove he *really* hadn't got his head on straight. Instead, she led him underneath the lifeboat station and out the other side, to the tiny scrap of beach beyond.

Dev slung his backpack on the sand and got out the bedspread and the bottle of Coke he'd picked up on the way, plus some packets of crisps. Ceri sniggered briefly at the bedspread before sitting down, her knees up in front of her so she could give them a hug.

"You ever seen 'em launch from here?" Dev asked, nodding at the lifeboat station. He unscrewed the bottle top and took a swig, wishing he'd left it a mo because most of what he got was bubbles.

"Yeah. Few times." She shrugged her skinny shoulders. "It's just a boat making a big splash." She took the bottle Dev held out to her, wiped the top with her palm and took a drink. "Saw them go out in a storm, once. That was scary. Uncle Jago was on it that time. My grandad took me down there to see them off."

"Yeah?" Dev could just imagine Jago on a lifeboat, ploughing through the waves, stony-faced, not knowing if he'd save lives or end up wading through wreckage and dead bodies. Huh. Maybe that was why he was such a miserable git.

"So what was this row all about?"

Ah shit. "Him telling me I ain't good enough for him." Dev let out a sad little laugh. "Think he's right."

"That's shite."

"Nah, 's true, innit? I mean, seriously, like I'm ever gonna have Kyle round to stay in my flat in Balham?"

"Never been to Balham. What's it like?"

"Well, it ain't like round here, that's for sure. You seen *EastEnders*, right? Lot of fucked-up families with no money, no education, and shit lives?"

"Yeah."

"It's a bit like that. Only less white. So yeah, we was in London yesterday, me and him. Just for the day. Got the plane from Newquay. And there's me and him outside my flat, and I bottled it. Couldn't let him come in and see the place."

Ceri took another drink, then handed the Coke back to Dev. "So? If he thinks he's too good for you, you should tell him to piss off."

Dev weighed the bottle in his hand before answering. "It's just . . . he never made me feel like that, you know? *Never*. So it came out of nowhere."

"Blokes'll say any old shite to get you into bed." She burped and didn't try to hide it, just like Tasha. "So what did he say?"

Squinting out to sea, almost blinded by the sunlight glinting off the waves, Dev frowned. "Uh . . ." Actually, now he came to think about it, all he could clearly remember was Kyle saying he *didn't* care about Dev having a crap job compared to him. "He said it wasn't a long-term thing, him and me. Like it should have been obvious. I mean, shit . . . I even said I'd move to be with him."

"And he still didn't want to know? Bastard. So you broke up then?"

"Nah . . . I had this phone call. From Tasha—you know, my sister? Foster sister." Dev told her the whole story, how Kyle had suddenly gone into legal superhero mode and basically saved the day.

"But it's like, I get it now," he finished with. "What he was on about. Him and me not being, well, long-term. I mean, I'd never seen him like that, had I? All professional and stuff."

Ceri had kicked off her deck shoes and was scrunching her bare toes into the sand. "Yeah, but he's never seen you doing your job either, has he?"

Dev frowned. "Well . . . a bit, maybe. I had a look over his car for him." He laughed softly at the memory.

"What?"

"That was the first time we shagged, wasn't it?"

"Had you over the bonnet, did he?"

"Nah, we was well civilised. Used a bed and everything."

"Boring."

"Oi, he's got a very small garage, all right?"

"First time I've heard it called *that*." She stared out to sea. "So what, you're worried it was just the thought of you in your greasy overalls with your tools out that got him in the mood? You think you're just his bit of rough?"

"What else? Ah, shit. I shoulda known he was way out of my league."

"No, he ain't. Having a posh accent and a law degree don't make him better than you. And he's a stupid git if he doesn't see that."

Dev wasn't going to carry on arguing with her. It wasn't like it'd change anything. And just thinking about it was doing his head in.

"Hey, you were in a good mood when I rang, weren't you? What's that all about?"

"Jesus, can't I be happy sometimes?"

"Not without spreading it about, babe." Dev made it sound extra cheesy.

"You can fuck off with the *babe*." She shoved a bony elbow in his side, but not hard enough to really hurt. Much. "I got some good news, didn't I?"

"Yeah?"

"Got a place on a catering course down in Newquay."

"Yeah? Props, babe." Delighted for her, Dev held up his hand for a high five.

"Fuck off." She high-fived him back, though. "Wasn't sure I'd get in, 'cos I applied late. You know. 'Cos of stuff. But they gave me a place for September. Mum's letting me have her car."

This, *this* was what really pissed Dev off about the care system. The way they seemed to think that once you got to eighteen you didn't need a mum and dad anymore, like the world wasn't full of parents helping their adult kids out in all kinds of ways. Total *bollocks*. But he wasn't going to say anything to make Ceri feel bad. "That's great. Seriously."

"Yeah. Mum and Dad are taking me out for a meal tonight. To celebrate."

"You're lucky, you are," Dev said without thinking.

Ceri slung a thin arm through his. "Yeah. I know."

The air was fresh and heavy with salt, with none of that sickly-sweet suntan-lotion-and-ice-cream smell he'd noticed on the prom. There was the constant whispering wash of waves against rocks. Sort of like traffic noise back home, it was so much part of the background he never noticed it now unless he actually thought about it. Sitting here on the sand, with only a few old cottages visible up on the cliff, it felt like it could have been any age. Any time. If a band of wreckers had come sneaking down the beach in *Poldark* costumes Dev wouldn't have been *that* surprised.

Of course, they'd probably be pretty baffled by the lifeboat station.

It struck him all at once that he'd never been to a place like this before—and he didn't want to leave. "If you could live anywhere in the world, where would it be?" he asked softly, and took a long swig of Coke.

"Honest answer? Or bullshite?"

"Honest."

Ceri shrugged. "Here, then. Or Wales, maybe. Bristol if it had to be a city."

"Where you've got family." Dev's chest felt tight.

"Not had much luck with friends, have I?"

"Oi, sitting right here, ta very much."

"Don't mean you." She nudged him again. "You gonna pass that bottle over?"

He passed it, and she had a good swig. Dev hesitated, then decided, *Sod it*. It'd been bothering him ever since he'd thought about it. "That one what . . . You know. Hurt you. Was he a Roscarrock?" Dev wasn't sure what he was gonna do if he found out he was related to that bastard.

"What? No. Why?" Ceri looked at him like he'd gone mad.

Dev felt a bit stupid. And a lot relieved. "Well, 'cos of what you said about them being bastards."

"Oh. No. They shafted us over Grandad's house when he died. They were his landlords."

"Oh. Right." Dev stared out to sea for a moment. It hadn't been the only thing bothering him, and seeing as how they were on the subject already . . . "That one, then. Who did it. He still here?"

Ceri shook her head vigorously. "Family moved away. Wanted a fresh start." She gave a bitter laugh. "Why? Planning to cut his balls off for me?"

"That sort ain't got no balls to start with. Nah. Just glad to know you don't have to walk around worrying you're gonna bump into him."

"Funny, isn't it?" she said, stretching.

"What?"

"I was just thinking, if things had been different, if you'd grown up here, we'd never have been friends, would we? You being five years older. Not like you'd have been asking me out, is it?"

"Could still have been friends."

"No. You'd always see me as that gawky kid with the squint and the braces."

"Yeah? Funny that. That's exactly how I see you now."

"Wanker." She scrambled to her feet.

Dev got up too. "Takes one to know one. So we off, then?"

"No. Just want to dip my toes in the water."

That sounded like a plan, so Dev pulled off his trainers and socks, then did his best to roll up his jeans. They were a bit too tight to get very far.

Ah, sod it. If Ceri could get her legs out, so could he. Dev undid his jeans and pushed them off, wished briefly he hadn't worn the naff stripy underwear today, and joined her in the sea.

The cold water on his feet and shins made him shiver, despite the rest of him still baking in the sun. Ceri smirked at him. "Nice kecks."

"Shut up. Didn't think to bring me trunks, did I?"

"Yeah, 'cos no one who goes to a beach ever ends up in the water."

Dev splashed her for that. She shrieked and splashed him right back, and it turned into an epic water fight that left them both drenched. Laughing like mad, they ran back to the beach and sprawled on the bedspread to let the sun dry them off.

It was good. It was just what Dev had needed. Something to take him out of himself and stop him obsessing over Kyle.

Bit of a shame, then, that after they'd eaten the crisps and sandwiches Dev had got at the shop, Ceri brought up the subject again. "So if you're breaking up with your bloke, does that mean you won't be hanging around here no more?"

Dev's gut, full of bacon, lettuce, and tomato sarnies, twisted. "I never said we was breaking up."

"So you're sticking around, then?"

"For another couple of weeks. But hey, you know we're gonna keep in touch, right? Me and you? We can text and stuff. And you gotta come up to London. I'll show you the sights, yeah?"

"What, of Balham?"

"Oi, don't knock it. Gateway to the South, innit? And you'll want to come, anyway, 'cos of Mal and Tasha. They're coming down tonight. You'll like Tasha. She's well cool. And Mal too. He's a laugh."

Ceri didn't say anything. Well, yeah, when Dev thought about it, he'd been there, done that too. Had friends swear blind Dev would fall arse over tit in love with whatever bloke they were banging on about—and then have him turn out to be just some boring tosser. "You'll love 'em," he said. "Just you wait."

She didn't say anything. She just kept staring straight ahead at the water.

Dev squeezed her arm. "I ain't gonna stop hanging round with you just 'cos me family's here. Promise."

"Two weeks."

He knew what she meant. "Yeah, but it ain't long till September. You'll meet new people. Better ones than those tossers round here, who won't be here anyway 'cos they'll have buggered off back to uni and good fucking riddance."

"What if they're tossers in Newquay?"

"Nah. Can't be. It's statistics, innit? There's only so many tossers you can meet in one lifetime, and you've had all yours already." He took a deep breath. "And anyway, you never know. Even if it don't work out with me and Kyle, I can still come back here to visit, can't I? It's dead quick on the plane, and it ain't even that expensive."

Ceri ducked her head. It could have been a nod, but Dev wouldn't have staked his life on it.

When they were more or less dry, Dev walked her home. He hadn't exactly planned to—she'd managed fine all the other times—but somehow he never got around to saying good-bye and heading off.

After a fair few winding country lanes that all looked the same, Ceri stopped outside a small, modern house. There was a potted shrub in the porch, and the sun gleamed off the outsize Christmas bauble stuck on a stick shoved into the pot. "This is mine."

Dev gave her a hug. She felt like a bundle of warm sticks in his arms, but she didn't push him away, which was something. "You working tomorrow?"

She nodded.

"I'll bring Mal and Tasha by the café, then. Not sure what time. Depends when I can drag 'em out of bed."

"Bye, then."

"Yeah. You have a good time tonight. Say hi to your dad from me."

She went in.

Walking back down the lane, Dev realised he didn't have a clue where he was and how to get back into town.

Time to send up a quick prayer to the gods of GPS that his signal would hold up long enough to get him home. Again.

When he got back to the B&B and there was still no sign of Mal and Tasha, Dev started to . . . well, not worry, exactly, but definitely start wondering where the hell they'd got to. He gave Mal a quick call, and waited impatiently until the phone was picked up. "Where are you, you slag?"

Tasha giggled down the line at him. "That's fucking charming, that is."

"Sorry. Forgot Mal was driving. So where are you?"

"Yeah, I had to get his phone out of his jeans pocket. It was well gross. I think I touched a bollock and everything." Dev could just hear Mal's laughter in the background. "Uh . . . we're somewhere near Taunton? The M5's been a real mare. Thought we were gonna be camping out in a traffic jam all night."

Great. "You'll be another couple of hours, then, at least. Call me if there's any more hold ups, yeah?"

"Yeah. So is it all sorted with your bloke, then? You're staying at his?"

Shit. "We'll talk about it when you get here, all right?"

It was still light when Mal and Tasha finally rolled up outside Mrs. Quick's, but it wouldn't be for long. Everyone was starving, so Dev took them out for fish and chips.

"We taking these back to the B&B?" Tasha asked, hugging the bag of food like some weird, limbless teddy bear.

"Nah, thought we'd have them down on the prom. Get some sea air in your lungs. Gotta watch out for the seagulls, though," Dev warned, as he handed over a twenty-pound note. "Give 'em half a chance and they'll have your haddock before you can blink."

"They're a menace, those birds," the woman behind the counter agreed, counting out his change. "Nothing but airborne rats."

Mal looked outraged and opened his mouth, probably to give the poor woman a lecture on how rat-ist that was or something, so Dev grabbed his arm and hustled him outside sharpish.

Tasha followed, cackling. "Your *face*, Mal!"

They wandered down to the seafront, which was fairly quiet this late in the day, and sat on a bench to eat their fish and chips. All the families had packed up and taken the kids back to their holiday homes for bed, and the beach was mostly empty except for a few dog walkers wandering across the sand and chucking balls for excited pets. The tide was about halfway up, Dev reckoned, and from the strip of smooth, damp sand by the water's edge, must be on its way out.

Even the seagulls seemed to be winding down for the evening, their shrieking somehow lazier. The sun was setting far over the sea, streaking the sky with pink and orange that scattered little sparkles of colour off the waves like a kaleidoscope Dev had had when he was a kid.

"Fuck me, that's pretty," Tasha said for all of them.

Did they get skies like that back in Balham? Dev couldn't remember seeing any. In the city there were always buildings in the way.

"Hey, Dev! Over here!"

Dev turned to see Chantal waving wildly at him from across the street. She was with Susie, both of them dressed up to the nines for a night of clubbing. He groaned under his breath.

Mal gave the girls a good long look as they hovered at the edge of the road, obviously trying to cross. "You been experimenting, mate? Could have done worse."

Dev had known Mal to take a walk on the bi side, every once in a while. "Don't go there, mate. Seriously. The loud one's got a bloke back home she's looking to cheat on, and the quiet one just does whatever her mate tells her to."

"How come my mates never do what I tell 'em to?" Tasha pouted.

"Because half of 'em have got more sense, and the other half are just shit mates."

"Fair enough." Tasha didn't take offence. "So what are these two hanging around you for?"

"Ain't got around to telling 'em I don't do girls, have I?"

Mal grinned. "Leave it to me, mate." He put an arm around Dev's waist just as Chantal and Susie made it across the road. "All right, laydeeze?"

Chantal gave him a frank look up and down. She seemed to like what she saw, because she was still checking Mal out when she spoke. "Hiya, Dev, who's your mates?"

"This is my sister, Tasha. And this is Mal," Dev said, leaving it there so Mal could do . . . whatever he was gonna do.

"Short for Malcolm?" Chantal asked flirtily.

Tasha cackled. "He wishes."

Chantal's eyes narrowed as she looked between Tasha and Mal. "So are you two an item?"

Tasha stifled another laugh. "No. Fuck me, no."

"Nah, I'm here to keep this one in line." Mal let his hand fall to Dev's hip and gave it a squeeze, pulling them closer together. "Can't trust him out on his own, can I, babe?"

Chantal's false eyelashes went wide, and her smile froze. "Babe?"

"Yeah, me and Dev, we been together . . . How long is it now, sweetheart? Five or six years, we been living together, innit? Course, sometimes he strays, but he always comes back home to his Mal, don't you, babe?"

The wanker. Dev gave in and made soppy eyes at Mal. "Yeah. Like a bad penny, ain't I?"

"Yeah, but you're my bad penny. And you're *very* good at some things, ain't you, love?" He gave Dev a sloppy wet kiss behind the ear.

Tasha had turned away and walked off a few paces, probably so they wouldn't see she was nearly pissing herself laughing.

"Right, well," Chantal said sulkily. "Can see you two got some catching up to do. Come on, Suse."

She grabbed her mate's arm and swung her away, and the two of them stomped off, high heels practically raising sparks on the prom.

Dev pulled away from Mal's hold and scrubbed at his neck, silently cracking up. "You wanker. Now they think I'm some kind of slapper."

Mal grinned. "So? Long as they know you're my slapper." He pulled Dev close again.

Dev pushed him away. "Fuck off, you cock. I don't want any more of your spit on me."

Tasha rejoined them, cackling. "That's just gross, that is."

"But, babe . . ." Mal pouted.

Then they all lost it, laughing so hard Dev's sides were literally aching. "Fuck, you two," he gasped. "It's good to have you here. I mean it."

"So, later, maybe . . ." Mal batted his eyelashes and made a circle with a finger and thumb, miming fucking it with another finger. Then he lost it again and doubled over, laughing. Tasha had already collapsed onto the low wall.

Dev loved them both. "In your dreams, mate. In your fucking *dreams*. Come on. Let's go get a drink."

Later, though, when they were back at the B&B after trying out the beer in half the pubs of Porthkennack, Dev couldn't help feeling something had been missing. Kyle should have been with them. Dev should have called him and invited him out with them.

He'd had the chance, too—early on in the evening, Tasha had asked him outright where his bloke was, 'cos she wanted to buy him a drink to say thanks. Dev could have given him a bell then and there. He'd bottled it, though. Just made some crack about Kyle having better things to do than hang around with a couple of pissheads like Tasha and Mal.

So sue him, all right? He'd just wanted one more night out before the axe fell.

"Tasha?" he asked, when they'd both got into bed and were lying there in the dim lighting, only a couple of feet from each other, just like when they'd been kids and insisted on sharing a room even though their foster mum didn't think it was right. Mal was off in the bathroom cleaning his teeth and doing whatever else he did that always seemed to take him half an hour a night—like seriously, was he putting his pubes in curlers or something?

"Mm?" Tasha didn't lift her head from her pillow, so all he could see of her was a floof of curls.

"What did you think of him? Kyle, I mean. Did you like him?"

"Course I like him. He got me out of jail. Well, he got his mate to get me out of jail, so same difference." She yawned. "So why ain't you with him now?"

"Don't need to be, do I? Mal's got a bed here." Mrs. Quick, bless her, had found a foldaway bed and managed to squeeze it into the room somehow, and said she'd only charge Mal for breakfast seeing as Dev had been paying for two people already all along. Dev had decided he was going to leave a bloody big tip, *and* he was getting on TripAdvisor the minute he got home to leave her the best review she'd ever had.

Mal had given him a funny look when he'd seen the bed, but he hadn't said anything.

"Yeah, we've all got beds, but there ain't no shagging going on in any of 'em."

She had a point, there. "Do you think it could work, me and him?"

"You mean 'cos he's posh and you're not?"

"It's not just that. He's, like, all educated and stuff. I barely made it through GCSEs. What would we even have to talk about?"

"Well, what do you talk about with him now?"

"I dunno, do I? All kinds of shit. But it's different, innit, when you've only just met someone."

Tasha made the sort of sound that could have meant anything. "It was sweet, him coming all the way to London. I mean, he could have just left his mate to handle it all. 'Specially him with his narcolepsy."

Dev propped himself up on an elbow to look at her. "He told you about it?"

"Yeah. Why not?"

"Dunno. He just . . . He didn't seem to want people to know, before." Had that changed? Or was it that he didn't mind Tasha knowing because she was Dev's sister?

"You ought to tell him he shouldn't be ashamed. Not his fault he got ill."

Dev had to smile. The number of times he'd told *her* that, when she was going through a rough patch about her diabetes in her early teens. "Yeah. I will. If we're still a thing."

Tasha yawned again. "Why are you asking me about relationships and all that shit, anyhow? You forgotten how the last bloke I slept with turned out to be a bloody drug dealer?"

Mal swaggered in from the bathroom in his boxer shorts, a towel slung over his shoulder. "Ain't you lot asleep yet?"

"Dev's pining for his bloke."

"No, I'm fucking not." Like anyone was going to believe that, least of all Dev.

"The posh tosser?"

"He ain't a tosser."

"No? So why ain't you sleeping with him tonight?"

"Christ, not you and all." Dev pulled his pillow over his head. "Just fuck off and let me sleep."

It must've sounded a bit muffled, but they seemed to get the message.

At any rate, the light went off and nobody spoke again.

CHAPTER THIRTY

Kyle woke up on his sofa in the early hours of the morning and rubbed his stiff neck while he checked his phone.

Still no message from Dev. Not that he'd really expected one. He'd last checked around 11 p.m., and he doubted Dev would risk waking him from a proper sleep just to message him, but the lack of contact was worrying. Of course, everything looked worse at four in the morning. But if Dev still wanted to be with him, why hadn't he been in touch all day?

Something twisted painfully inside him. The obvious answer was that Dev didn't need him anymore. He had his sister and his flatmate with him now.

The flatmate Kyle still hadn't met. Dev had mentioned Mal's return from Portugal—and had apparently totally forgiven him for going there in the first place rather than coming to Porthkennack with Dev. Granted, they'd had a plane to catch, but it still seemed a little odd that Kyle had been hurried away from Dev's flat before he could even set foot inside.

It was almost as if Dev didn't want him to meet Mal—but that couldn't be true, could it? After all, if Mal was coming down to Cornwall with Tasha, how could they avoid meeting?

On present showing, the bitter 4 a.m. voice whispered, *quite easily*. After all, he still hadn't met Ceri yet, had he? But then, why would a young, active man like Dev want his friends to have to spend time with his older, chronically ill lover? If Kyle even qualified as that any more. Was Kyle really anything more than an embarrassment to Dev—better than being alone, perhaps, and useful in a crisis, but not worth wasting time on when there was better company to be had?

Kyle had a glass of water and a couple of paracetamol for his headache, then undressed and went to bed in the hopes of fooling his body into sleeping when it ought to.

He managed a couple of hours and got up at eight, feeling hardly rested but unable to stomach any more time in bed. Still no message from Dev. Kyle wondered bitterly if he was ever going to hear from him again.

After forcing down some breakfast, he thought to hell with it and grabbed his phone to call Dev. Then he hesitated. It was still early, bearing in mind that Dev had quite likely been out late with his friends last night. Just because Kyle hadn't been able to sleep didn't mean that Dev wasn't enjoying a lie-in. Waking him up wouldn't get them off to a good start, would it? And even if he was already up . . . what if Kyle just got the brush-off over the phone? That would be that, wouldn't it? He'd have no chance to talk Dev round.

Instead, he bit the bullet and called Jeffrey. He'd held off yesterday, thinking it might be better to—hah—sleep on it, but now, all he wanted to do was get things moving.

Have one more achievement to bolster his confidence when he finally got to speak to Dev.

Jeffrey picked up almost immediately. "Kyle? Well, hello, stranger."

"Can you talk?"

"Of course. You know my routine." Kyle did. At this time in the morning, Jeffrey would be at the gallery preparing to open up.

"I'm coming back to Surrey."

There was a pause. "You want to move back in?" Jeffrey's tone was wary, and for a moment Kyle toyed with the idea of saying yes, just to hear Jeffrey's attempts to squirm out of it.

"No. But I will need somewhere to live, so I won't be able to afford to keep paying my half of the mortgage. We'll need to do something with the house."

Another pause. "Didn't you get the letter?"

"What letter?"

"The one from my solicitor. I've been trying to call you about it for *weeks*. I'm buying you out—I trust that's agreeable?"

Ah. That would be the letter postmarked from Surrey that he'd tossed on a pile of similarly unopened correspondence to deal with sometime after never.

"And F-Y-I," Jeffrey continued, "you haven't been paying the mortgage. I told them to cancel your direct debit when you left. I'm not a monster, Kyle. I wouldn't take your money when, well, you're going to need it, aren't you? What with all the cuts to disability benefits—"

"I'm not on benefits, Jeffrey. In fact, I'm going back to work." Although why he thought Jeffrey needed to know that, Kyle wasn't sure. And had it really been that long since he'd checked his bank account online? God knew the paper statements had been going into the "ignore" pile.

"Oh. Good for you." Jeffrey was clearly trying to sound as if he meant it, but it still came out with a rising inflection at the end, as if there were a silent, *Are you really sure that's wise?* appended. "So . . . you're better, then?"

"Narcolepsy doesn't get better," Kyle reminded him, struggling to keep his patience. But for God's sake, they'd been together for years, yet Jeffrey hadn't bothered to inform himself about Kyle's condition. Dev had found out more than him in a matter of *days*.

"Oh. Anyway, we've boxed up all your things, so—"

"'We'?"

A deep intake of breath. "Martin. You remember him from the Dutch exhibition? Anyway, he's, ah. He's moved in."

"You don't hang about, do you?" Kyle snapped, then reflected he didn't really have a leg to stand on.

"Oh, come on. You know as well as I do that our relationship was dying by degrees long before you moved out."

Yes, because you didn't take at all well to me no longer having the energy to go out, you refused to sleep in the same bed any longer, and you had a hissy fit every time an unplanned nap happened. And as for sex . . . most of the time you didn't want to bother in case I had a cataplexy attack, because it was so creepy. Kyle didn't say it.

"If I hadn't had the guts to call it a day . . ." Jeffrey left it hanging.

Trust him to make a virtue out of a rejection. But he'd been right, Kyle knew that now. It could never have worked between them.

And besides, if they'd stayed together, he'd never have met Dev. "I'll come by and get my things when I have a place," he said. "And I'll look for that letter."

"Good. But call ahead before you come, please. We don't want anyone to have any unpleasant surprises."

"Fine." Kyle hung up. He hadn't said what he'd meant to about Jeffrey telling tales to his mum, but in the end it just hadn't seemed important anymore.

At least now that chapter of his life was finally over.

Time to gather all his courage and start work on the next one.

Kyle set out for town straight away. It was still early to drop in on Dev, but if he was honest, Kyle was a little paranoid he might lose his nerve, or worse fall asleep, if he didn't get moving. He could always stop en route at the Square Peg Café. Their coffee and scones hadn't been too bad the other morning. And more to the point, he'd hopefully get a look at Ceri at last. Kyle was sick of not knowing the people in Dev's life.

It was another sunny day, the gentle breeze coming in off the sea bringing with it the strong scent of seaweed mingling with the briny smell of the water itself. Low tide, then. Strange, how quickly he'd got used to this place. Kyle was going to miss it when he moved back to Surrey.

But then again, he had a feeling Porthkennack would wait for him to come back. And he would, he knew, no matter what happened today with Dev. It was in his blood—or perhaps it was truer to say it was in his soul.

The walk, instead of tiring him, seemed to wake him properly, clearing the fug from his head. Reaching the café, he hesitated—should he go straight on, after all, to try to catch Dev before he left the B&B for the day? Standing, irresolute, by a seat at an outside table, Kyle was startled out of his indecision when someone spoke to him.

"You meeting Dev here?"

Kyle looked around, startled, to see a small, skinny waitress with long, straight hair. "Ceri?" he guessed. She wasn't what he'd expected, somehow. He'd pictured someone . . . larger. More confident.

More like Dev.

This girl was fragile looking, almost birdlike. Kyle sat down, more to stop himself from looming over her than anything else. She nodded without smiling. "You gotta order something if you're staying."

"Do you do iced coffee?" He hadn't had one in ages. Just the thought of it brought back memories of Rome with Jeffrey . . . Abruptly, Kyle lost the taste for the drink. "Never mind. I'll have a white filter coffee, please. Decaff," he added with a sigh.

She didn't move. "You ain't too good for him, you know."

"*What?*"

"You, with your money and your posh voice and your career and all that. Don't make you no better than Dev."

Oh God. This was exactly what Dev had been saying, just before his sister rang. Did he really still think Kyle, what, looked down on him? Why, in God's name? Because he had a trade, instead of a profession? "I know it doesn't," he said, but it sounded weak even to him.

She stared at him. Then she sat down in one of the free chairs at the table. "Don't you mess with me," she said in a low voice. "Nor him, neither."

"I'm not." Kyle took a deep breath. "The only thing I'm worried about is how my condition will affect him."

God, that was embarrassing. But she'd seen him collapse at least once, and presumably Dev had talked about him. She must know there was something wrong with Kyle.

"Not how he tells it. *And* you got him thinking you're right."

Oh. That was discouraging. Kyle had thought all he'd have to do would be to reassure Dev his fears that Kyle looked down on him were groundless. Well, that and convince him he wasn't going to be stuck with a virtual invalid. If Dev had decided their backgrounds were too different . . .

Damn it. He'd just have to work that bit harder to show him it was nonsense, that was all. "It was a misunderstanding. I'm hoping to see him today and tell him that. I, ah, don't suppose you know what his plans are for today?"

"He said he'd come here. Bring his sister and his mate to meet me. That's why I thought you were meeting him. You've not heard from him, then?"

"No." It was a painful admission. The thought of hanging around waiting to crash Dev's plans with his friends was even worse. "Look, forget the coffee. I'll see him later. It was nice to meet you," he remembered to add as he stood.

Kyle turned away from her unreadable expression and threaded his way through the tables to escape.

As he passed by the bench he'd collapsed on that first day of knowing Dev, he was startled when a young woman who'd been sitting on it jumped up and grabbed his arm. She was pretty, with long blonde hair and big sunglasses, and another young woman hovered by her with a worried look on her face. Kyle was positive he'd never seen either of them before.

"Are you a mate of hers?" the blonde woman asked while Kyle was still concentrating on making sure his legs didn't fail him. She had a strong Birmingham accent.

"What?"

"That waitress. Ceri. You a mate?"

"I, well . . ." He cast a glance back at the café, but Ceri had disappeared inside.

The blonde girl didn't quite roll her eyes at him, but he could see it was a close thing. "See, there's this problem. Her fella's been cheating on her, and we didn't know if we should say anything, did we, Suse?"

"Her fella?" Kyle was probably sounding less and less intelligent by the minute.

"Yeah. We met him down on the beach. Dev, his name is. From London."

Seriously? She thought Dev was going out with Ceri? Then again, Kyle had wondered too, hadn't he? Just for a moment. He'd never seriously thought Dev was cheating on him.

He was suddenly glad he'd had that conversation with Ceri a few minutes ago, even so.

"He's a looker," the blonde girl was saying. "But I always said— didn't I say, Suse?—I wouldn't trust him far as I could chuck him. And get this: we saw him last night, down on the front, and he was with this fella. His *boyfriend*." She said it as if there should have been dramatic music playing.

Kyle blinked. "I think there's been a misunderstanding."

"*No*. See, we went to talk to them, 'cos this fella Dev was with wasn't bad looking, neither, and he said it straight out. Been living together for years, haven't they? So what we was wondering, was—"

"Mal?" he interrupted her.

She frowned. "Yeah, that's his name. How d'you know?"

"You've got the wrong end of the stick. They're just flatmates."

"Uh-*huh*? So how come this fella's all, 'I'm with Dev here, ain't I, babe'? And then he *kisses* him. *And* he says Dev's a player, which I tell you what, I wouldn't put up with like he does, but he always goes home to his fella. So what I thought is, that Ceri girl ought to know about this. And we was going to tell her, but then we saw you talking to her and I thought, it'd be better coming from a mate, right?" She gave a smug little smile at the end.

God. Kyle felt suddenly chilled. It made a horrible sort of sense, no matter how much he wanted to doubt the veracity of everything she'd said on principle. Dev's reluctance to let him into his flat to meet Mal; his lack of contact since then . . .

Not that any of it was this girl's business, in any case. "I'll make sure Ceri hears about anything she needs to know," he said coldly. "It was kind of you to be concerned for her."

He was pretty sure the sarcasm flew straight over the young woman's perfectly styled head.

Not the friend's though, perhaps. She'd gone red and was tugging at the blonde's arm.

"Good-bye," Kyle said, pointedly disengaging his arm from her grasp.

She didn't reply as he walked off, and he didn't look back.

Not quite sure what to do now, Kyle turned his steps towards the seafront. His plan to go and see Dev now looked like it might just end in bitter humiliation. But he couldn't leave it like this. Perhaps the girl's comments were simply malicious, maybe to avenge some imagined slight on Dev's part?

Kyle's stomach churned. He had to know the truth. Dev had to be given the chance to tell his side of the story. No matter how much nerve Kyle was going to have to work up to go through with it.

He had just about convinced himself to head out to the B&B when, with a jolt that made his heart stop for a moment, he caught sight of Dev himself not ten yards away, walking along the promenade.

There was a young man with him, who turned at that moment to say something with a laugh. He was white, good-looking in a knowing way, with sharply cut light-brown hair and the sort of smile on his face that made Kyle instinctively distrust the bearer. He'd seen plenty of young men like that in court, standing up in the witness box to cheerfully perjure themselves, then throwing a cheeky grin in the direction of the jury as if to say, *Who, me?*

This must be Mal.

He wore a pair of ripped jeans with a tight grey T-shirt and was walking way too close to Dev, their shoulders brushing with every step. God, their *hips* were practically touching. Kyle felt a sick, plummeting sensation in his stomach. Mal was far more suited to Dev than Kyle was, that much was clear. They were the same age, from the same sort of background—not that Kyle gave a damn, but from what Ceri had said, it seemed Dev might.

And Mal almost certainly didn't fall asleep while in company. Tired beyond belief, Kyle turned away and headed for home.

Three steps later he stopped dead, and turned around.

No, damn it. He wasn't going to give up and fade into the background. And if his own experience had taught him anything, it was that things weren't always what they seemed, or even what people said they were.

His heart pounding in a rib cage that felt suddenly, painfully tight, Kyle strode down towards the seafront to confront them.

And prayed he wasn't about to have a cataplexy attack.

CHAPTER THIRTY-ONE

Dev wasn't sure how to feel when Kyle caught up with them wearing the sort of expression that . . . well, Dev wasn't certain what it meant, but it definitely didn't promise anything good. His guts seemed to be making the decision for him, twisting themselves up in painful knots.

"Hey," he said when Kyle reached them. "So, uh, this is Mal."

"Your flatmate." Something about the way Kyle said it rang alarm bells, and Dev wasn't even sure why.

It wasn't like Kyle was accusing him or nothing. Just . . . waiting.

Which maybe was an accusation in itself.

"Yeah."

Mal stepped forward, holding out a hand like this was some kind of business meeting. Dev stared at him. "You're Kyle, right? Good to meet you."

Kyle shook Mal's hand, still looking wary. "Likewise. You, ah, had a good trip down?"

"Yeah, not so bad. Traffic on the M5 was a bit of a mare, though. Dev says you got a house round here?"

"Yes—over the other side of the headland. Up on the cliffs."

Christ, any minute now they'd start talking about the weather, and then Dev was literally gonna explode. He cleared his throat and interrupted them with, "So, uh—"

He said it at the exact same time Kyle came out with, "Dev, could I have a word with you in private?"

There was an awkward silence. Mal backed off, smiling, with his hands up. "Don't mind me. I'll go and see if Tasha's dragged her lazy arse out of bed yet. She's gonna be gutted she missed breakfast. See ya at that caff."

Dev watched him go, then turned back to Kyle. "Hey, so . . ."

"I just heard something interesting, over at the Square Peg Café."

"You been talking to Ceri?" Dev wasn't sure how he felt about Ceri and Kyle talking about him.

"Yes, actually, but it wasn't from her. A blonde girl. From Birmingham."

Okay, he was definitely sure he didn't want Kyle talking to *her* about him. "Chantal? What the hell did she have to say to you?"

"You do know her, then? Well, the gist of it was that you apparently told her you and Mal were a couple." Kyle made an awkward gesture that was less a shrug and more sort of hunching in on himself. "And, well, after what happened in London . . ."

Dev's stomach lurched and he stared, horrified. Christ, how had he been so fucking *stupid*? He'd basically told the bloke, *Hey, guess what, my flatmate's turned up unexpected so we're pissing off right now so you don't get to meet him.*

How the hell had it not even *occurred* to him what that had to look like? Like he was getting the mistress the hell out of Dodge so the wife wouldn't see her, that's what. And then, *then*, him and Mal have to go spreading it about that, yeah, they're shagging and have been for years.

"It's not . . . It's not like that. Shit. I wouldn't do that to you. To anyone." Dev ran a hand through his hair. "You gotta believe me."

"So you didn't tell her you and Mal are together?"

"Well, yeah, we did—but we're not, honest. I mean, yeah, sometimes we've—" Dev broke off, horrified at the way his mouth seemed to want to fuck up his chances with Kyle. "We're not a couple. It was just Mal's idea to stop them trying to chat us up." He desperately searched Kyle's face for some sign that he'd been believed. "Look, shit, I'll call him, okay? He can tell you himself."

Dev pulled out his phone, but Kyle shook his head.

He was smiling. Not, like, a big cheesy grin or anything, but there was definitely a smile there. Thank fuck.

"It's all right. I believe you." He looked down and then back up at Dev again. "I've been doing some thinking."

Dev gave a nervous laugh. "Okay, that don't sound ominous or nothing." Was this where Kyle said, *Cheers for not cheating on me, but I'm dumping your working-class arse anyhow?*

"It . . . shouldn't. I'm moving back to Surrey, and I'm going to see if I can manage some part-time legal work."

"Yeah? That's great. Uh, that is great, innit?"

Kyle nodded. "Not sure if it'll work out, but I'm going to see what the doctors can do to help too."

"Yeah? Good on you, mate. So, uh . . ." Dev wasn't quite sure what to say.

"So . . ." Kyle stopped. Maybe he was having the same problem. "It shouldn't be too hard for us to keep seeing each other. If that's what you want."

Dev could feel his face spreading into a huge, relieved grin. "Yeah. That's what I want. And, uh, shit. I'm sorry about not letting you in my flat. I panicked, all right? It's a bit of a shithole."

"Does it have slug trails all over the carpets and mouse droppings in the cupboards?"

"What? No way. That's well gross."

"Then it's better than some of the places I lived as a student."

"Yeah, but it ain't what you're used to now."

"Dev, it doesn't matter. So you don't earn as much as I used to. So what? Neither do I, and I'm never likely to again." Kyle closed his eyes briefly, and Dev automatically put a hand out to steady him in case he needed it. His eyes snapped open, and he took a deep breath. "If you can stand being with someone who's never going to have a normal life or a proper sleep cycle, and who's likely to only be able to work part-time at most for the rest of his life, and—"

"Oi, that ain't your fault. None of it."

Kyle shook his head. "It's still a lot to ask you to put up with. You're young, you're fit—"

Dev grinned. "You looked in a mirror lately? 'Cos you're pretty fit yourself."

"That's not what I—"

"I know it ain't. Stop talking like . . . like I dunno what I'm doing. I know you're ill. So what? We can handle it. See these eyes? Wide open, mate. I know it ain't gonna be easy sometimes. But we'll deal. Together."

Jesus, the look on Kyle's face. Like he really wanted to believe—but just couldn't let himself. Couldn't shake the feeling he was going to be, what, some kind of burden to Dev? And that was all kinds of stupid. He wasn't a fucking burden. He was *everything*.

"But—"

Dev didn't want to hear any more. Nobody got to do Kyle down in front of him, not even the bloke himself. *Especially* not the bloke himself. So he stepped up close to Kyle, and shut him up with a kiss. And, yeah, that was definitely one of his better ideas. Dev added a bit of tongue and pulled Kyle in tight, and Christ, that hit the spot.

He wasn't sure how long they were kissing for, but long enough for a fair few wolf whistles and cries of "Get a room!"

Dev was grinning madly when they drew apart again, and Kyle . . .

Kyle looked happier than Dev had ever seen him.

Standing on the other side of the road were Chantal and her mate, watching them with scandalised expressions.

Laughter bubbling up inside him, Dev couldn't help himself. He made a helpless gesture in their direction. "What can I say? I'm a total slapper."

All he needed now was Demelza-like and her mates turning up so Dev could . . . do something to get revenge on Ceri's behalf, although he didn't have a clue what.

Then he thought, no. Why waste his time on those losers?

He had better things to do. Smiling, he pulled Kyle back in for another kiss.

EPILOGUE

Sitting on the beach shivering in the icy December wind, Dev couldn't believe how much Ceri had changed in a few short months. The dark circles under her eyes were almost gone, and she'd done her hair up in dreads that floated crazily around her head as she ran along the sand, like she was Medusa or something. Was she wearing makeup? Yeah, a bit of mascara and lippy. She'd put on some weight too, and her arms didn't look like they'd snap anymore if she lifted anything heavy. She seemed happy. More than that. She seemed proud—proud of herself. Her and Tasha had been walking around arm in arm like they owned the fucking world.

That was another thing. Tasha had stayed in Porthkennack after Dev's three weeks were up. Which Dev hadn't been all that keen on, first off, but like she'd said, she needed a new job and a place to live, and where better to find both than a seaside resort? And it'd turned out that Ceri's mum or dad, Dev wasn't sure which, had known someone in charge of hiring at one of the big hotels, so she'd been sorted until the grannies' coach parties dried up. By which time she'd sweet-talked Ceri's Uncle Jago into taking her on at the pub, replacing Mrs. Jago, whose knees weren't getting any younger. Tasha liked to say he was a right bastard to work for, but she said it with a smile, so Dev reckoned he just didn't take any of her shit.

And at least she'd never have to see that drug-dealing wanker Matt again. The police had dropped all charges against Tasha, thank God. Dev didn't know how much of that was down to Kyle and his mate, and he didn't care. He still wasn't exactly *happy* about his little sister being so far away, but he'd been feeling a lot better about it since the first time Tasha complained about Ceri nagging her about her blood sugar.

They'd joined the girls in Porthkennack for Christmas, him and Kyle, seeing as Tasha was Dev's only family and Kyle's lot were the other side of the world. Not that they hadn't been invited over to Perth, both of them, but it'd felt a bit too soon for the big family Christmas, seeing as he still hadn't met them yet. And the jetlag would've been a bastard for Kyle. His mum and dad were going to come and visit in a few months, and Dev was looking forward to meeting more of Kyle's people. Honest. After all, it wasn't like Kyle's mate Sujata scared the crap out of him . . . Oh. Wait.

Mal had come down on Boxing Day, 'cos his mum would've gutted him with a carving knife if he hadn't turned up for her Christmas turkey. The three of them were staying at Mother Ivey's Boudoir, which put a bit of a cramp in Dev and Kyle's style, but like Mal said, now they were living together they could shag any time they wanted, couldn't they?

It'd maybe been a bit soon to move in together, time-wise, but Dev had been sick and tired of losing half Kyle's awake time to travelling. And it felt right, them in the little house they'd found together on the edge of Epsom. Dev had thought maybe he'd miss London, but they were close enough he could go in and see his mates any time he wanted to.

It'd been easier than Dev had thought, getting a job down in Surrey. Masood had bitched at him for weeks when he'd said he was leaving—and then he'd got in touch with someone he knew, who was something like his brother-in-law's father-in-law's sister's cousin's best friend, fuck if Dev knew, and pulled a few strings, and given Dev a seriously awesome reference on top. He was definitely getting to work on a better class of car now. Well, if he didn't count Kyle's Fiesta, which against all odds was *still* going strong. And Surrey was a good compromise, for now. Him and Kyle had agreed: in a few years, once Kyle was sorted with his new line of work and his meds, they'd be moving somewhere by the sea.

Maybe not to Porthkennack. But they hadn't ruled it out, either.

The girls were running around, with Kyle throwing a ball for his new chocolate Labrador, Zelley. Well, she was technically Dev's too, but she was more Kyle's really. He was the one who mostly took her for walks, went to puppy-training classes with her, and cheerfully cleared up her messes, even though some of them had been pottery-related in the beginning, before they'd got used to putting stuff out of reach.

Mal, looking a bit puffed out, came and sat down next to Dev. "So are them two together now, or what?"

"What, Tasha and Ceri?" Dev shook his head. "Nah. Least, I don't think so. They're just mates. Probably."

Mal put his head on one side. "If they *were* together, Tasha would definitely be the bloke."

"Okay, leaving out the fact they're both *girls*, how d'you work that one out?"

"Easy. She's the irresponsible one."

"Way to gender stereotype, bruv. So which out of me and Kyle is the bloke, then?"

"Neither. You're both responsible and boring."

"I think the word you're looking for is *adult*."

"Nope. I was spot-on with *boring*." Mal grinned, then gazed at Kyle for a moment, a weird look on his face. "Funny how it all turns out, innit? This could have been, like, your epic tragic love story. Like *Romeo and Juliet*."

Dev stared at him.

"What? Like I never seen Shakespeare? It was on telly when I was off work with that flu bug. It was well tragic. He thinks she's dead and he tops himself, and she wakes up like three minutes later being snogged by a stiff. And then she tops *her*self. Fucking tragic, bruv. Like, she wasn't even legal when it happened. Not even *close*. Thirteen, man. I mean, come on. My sister still had like a million soft toys on her bed when she was thirteen, not some older dude fresh from a gang fight. If I'd caught that bastard climbing in her bedroom window, I'd have beat the crap out of him."

Dev snorted. "No, you wouldn't. For a start, you were ten."

"Hey, I'd have wanted to. It's the thought that counts, innit? But anyway. Epic tragedy, bruv."

"So let me get this straight. You're saying me and Kyle are like a suicidal teenage pedo and his victim? Do I wanna know which of us is which? Seeing as we're both apparently girls anyway?"

"You're Romeo. He's gotta be Juliet, 'cos of the whole Sleeping Beauty thing."

"Okay, now you've seriously lost me. I thought you were talking about Shakespeare, not Disney."

"Yeah, but there's parallels, ain't there? Juliet on her balcony, Sleeping Beauty in her castle." Mal grinned. "And they both get shafted by some prick."

"Oi, you calling me a prick, you wanker?"

"Takes one to know one."

"What are you, five?"

Mal stuck out his tongue and made wanking off gestures.

"Have I missed something?" Kyle called out, walking over to them.

Dev took a mo to drink in the sight. Kyle looked a lot fitter than he had in the summer, which, since he'd been pretty fit then, meant he was fucking gorgeous these days, and sometimes Dev had to pinch himself 'cos he couldn't believe his luck. Kyle had kept the beard, though he was working a bit now, and he looked even better in a suit, although not as good as he looked naked. The meds had helped a lot, once him and his specialist had sorted out the ones that really, really didn't.

Mal answered for them, which was just as well as Dev had sort of forgotten Kyle had asked a question. "Just discussing classic literature, mate."

Kyle raised an eyebrow. "Do I want to know?" He sat down next to Dev and slung an arm over his shoulders. "Have you decided what you're going to do about your dad yet?"

Dev nodded. "Yeah."

Mal gave him a frankly nosy look. "What's all this, then?"

"You know I got my dad's name and his old address from *her*, right?" Dev jerked his head towards the cliff and Roscarrock House.

He hadn't seen her since that time at the PEBBLE thing, but she'd kept her promise and emailed him the info. It still hurt, thinking about her, but Dev had accepted she wasn't going to have a change of heart, and he was fine with it. Most days.

Mal nodded.

"Well, I found out where he's living now, and I wrote to him." Dev paused, mostly for effect. "And last week he wrote back."

"You're shitting me! What did he say?"

"Loads of stuff. Like he's always regretted what happened, and he didn't know how old my . . . m-mum was, and he panicked big time when he found out. And if he'd known about me, things would've been different." Dev took a deep breath. "He wants to meet me."

"You gonna? I mean, you believe him?"

Dev took a mo to answer. "Dunno if I believe him or not. I mean, he's never gonna admit he knew she was only fifteen, is he? Or that if he'd known I existed he'd have just left me in care. But yeah, I'm gonna go see him. But not 'cos I'm looking for a family. Not anymore. I mean, yeah, I wanna know where I came from, but well."

He glanced around, at Ceri and Tasha petting Zelley with their heads so close together Tasha's curls were getting crumpled, at Mal himself, and finally, at Kyle by his side, his hair ruffled by the wind and the sort of look in his eye that made Dev feel all warm inside despite the wicked cold breeze.

Dev smiled. "Got my family right here, haven't I?"

AUTHOR'S NOTE

Lines of poetry in chapter twenty are taken from "The Love Song of J. Alfred Prufrock" by T.S. Eliot.

Explore more of the *Porthkennack* universe:
riptidepublishing.com/titles/universe/porthkennack

a PORTHKENNACK CONTEMPORARY

Broke Deep
Charlie Cochrane

House of Cards
Garrett Leigh

Foxglove Copse
Alex Beecroft

Junkyard Heart
Garrett Leigh

a PORTHKENNACK HISTORICAL

A Gathering Storm
Joanna Chambers

Count the Shells
Charlie Cochrane

Dear Reader,

Thank you for reading JL Merrow's *Wake Up Call*!

We know your time is precious and you have many, many entertainment options, so it means a lot that you've chosen to spend your time reading. We really hope you enjoyed it.

We'd be honored if you'd consider posting a review—good or bad—on sites like **Amazon, Barnes & Noble, Kobo, Goodreads, Twitter, Facebook, Tumblr,** and your blog or website. We'd also be honored if you told your friends and family about this book. Word of mouth is a book's lifeblood!

For more information on upcoming releases, author interviews, blog tours, contests, giveaways, and more, please sign up for our weekly, spam-free newsletter and visit us around the web:

Newsletter: tinyurl.com/RiptideSignup
Twitter: twitter.com/RiptideBooks
Facebook: facebook.com/RiptidePublishing
Goodreads: tinyurl.com/RiptideOnGoodreads
Tumblr: riptidepublishing.tumblr.com

Thank you so much for Reading the Rainbow!

RiptidePublishing.com

ALSO BY
JL MERROW

One Under (March 2018)

Lovers Leap
It's All Geek to Me
Damned If You Do
Pricks and Pragmatism
Camwolf
Muscling Through
Wight Mischief
Midnight in Berlin
Hard Tail
Slam!
Fall Hard
Raising the Rent
To Love a Traitor
Sex, Lies and Edelweiss
Trick of Time
Snared

The Plumber's Mate Mysteries
Pressure Head
Relief Valve
Heat Trap
Blow Down

The Shamwell Tales
Caught!
Played!
Out!
Spun! (July 2017)

The Midwinter Manor Series
Poacher's Fall
Keeper's Pledge

ABOUT
THE AUTHOR

JL Merrow is that rare beast, an English person who refuses to drink tea. She read Natural Sciences at Cambridge, where she learned many things, chief amongst which was that she never wanted to see the inside of a lab ever again. Her one regret is that she never mastered the ability of punting one-handed whilst holding a glass of champagne.

She writes across genres, with a preference for contemporary gay romance and the paranormal, and is frequently accused of humour. Her novella *Muscling Through* was a 2013 EPIC Award finalist, and her novel *Slam!* won the 2013 Rainbow Award for Best LGBT Romantic Comedy. In the 2016 Rainbow Awards, her fourth Plumber's Mate Mystery *Blow Down* came second in the Dorien Grey Award for Best Gay Mystery/Thriller, and was a runner-up for Best Gay Book, as was her historical romance *To Love a Traitor*.

JL Merrow is a member of the UK GLBTQ Fiction Meet (ukglbtfictionmeet.co.uk) organizing team.

Find JL Merrow online at: www.jlmerrow.com, on Twitter as @jlmerrow, and on Facebook at facebook.com/jl.merrow.

Enjoy more stories like
Wake Up Call
at RiptidePublishing.com!

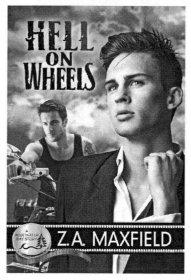

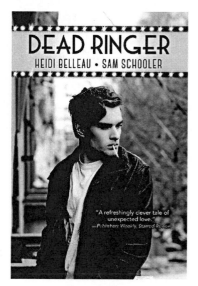

Hell on Wheels
ISBN: 978-1-62649-173-1

Dead Ringer
ISBN: 978-1-62649-338-4

Earn Bonus Bucks!
Earn 1 Bonus Buck for each dollar you spend. Find out how at
RiptidePublishing.com/news/bonus-bucks.

Win Free Ebooks for a Year!
Pre-order coming soon titles directly through our site and you'll
receive one entry into a drawing for a chance to win free books for
a year! Get the details at RiptidePublishing.com/contests.

CPSIA information can be obtained
at www.ICGtesting.com
Printed in the USA
FSOW01n0001150417
33149FS

9 781626 495418